Star Touched

by
A. L. Kaplan

Copyright August 2017

ISBN: 978-1-940758-62-6 Paperback
ISBN: 978-1-940758-63-3 EPUB
ISBN: 978-1-940758-64-0 Mobi

Cover Design: Ryan Anderson

Published by:
Intrigue Publishing, LLC
11505 Cherry Tree Crossing Rd. #148
Cheltenham MD 20623-9998

Star Touched

Chapter One

Tatiana

"Hurry. The ceremony's gonna start soon." The dark-skinned girl tugged her mother through the town square.

A hard lump formed in Tatiana's throat as she watched them. She'd give anything to spend time with her mama again, but the Cataclysm had ripped that possibility away. The teenager bounced on the balls of her feet and craned her neck to see over the crowd. Her hand waved for her mother to catch up.

"Clear Sky Day isn't going anywhere," said the mother.

"But, Mom," the girl's voice rose in pitch. "I want to get a good spot."

"All right, all right. You can go on ahead, but keep your wits about you. You've heard the rumors."

"I will. I promise."

She pecked her mother's cheek and ran off. The woman smiled, but her gaze darted across the town square as if expecting an imminent attack. Already taut knuckles tightened their grip on her cloth shopping bag. Worry lines creased her face. Still scanning the merchants and shoppers, she hurried to follow her daughter.

Tears stung Tatiana's eyes as the two vanished into the crowd. No one had worried about her since the Cataclysm eight years ago. She pushed her feelings back, something she wished she could do with those around her. A maelstrom of emotions bombarded her from the crowd: excitement, happiness, fear, joy, anger. Even after years of struggle to keep them out, other people's strong emotions still leaked into her mind like a winter's chill. Her empathy had its uses, like knowing who was too angry to approach, but sometimes the feelings were so overwhelming that she wanted to run off and hide.

A pair of guards strutted by, and Tatiana made herself as inconspicuous as possible. Unlike the people who had watched Atherton's walls during her last visit to town four years earlier, they 'felt' cruel. Hired thugs doing a job. Not citizens guarding their homes. One of them, a dirty-looking man with greasy hair and a half-buttoned uniform, grabbed a loaf of bread off a cart without pausing. The merchant said nothing, but Tatiana saw the muscles in her jaw twitch.

An old man with clothes as worn and patched as Tatiana's glared at the guard. "Damn mercenaries. They think they own this town."

His companion nudged him. "Shh, they'll hear you. Besides, their boss already does own most of Atherton. Just be glad they haven't come after us."

The old man wrinkled his nose. "We should leave."

"And go where, Pops? Long Island's under water. Most of New Jersey is a ghost town. I know northern Kentucky isn't your idea of home, but we have family here."

"Humph. There should be an American flag flying in this square."

"Pops, it's time to accept there is no more USA. Cataclysm killed it."

The voices faded as they walked away. Tatiana held Fifi close, adjusting the sling that held the tiny white poodle. Fifi was more than capable of taking care of herself now, but her size and coloration drew too much attention. It was better she remained hidden.

"Look, they're coming!"

A procession of cloaked figures exited a large white building to the slow, rhythmic beat of a drum, like a death march. The figures moved toward the center of the town square where a tall pole stood shrouded in gray cloth.

Tatiana watched from a distance, away from the milling crowd, knowing what would transpire. She'd seen similar Clear Sky Day ceremonies in other towns. Ten ribbons wove around the pole, each representing one of the ten months the sun had been blocked after the Cataclysm. Still in their gray cloaks, the dancers began to step around the pole, unweaving the ribbons as the drums intensified their rhythm. The crowd began to clap and stomp their feet to the tempo, spurring the dancers to pick up their pace. Bit by bit the ribbons came unwound until the cloth on top fell free, revealing a gold-painted sun sculpture. At the same time, the dancers tossed off their cloaks. Waves of joy rode on the crowd's roar as the noonday sun glinted on its land-bound model.

Tatiana closed her eyes, fighting back tears. Clear Sky Day meant different things to different people. It was a rebirth of life, as miraculous as a woman's womb. But for Tatiana and others, it also meant the beginning of isolation, fear, and loneliness.

A voice rang out right next to Tatiana. "The Day of Reckoning destroyed our old world eight years ago. The miracle of Clear Sky Day gave birth to a new one. Celebrate our renewal with a Clear Sky Day sweet."

The man pressed a sticky egg-shaped confection into Tatiana's hand before she could react, then continued dispensing treats through the crowd. Her chest tightened. It wasn't the blue pants or plain cotton shirt he wore that made Tatiana's breath catch. She ducked behind a tree. Her vision blurred, but the neatly painted yellow and orange star on the man's forehead was already etched in her mind. She'd seen more of that brand on both men and women over the last few years. Would He be with them? Would He be right behind her, that haunting shadow she'd dodged for nearly four years?

A warm wet tongue touched her hand, soothing her mind. The panic withdrew. Tatiana glanced down. She didn't remember sticking her hand into Fifi's sling. It used to be Tatiana calming and caring for the sickly pup, but that was a long time ago. Honey from the sweet oozed between the fingers of her other hand, crushed and forgotten. She stuffed it into the sling for Fifi. One of them should enjoy it, and her stomach was too knotted to eat.

Hands clasped her shoulders as she stepped away from the tree. A body pressed against her back, a hard bulge making clear both gender and desire. One filthy arm slipped across her chest and held her tight. Another hand slid down her side and began to claw at her skirt.

"You're a sweet little thing. My kinda Clear Sky Day treat."

His words slurred together and the smell of booze was

seconded by that of old sweat. Images again blurred Tatiana's vision, memories that refused to die. Memories that made her stomach twist. She kicked back and caught the man in the knee, loosening his grip enough for her to slip out of his meaty grasp and turn. Tatiana expected to face a drunken townsperson. Instead she found herself face to face with a guard in a stain-splattered dusty-green uniform. Her throat tightened as she backed away. The man's face flushed, and he teetered for a moment, then he lunged.

Tatiana dodged, bumping into a passerby. People looked and hurried away. No one intervened. She clutched Fifi tightly, hoping no one could hear the dog's growing snarl. Energy tingled her fingers, and she felt Fifi tremble beneath her hands.

"What the hell do you think you're doing, soldier?"

The newcomer, a scar-faced man with a metal star on his sleeveless uniform, smashed his fist into the drunken guard's head with cold efficiency. The eagle tattoo on his bulging right bicep flexed as he bent down and whispered in the drunk's ear. Sun glinted off his shaved head.

At a flick of his hand, two guards grabbed the drunk and dragged him off. People around them scurried away, eyes averted. The scar-faced guard vanished. Tatiana tried to still her trembling hands. It wasn't too late to flee this place.

So much had changed in this town since her last visit, on a cold November day four years ago. The small northern Kentucky town had been just a few blocks of patched-up buildings and farms then. Now it bustled, nearly a mile wide, not counting the fields. It was bigger, prospering, yet something didn't feel right.

Tatiana's knowledge of wild foods, a legacy from her parents had allowed her to forage successfully after the Cataclysm. But Fifi had been sick and needed meat, so in desperation, Tatiana had ventured into Atherton to beg door to door. Fourteen years old, ragged, bruised, and barely hanging on. Only the need to help Fifi had kept her going when she was refused aid. One door hadn't closed.

People jostled around Tatiana as she moved out of the tree-lined market square toward the person who had restored her faith in humanity. It was long past time to repay him. She kept her eyes downcast, hoping no one would notice her. If only she could throw her shawl over her head, but the summer's heat dissuaded that idea. Instead, the threadbare cloth was tied around her waist. Her hand slipped unconsciously into one of the deep pockets of her dress to finger the small gold coin hidden there. Flashing lots of gold wasn't a smart idea, so she had taken only one coin from the cache she had discovered years back. The rest she left to slow down the man who followed her. Always her intent had been to repay the man who had given her that small can of food. This was the first chance she'd had to return since the riots had ended. Hopefully it was safe to stay for a short while.

She slipped into the shadows between two buildings across the street from her destination and closed her eyes until the fear subsided. Pleasant thoughts filled her mind, like the day she first met Gareth in his cluttered store and bar. Lit only by candlelight, it had felt like walking into a warehouse, a blessedly warm warehouse. Even then he reminded her of her papa. If only she could have stayed.

Would he remember her? Four years was a long time to recollect one young beggar girl. Tatiana brushed the wrinkles from her patchwork dress and ran her fingers through her long raven mane. Only the sign outside the brick building where she had once been offered food had changed. Gareth's Odd Shop and Bar now read Gareth's Tavern. To the left stood a new addition proclaiming itself Gareth's Store. The two-story structure was wider than the brick building and stood in what had been an abandoned lot.

A smile crept across her face as she watched people go in and out of Gareth's store. It was good to see his business flourish. Groups of raucous Clear Sky Day revelers entered the tavern. Tatiana didn't like crowds, especially rowdy ones, but she'd been drawn to today's celebration. Such a large business couldn't be run by one man alone. She had hoped to ask for a job but wasn't sure if he would need more help or even want it.

Tatiana took a deep breath to calm her nerves as the last of his customers left the store, then hurried across the street, entering with the sun setting behind her. A lantern flickered on the counter. Gareth looked up as the bell above the door jingled and reached for the shotgun on his back with the ease of a warrior. He squinted with the sun's glare in his eyes.

"Sorry, but we're closing for the Clear Sky Day celebration. You'll have to come back tomorrow."

Tatiana paused. Had she waited too long? Gareth sounded tense, as if expecting trouble. A well-trimmed beard covered his face, and his hair looked a touch grayer than she remembered. She continued forward into the light, noting his grip tighten on the gun. His mouth parted in surprise as she came closer and his eyes widened with recognition.

"You came back."

"To thank you and pay you back for your kindness," Tatiana pulled the gold coin from her pocket and held it out. "The food you gave us kept us alive. We are indebted to you."

"It was only a tiny can of dog food. I...I didn't expect to see you again."

Tatiana lowered her eyes, confused by the shy emotions welling up inside her. "It was enough to give us strength to find more food. I promised to pay you back."

"Yes, you did," said Gareth. He took the coin without looking at it and placed it on the counter next to the lamp. "But, well...these days...It's good to see you," he said at last. "I never asked your name."

Tatiana's voice dropped to a whisper. "My name is Tatiana, Tatiana Lenusy. I'm looking for work. All I ask in return is a place to sleep inside and a little food to eat."

Gareth's hand gently lifted her chin until their eyes met. "I don't know where you've been or how you survived these past four years, but you are welcome to stay."

"Fifi, too?" she asked, a little fearfully. Not everyone liked dogs.

Fifi poked her small white muzzle out of the sling. A second later an equally petite fuzzy head and two delicate white paws followed. Tatiana scooped the tiny creature into her hands and held her up for Gareth to see. The dog's fur gleamed like freshly fallen snow in the sun. Fifi stood on Tatiana's hand with one paw raised and gave Gareth a pathetic, pleading look.

Gareth scratched his head and stifled a laugh. His brows rose with a mixture of wonder and skepticism. "Didn't think that pup would live. Looks kind of fragile."

Tatiana smiled and the dog's tail fluttered. They were used to that kind of reaction. "She survived because of your kindness. Fifi's really no bother and eats very little. She's always clean and does tricks as well. Perhaps she can entertain your customers."

"I'd like to hear what you and Fifi have been up to," he said. "And why you were running. You can tell me all about it once you're settled in."

Relief flooded Tatiana. "Thank you, sir."

"Oh, don't thank me yet, Tatiana, and call me Gareth. There are some rules you should know about first. No private business is allowed with the customers and no visitors in the sleeping quarters. Unless you're cleaning or delivering food or messages, the guest rooms are off limits. I'm not running a brothel here. Treat every customer with respect. No foul language, absolutely no drugs, and keep yourself clean. Sabrina has seniority and assigns daily chores. Everyone takes a turn working the generator each night. Stealing or cheating gets you thrown out. No second chances. Do you understand?"

"Yes, I understand,"

"Good, go back there." Gareth pointed to a door at the back of the room just as a nineteen-year-old woman poked her head in. Wavy red hair framed her fair skin and a frown creased her face.

"Gareth," she said with an exasperated southern drawl. "Your nephew's here and he's already drunk."

Gareth mumbled under his breath. "He hitting on you again, Bobby Sue?"

"Like a baseball bat."

Gareth let air hiss from his mouth. He closed his eyes. His voice sounded strained. "I'll be right there. Send one of the others in for now and help Cook in the kitchen."

"Thanks, Gareth. I'll let Sabrina know."

"Bobby Sue, I'd like you to meet Tatiana. She'll be working here. Point her in Sabrina's direction for me."

"Welcome to Gareth's place, Tatiana," said Bobby Sue. A warm inviting smile filled her freckled face. "That's the smallest little thing I've seen short of a newborn kitten," she said, pointing at Fifi, before wiping her hand on the apron that covered her calf-length skirt.

"Her name is Fifi," said Tatiana, taking the offered hand. Fifi's tail beat rapidly.

"Well, welcome to Fifi as well. Y'all just follow me."

"Tatiana," said Gareth, "tell Sabrina you're the new hire and to find you a place to sleep and clean clothes to wear."

"Yes, Gareth."

Tatiana followed Bobby Sue into a small sitting room.

"Y'all new to Atherton?"

"Yes," whispered Tatiana. "We arrived today." She left out the part about sneaking into town before dawn so she wouldn't have to deal with the creepy-looking guards at the gates.

"I've been here about two years now. It's a pretty fine place." Bobby Sue frowned. "Most of it anyway. Stay away from the west side of town, especially to the south. That's where Mako and his goons hang out. Rough neighborhood. Some of those bastards tried to drag me into his brothel last year."

A chill ran down Tatiana's back. Memories haunted her, faces, laughing, jeering. "Who's Mako?" she asked, careful to keep her voice neutral.

Bobby Sue's face wrinkled as if she were sucking on a sour fruit. "Mayor Mako Scaffeld. That slime moved into town a little over a year ago. Turned his house into a brothel and sweet-talked his way onto the town council. Frankly, I don't know how he got elected mayor. You know Gareth pulled this whole town together after things fell apart. He started that council. Used to head it up before Mako. Now we have all sorts of troublemakers runnin' around, drugs, and some rough-necked mercenary runnin' the militia. I swear it's not safe to go out after dark anymore.

"Anyway, enough gloomy talk. It's almost time for evenin' assignments so y'all better hustle up those stairs and to the right. Sabrina always checks the linens this time of day. You can't miss her. Oh, and you better hide that cute critter for now. Sabrina has a nasty temper and hates dogs. I think she's scared of them or somethin'."

"Do you want me to tell her about Gareth's nephew?"

"Danged. I almost forgot 'bout that with all our chit-chatting.

Yes, please tell her."

Bobby Sue dashed off, leaving Tatiana by the stairway door. She placed a hand on the knob and took a deep breath. Memories of the Cataclysm flashed through her mind and her palms began to sweat—a giant ball of fire across the sky, massive floods and earthquakes.

Would this place be any different from the others she had visited since the Cataclysm? There was only one way to find out. With Fifi carefully stowed in her sling, Tatiana pulled the door open and climbed the stairs.

Chapter Two

Gareth

Almost all nine of the sturdy round tables and chairs around the room were filled with laughing and talking revelers when Gareth entered his tavern. Everyone had a drink of some kind, and a few had bowls of Karen Cook's stew. Gareth couldn't help but smile as he scanned the room. His late wife, Margaret, would have liked the friendly bantering going on. A far cry from the cluttered and dismal mess it had been when he first opened, the walls were now painted a soft cream and paintings ringed the room. All of them were reproductions Margaret had painted before she died. Landscapes of daubed colors, soft brushstrokes of women and children, these creations by Monet and Renoir generated a feeling of windows into another time. It added cheer to an otherwise troubled world. Lights also hung from the ceiling, real electric ones, not lamps and candles, thanks to his generator.

Only two things spoiled his view of the bar room—Margaret's absence and his nephew Joe's ragged figure in a drunken stupor, making lewd gestures at the other patrons. Clear Sky Day wasn't universally observed or even liked, but most in Atherton enjoyed celebrating. Joe wasn't one of them. The other guests had slid farther down the bar to escape his ridicule, doing their best to ignore his ranting. Joe looked at Gareth with bloodshot eyes, took a swig from his mug and slammed it onto the wooden bar.

Gareth scowled at him. "I think you've had enough, Joe. And I've talked to you about bothering Bobby Sue. She's not interested."

Deep furrows creased Joe's brow below his receding hairline and he hunched over his drink. Too much booze and a hard life had taken their toll on Joe, leaving his twenty-eight-year-old skin wrinkled and dry. His face wore a constant frown and a long, greasy brown beard. A smattering of gray peppered the oily dun-colored ponytail. "Damned Clear Sky Day. All it ever did was bring those freaks."

Joe's voice rose as he spoke, making several heads turn. Gareth's jaw tightened. Those 'freaks' were heroes to some. It seemed as though most people were either strongly for or against the star-touched. Joe seemed to take their existence as a personal affront, although he'd never explained why. Gareth wasn't sure where he stood himself regarding the star-touched. He'd heard some wild stories about the things they could do. On one hand, they could heal injuries and illness, but they had also been said to cause things to burst into flame. That idea made him shudder. The fact remained, though, that even during the riots, when they were being persecuted, many star-touched had stopped to help the injured.

"Joe, we were headed for another ice age. Seeing the stars for the first time in ten months was beautiful."

Joe clutched his mug. A mixture of fear and loathing filled his narrow face, causing his upper lip to curl up on one side. "Beautiful?" His face grew red and his jaundiced eyes narrowed. "Those monsters showed up at the same time."

Gareth wiped away the bits of saliva that had splattered from Joe's mouth onto his apron and tried not to sound too patronizing. "If it weren't for them a lot more folks would be dead."

He gave Gareth a nasty look and shoved his empty mug so hard it would have flown off the counter if Gareth hadn't caught it. "If it weren't for them damned star-touched, a lot of folk'd be alive as well. I'm telling you, Uncle, they're demons, monsters, they'll burn us all alive."

Gareth placed the mug in the dirty dish bucket and gave Joe a hard look. "It's talk like that that started the riots and got thousands of people killed. Do you really want to start that up again? Like it or not, the star-touched are here to stay. We may as well let them do their stuff and help people. There's been enough death."

"You sound like one of those wackos telling everyone the star-touched are sainted gifts from God." He wiped a dirty sleeve across his mouth. "Damned floods, earthquakes, and volcanic eruptions. Was the Cataclysm nothin' but God's punishment?"

Gareth shook his head. League of the Stars disciples were everywhere these days. They were easy to spot because of the bright yellow and orange stars painted on their foreheads.

"The only thing I'm sure of right now is that I survived the worst nightmare mankind has ever faced, and if we're going to survive in the future we need to work together. We gotta stop killing each other over stupid things."

"Whatever." Joe tossed a few coins on the counter as he pushed his stool away from the bar. "See you around, Uncle."

A few of the other patrons nodded as Joe stumbled to the door and slipped out. Family was still family, no matter how damaged, and Joe was his only living blood relative. Gareth's sister was almost killed by Joe's dad during one of his drunken rages before she threw him out. Some folks didn't even have that these days.

The tavern door swung open, jingling the bell above it. Gareth tensed as soon as he saw the figure saunter in, and he wasn't the only one. Marlo P. Snider, the man Mako had hired and appointed as head of the militia, called himself a commander, but Gareth doubted he had ever been in a real military outfit. If he had, it probably wasn't out of any sense of duty like Gareth had done. Snider came across as the kind who would have joined the military just to kill people. Gareth had seen him kick a cat that had been foolish enough to walk too close to him and then crush its head. An almost cheerful snarl had been on his face when he killed that cat. Snider's dark brown, almost black eyes, surveyed the crowd now as he approached Gareth. They were cold calculating eyes, the eyes of a killer, and everywhere they passed, silence followed. A scar drew a pale stripe across his face. It took all Gareth's self-control not to reach for his shotgun.

"What do you want?" said Gareth, barely keeping the distain out of his voice.

Snider's eyes narrowed, then he slapped a coin on the table. "Let's start with a beer."

The metal disk glimmered on the table, but Gareth didn't care if it was a steel washer or another rare gold coin like the one

Tatiana had given him. Damned if he was going to be intimidated in his own tavern. Neither of them moved for a long while, as the rest of the room held their breath.

"Whatever," said Snider. He turned to the man next to him at the bar and glared until the guy scurried away, leaving his mug behind. Snider picked it up and drained it in a single gulp.

"Get out, Snider."

"Sure." Snider stepped away from the bar, then returned, pulling something from his pocket. A smirk twisted his face. "After I deliver this and get your reply." He slapped a folded piece of paper on the counter next to the coin.

Gareth looked at the document, recognizing the shark-shaped wax seal right away. "Never pictured you as Mako's delivery boy."

Snider just shrugged as Gareth broke the seal and began to read. He felt his face flush as he rescanned the words before crumpling the paper into a tight ball. "Tell your boss to forget it, Snider. And get off MY property."

"I'd reconsider if I were you, Gareth. It's a mighty generous offer."

"Not a chance. This is one property Mako's not getting his grubby little paws on."

Snider's smile ended at his lips, never reaching further than a superficial mask. Every eye in the place followed him to the door. Even after he was gone, the joviality never fully returned.

Chapter Three

Five Years Eight Months ADR – April

Tatiana brushed away the tears that blurred her vision as she raced ahead of the mob. How many places would she have to leave because of what she was? She and Fifi had been in the tiny village less than a month. All she'd done was heal the boy's broken back so he could walk again. She'd been trying to help, but using star-touched power was against their beliefs; it was evil. The star-touched were evil.

Maybe they were right; maybe the star-touched were cursed. Every time people found out about her someone got hurt. As soon as they realized what Tatiana had done, the preacher had ordered the boy killed. Tatiana's hands trembled as she held Fifi close, the image of the boy's father cutting his son's throat burned in her mind. Bile churned in her gut. She hadn't been fast enough to stop them. How could healing the injured be wicked?

Someday she'd find a place to call home. Someday she'd find people who wouldn't cringe in horror at the power she possessed. Maybe someday she'd stop cringing from that same power herself.

Tatiana

Cheerful humming echoed in the hall as Tatiana reached the top of the main stairway. The words and title escaped Tatiana's memory, but the music reminded her of happier times. A young woman stood in front of a closet down the hall. With each mark on her clipboard, the woman's deep-blue chintz dress rippled.

"That's a very pretty tune," said Tatiana.

The woman nearly dropped her clipboard as she turned. Her long black hair whipped around. A frown creased her forehead when she caught sight of Tatiana, and her hazel eyes narrowed.

"Who the hell are you?"

Tatiana lowered her eyes. Apparently Gareth's rule didn't apply to everyone. "I'm sorry, I didn't mean to startle you, but your humming was nice. You must be Miss Sabrina. My name is Tatiana. Gareth told me to tell you that I was the new hire and to find me clothes and a bed."

"Not another one." Sabrina grimaced as she studied Tatiana. "Things are tight enough with Mako taking away business. You're thin as a twig. I bet you couldn't even lift a piece of firewood."

Sabrina stalked around Tatiana like a predator sizing up its prey, finally grabbing her by the chin and turning her head this way and that. The scowl didn't leave Sabrina's face as she examined Tatiana's teeth. Tatiana endured the inspection without complaint. It wouldn't be the first or last time she had been examined like a piece of meat. Sabrina continued to poke and mutter under her breath.

"Well, you look healthy enough," said Sabrina. "Have you any skills? Can you read? Do numbers? This is a business. We have no room here for slackers."

Tatiana kept her head turned down, her voice soft and wispy. "I'm stronger than I look and more than willing to do my fair share of work. My math skills are good and I love reading. I can also sew, cook, and I'm well versed in herbs and herbal remedies."

Finally, Sabrina's ego appeared to be curbed. Tatiana held her breath as Fifi squirmed in her sling. The movement shattered the brief calm.

Sabrina jumped back, a panicked look on her face. "What the hell is that thing?"

Fifi poked her head out of the bag and tilted it to the side, examining Sabrina with an unhappy eye. The dog's ears were cocked up and forward, listening intently. Sabrina frowned, and Tatiana felt the woman's fear rise. "That thing is not staying in my house. Get it out of here this second!"

Stay calm, Fifi.

The thought was aimed at Fifi, but Tatiana steeled her own emotions. There was no way she and Fifi were going to be separated. Tatiana's head didn't move, but her eyes peered up through her thick dark lashes, steady and unwavering. "Gareth said Fifi could stay."

For a moment Sabrina gaped at her. Anger boiled, spinning like a twister around the room. Sabrina's hands clenched and unclenched at her sides.

"Damned old fool," Sabrina muttered. She brushed past Tatiana and began to march down the hall, then turned, her upper lip curled in distain. "Hurry up and follow me. I don't have time to waste. It's almost time for assignments."

Tatiana followed Sabrina through the winding hallways. Every so often, Sabrina pointed at a door or down a hallway giving directions. It seemed an unusually long tour, especially when Sabrina circled the second floor three times, twice before going upstairs and again on the way down.

Back on the ground floor, Sabrina handed Tatiana a shapeless, dull-gray cotton dress. "Wash up here, put your things in the last room on the third floor, and report to the common room in fifteen minutes. If you're late, you will be locked out of the room and given extra duties as punishment."

"Yes, Miss Sabrina," said Tatiana. She kept her face neutral, but her irritation brewed at the woman's attempt to intimidate her.

"We're going to have to hustle, Fifi," said Tatiana after Sabrina left them standing in the doorway.

She ducked into the washroom, quickly stripped out of her threadbare clothes and scrubbed down using the lukewarm water in the sink. With only a few minutes to spare, she and Fifi sprinted up to the third floor, left their things, then raced back down. A locked door barred their path, forcing them to run for the second entrance to the common room. Sabrina stood just inside the door as Tatiana rounded the corner. The woman's jaw dropped when she saw them and her eyes narrowed.

Sabrina slammed and locked the door, which left only one route, the longest. Anger boiled just below the surface in Tatiana's mind. Energy bubbled up, lending speed to her feet as she raced back up to the second floor and down the steps on the other side of the building. She and Fifi reached the third door ahead of Sabrina, threw it open, and brushed past her without comment.

Sabrina grabbed Tatiana's arm just above the elbow and spun her around. "How the hell did you do that?"

Tatiana glanced at the fingers digging into her arm, then looked at Sabrina. While her heart beat rapidly, Tatiana was far from out of breath. Energy still coursed through her, and she could feel Sabrina's heart skip a beat, see the fear and inadequacy that drove her hunger for power. Such a beautiful person. Such a sad and ugly heart. But giving in would change nothing.

"You told me to hurry. I did," Tatiana said, letting a steely tone slip into her voice. "Release me."

Sabrina stared at her, instinctively loosening her grip. Her other hand, ready to deliver a slap, halted at the sound of a growl. The unusually deep noise emanated from the minuscule canine at Tatiana's feet. Fifi's teeth gleamed menacingly. Nervous laughter burst out of Sabrina's mouth. She snapped her foot at the dog only to meet empty air. Thrown off balance, she grabbed at the nearest wall for support.

Too late, Tatiana noticed Fifi pull in more energy. *No, Fifi, not now!* Before Tatiana could act, the tiny poodle began to change, transforming into a two-hundred pound behemoth with dark, bristling fur and a mouth big enough to hold Sabrina's head. Sabrina stood frozen in terror, staring at the two-inch-long teeth as Fifi's hot breath beat on her face. Tatiana wanted to cry.

"Fifi, come," she said, then hurried down the hall toward the common room fighting back tears. Would they even last one night before being thrown out?

Companion, friend, bonded... But right now all Tatiana felt for the little dog was anger. She rushed into the common room without looking back. The two way door closed with a soft swish. How long would it take for Sabrina to tell Gareth? Faces looked up as she entered, forcing Tatiana to bury her emotions. The effort left an ache in her throat.

Bobby Sue grinned. "Look at you all cleaned up, Tatiana. You look like one of them beautiful princesses in a fairytale, even in that sack Sabrina picked for you. If she ain't jealous yet she will be. Now don't you go a'blushin' on me." Bobby Sue barely took the time to breathe before she continued. "We were sort of takin' bets on whether you would make it back here in time. We've all been through Sabrina's dizzyin' tour. Glad to see I won. Don't be shy. Y'all come here and meet everyone."

Still reeling from the confrontation with Sabrina, Tatiana moved closer to the five people in the room. Several of them looked around nervously at Bobby Sue's words. The youngest, a grim-faced fifteen-year-old wearing oversized denim pants and a t-shirt, was the first to shuffle over. Barely five feet tall, with chocolate-colored skin that glistened, it wasn't until the teen spoke that Tatiana was certain of her gender.

"Jill," the girl said, through pursed lips, as she eyed Tatiana. "You have no idea how glad I am to have a newbie here."

"Jill here's only been with us a few months," said Bobby Sue, as Tatiana shook Jill's hand. Bobby Sue's smile faded, a sad tone of disapproval slipped into her voice. "Sabrina likes to make life miserable for any newcomers just to show she's in charge, so be prepared. Gareth doesn't know. She's the sweetest glass of tea when he's around."

"Got him wrapped up round her little finger, that one does," Jill said.

"Hush, she'll hear you," said a woman in her thirties with bouncy brown curls. Her round face looked pinched and she glanced over her shoulder down the hall, twisting the end of her apron into a knot.

"Take it easy, Cook," said Bobby Sue, "or you'll scare Tatiana away. Don't you worry 'bout Sabrina, Tatiana. She's a pill but Gareth is a great person to work for. The pay is good and he's never laid a hand on anyone. In fact, he's downright protective. Sort of like mom and dad all wrapped in one."

"Yeah," said Jill. "You just have to deal with the wicked witch of the west. Now where's that little dog Bobby Sue keeps talking about?"

Tatiana's eyes searched the room until she spotted Fifi hiding under an armchair in the corner, ears and tail drooping.

One of the other women spotted Fifi a moment later and scooped her up like a toy. Fifi's fluffy tail whipped back and forth, drinking in the attention like a thirsty alcoholic. Tatiana watched them coo over the little dog, trying not to panic as Sabrina marched into the room, tension etched on her face. Everyone focused on the head woman, although Jill ducked her head and stuffed her hands in her pockets. An uneasy silence fell on the room. Cook continued to twist the end of her apron. Only Bobby Sue actually met Sabrina's eyes. A greenish cast filled Sabrina's face when she saw Fifi, and she grabbed the back of a chair, avoiding Tatiana's eyes.

"You feeling okay, Sabrina?" asked Bobby Sue. "You look real pale."

Sabrina glared at the woman. "I'm fine," she said with a sharp snap. "Just a little tired. Jill, take the new girl and show her how to run the generator and mop the floors. Keep her away from the customers. Bobby Sue, go to the bar. The rest of you have the same assignments as last night. Now get to work!"

Jill rolled her eyes, took Tatiana's hand, and mumbled under her breath. "So much for a reprieve from the slop jobs. Come on."

Reprieve indeed, thought Tatiana as everyone scurried to follow Sabrina's orders. How long? How long would it take for Sabrina to convince Gareth to throw her out? Would there be a lynch mob as well? Tatiana bit her lip as she followed Jill, hoping the girl wouldn't notice her shaking hands. All she wanted was to live an ordinary life like anyone else.

"But you're not like everyone else." Shivers ran down Tatiana's spine as the voice echoed in her mind.

19

Chapter Four

The Day of Reckoning, or Cataclysm as some people call it, began when a rogue meteor struck the Atlantic. The horrific tsunamis, earthquakes and eruptions it spawned redrew our landscape and our old way of life. So began our new dawn.
William Darwinian
Official Chronicler for the League of the Stars

Bobby Sue

"Lazy, no good slob," said Sabrina. "Go tend to those chickens."

Bobby Sue jumped out of the way as Sabrina stormed out of the tavern dragging Jill by the ear. Several dirty sheets spilled out of her basket and she hurried to pick them up before Sabrina noticed. The woman had been on a worse rampage than usual this past week. Poor Tatiana limped for a day after working the generator her first night. An hour on that bike contraption was tough. Four hours was cruel, even for Sabrina.

Jill grimaced. "Let go. That hurts."

"Quit complaining and shut up," said Sabrina. "You better gather all of the eggs today. I won't stand for any more waste."

"I did the best I could. That rooster is crazy."

Sabrina spun around and glared at the girl, still keeping a tight grip on her ear. Before Bobby Sue could slip away, Sabrina's eyes glowered in her direction. The woman's nose wrinkled, accentuating her scowl. "What are you staring at? Put those filthy sheets in the washroom and get back here now."

"Yes, Sabrina."

"And you," Sabrina said, turning back to Jill. "Better start doing what you're told."

"I was," said Jill, a bit too forcefully. "You told me to mop the floor."

Sabrina's hand struck Jill's face with a sharp thwack. "Any more of your sass and you'll sleep in the gutter. That floor should have been done an hour ago."

Jill's face looked pinched, but she didn't yelp. "Yes, Sabrina."

Bobby Sue bit her lip to keep from correcting Sabrina. There was no point in mentioning that Jill was sent to clean the floor only fifteen minutes ago. All that would do is make her crankier.

"Make sure this child does as she's told," said Sabrina, shoving Jill at Bobby Sue. After she's finished gathering eggs she's to do the laundry with the new girl."

"I thought you wanted me to do the washin' today?" said Bobby Sue.

Sabrina's eyes narrowed. "There's been a change. Gareth is busy fixing the roof. Watch the store while I take care of some business in town. Do. You. Understand?"

"Yes, Sabrina," said Bobby Sue.

"Where is that girl, anyway?"

"Who, Tatiana?" Bobby Sue asked. "She's been up since early this mornin' cleanin' and helpin' Cook in the kitchen."

"That's not her job," snapped Sabrina. "Make sure she does her chores instead of loafing about."

Sabrina didn't wait for a response before turning away. Once the door swung shut behind her Bobby Sue let out the breath she'd been holding.

"Gees, Jill," said Bobby Sue. "You tryin' to get kicked out."

"No," mumbled Jill. "I was doing what she told me to do. Not my fault she keeps changing her mind. Why she gotta be so mean?"

Bobby Sue shrugged. "Insecure I guess."

"Don't know why she's worried. Gareth treats her like his kid."

"He cares about all of us," said Bobby Sue, guiding Jill into the kitchen.

Karen, who went by the name Cook, stood at the counter preparing biscuits for the morning meal. Her petite five-foot-four figure twisted as she worked, directing several of the other women in the kitchen with practiced experience.

"Maybe," said Jill. "But not like her."

"I think Sabrina's extra special 'cause she was the first one he took in. I overheard him mention that he hired Sabrina only a few weeks after Tatiana came through Atherton the first time. Said he couldn't stand any more kids beggin' or trying to sell themselves for food."

"What was that about Tatiana?" said Cook.

"Actually, we were talkin' about Sabrina and Gareth," said Bobby Sue. "She really doesn't like Tatiana for some reason. Sabrina changed the duty list again."

"Of course she did." A baking sheet of dough balls sat on the counter along with a bowl of cheese cubes. Cook pressed one of the cubes into some dough, sealed it with a twist, and put it on the baking sheet. "Just sent Tatiana out with some compost. Hope Sabrina eases up soon. That girl is a hard worker. I'd hate for Sabrina to drive her away."

"Her dog is cute too," said Jill. "But boy is that girl shy."

"I'll get her out of her shell," said Bobby Sue. "Mark my words."

Cook smiled and continued to work. "I don't doubt you, Bobby Sue. You have a special way with people. Even Sabrina isn't as nasty to you."

"You ever meet Gareth's wife?" asked Jill as she reached for a cube of cheese.

"No," said Cook, gently slapping Jill's hand away. "She died long before the Cataclysm. Cancer, I think. They never got to have any kids."

"And now he's got a bunch of daughters to make up for it," said Bobby Sue.

A grin filled Jill's face. "And one evil witch."

"Jill!" Cook's face turned as pale as the flour."

"You sassy little imp," said Bobby Sue, struggling not to smile. "You best get out there and gather them eggs before Sabrina gets back."

Jill snagged a chunk of cheese as she ran out the door. "I'd like to see Sabrina gathering eggs and moppin floors."

"Wouldn't that would be a sight," laughed Bobby Sue.

Cook shook her head. "Jill has a lot of spirit."

"She does indeed," said Bobby Sue. "Sure hope it doesn't get her in too much trouble. I best get to the store. Tell Tatiana she and Jill have laundry duty when she comes in."

Chapter Five

Three Years Three Months ADR – November

Tools lay scattered haphazardly on the floor around the man in the worn dungarees. A small glass bottle was stuffed in his back pocket. The smell of sweat and alcohol almost made Tatiana turn back, but she inched closer. The Abuda Orphanage opened two years ago, a year after the Cataclysm. It was supposed to be a school as well, and Tatiana was determined to learn as much as she could, but in the three months since she had arrived, little teaching had occurred.

"What the hell do you want?" his voice was slow and slurred.

The man's bloodshot eyes looked Tatiana's way, but it was unclear how focused they were. She stepped back and lowered her gaze. People were uneasy when she looked at them. At thirteen Tatiana liked to pretend she was a child like any other, but the Cataclysm and Clear Sky Day had changed that. Did the people here know what she was? What she could do?

"I'm sorry to disturb you, Sir. I just wanted to watch and learn how to fix things."

"You the one that hangs out with the creepy little brat. I don't want you staring over my shoulder. Go read one of your books if you want to learn."

As soon as Tatiana turned away, she heard him take a swig from his bottle. Read a book he had said. She didn't want to tell him she already had, that she knew exactly what was wrong with the generator. Words on a page had always been magic to her, the kind of magic that holds on and never lets go.

Tatiana

Each work day started before dawn and lasted well into the

night. Since arriving, Tatiana had already scrubbed the floors seven times, sanitized the outhouse and bathrooms twice a day, washed pots almost nonstop and run every little errand that Sabrina could think of. Then there was the generator. She and Jill had ridden the stationary bike Gareth had rigged to the thing for four hours that first night and every night since. The exhausting work wasn't unexpected. Tatiana had worked harder in worse places. At least here most of the people were nice. In fact, Sabrina remained the only one Tatiana didn't care for.

Fifi sent her an image of Gareth with his scruffy face, balding head of gray-streaked hair, and tall stocky build. Gareth smiled and laughed. Even his eyes twinkled, making Fifi's tail wag rapidly. Did he know how Sabrina treated the other employees? She was quite the actress when he was around and Gareth seemed too blinded by his paternal love for her to see her darker side. It wasn't all fake, however. Tatiana could sense genuine affection from Sabrina for Gareth.

"Yes, Fifi, I like Gareth, too. But more importantly, Gareth helped us when no one else would. He could have chased me off, like so many others had, but he didn't. You would have died without his help. Something is making him feel unhappy. We're going to change that, but to do so we need to be as low key as possible."

"If it's not too late already."

Tatiana bit her cheek. That voice popped into her mind more each day. It took a moment to shake off concerns of what that may portend and refocus on Fifi. The little dog whimpered and lowered her head. A pair of red bows adorned her ears, but Tatiana had no idea where they came from. She ruffled Fifi's fur, careful not to disturb the ribbons, and stood. She needed to get back to the house before Sabrina noticed how long it took her to throw out the trash. There was only so long she could sit in the corner of the yard near the compost heap without being missed.

On her way back to the kitchen, she noticed a proliferation of weeds in the vegetable garden. If there was time she would add weeding to her early morning list. The herb garden near the house was lacking in content but looked better cared for. Tatiana brushed her hand across the rosemary bush as she passed, letting its aroma bring back pleasant memories. Growing up with a botanist who specialized in herbal remedies, Tatiana had never taken any over-the-counter medicine or drugs. Mama always had a natural concoction for every ache, pain, or illness and she'd passed on her skills to Tatiana. A sharp twang of sadness rippled through Tatiana, causing her stomach to knot. She missed Mama.

"You miss a lot of things." hissed the voice.

The sound of clanking pots and chopping knives emanated from the kitchen as Tatiana returned to the house with the empty compost bucket. Bacon sizzled and its scent wafted through the air, making her mouth water. Even Fifi's tongue had begun to drip.

"You've been reassigned," said Cook as soon as she entered the building.

Tatiana sighed. She'd been looking forward to helping in the kitchen today. "What am I scrubbing this time?"

"Laundry with Jill. I'll send her to you as soon as she gets back from gathering eggs."

Loud shrieks and squawks shattered the morning stillness, making Tatiana's heart jump. Without hesitation, both she and Fifi dashed back outside toward the small chicken coop on the other side of the storage shed before anyone else could react. Jill lay curled in the center of the coop surrounded by smashed eggs. A wicker basket sat trampled in one corner. Old Henry, the rooster, scratched and pecked viciously at the poor girl. Bloody patches stained Jill's clothes and skin where the bird had pecked out bits of flesh.

Transforming in mid-air, Fifi pounced on the fowl the second Tatiana opened the gate. The dog's huge mouth held most of the bird's fluffed out body, hauling him to the other side of the coop while Tatiana scooped up Jill and carried the terrified girl to the house. Energy coursed through Tatiana, creating a prickly sensation in her fingers. Flustered and confused, Old Henry lay where Fifi tossed him, staring as the dog kicked the door closed.

They neared the kitchen door as the other employees rushed out. Bobby Sue, the first to reach them, cleared a path into the building. Jill shook and cried as Tatiana placed her gently on the floor near several sacks of flour. Blood streamed through her fingers, which she held tightly clamped over her left eye.

"Good Lord," exclaimed Bobby Sue. "What happened?"

"Old Henry attacked her," said Tatiana, taking the dishtowel Bobby Sue held. "Get me some clean bandages and hot water."

Tatiana did a quick survey of Jill's wounds while Cook saw to the water and another girl ran to the storeroom for bandages. She ran her hands over the multitude of cuts and gouges marring Jill's rich brown skin, painfully aware of the other women hovering around nervously. Most of the wounds were superficial but many would leave scars. Once she managed to pry Jill's hands away, she saw the deep cut over the eye, which reached down toward her eyeball. Blood oozed out of the wound and the eyeball itself tilted at an odd angle. Tatiana's heart beat rapidly and the voice echoed in her head.

"You need to heal her or she'll lose the eye."

"If the others see," she thought back, *"they'll know."*

"Then hide it."

Fifi began to whimper. Tatiana needed to act before anyone else saw the extent of the injury. Her throat felt tight, but she knew what needed to be done. Instinct took over.

"Bobby Sue, I need the small gray bag under my bed. It's in the brown backpack. And clear the room."

The urgency in her voice left no room for questions. Everyone left immediately, even Cook, twisting the corner of her apron as she did. As soon as they were alone, Tatiana placed her hand over Jill's eye and took a deep breath. She could feel the energy bubbling and building like syrup in a pot. The power always rested near, carefully bottled, but this time Tatiana let it go. Tingly warmth flowed through her arms and hands. Beneath those hands, Jill's panicked breathing eased and her body went limp, as if she were sleeping. Tatiana's mind sank deep inside the wound, carefully cleaning and knitting the flesh back together. She was only vaguely aware of Fifi watching, waiting, guarding. How many times had she used her powers to heal? Tatiana couldn't remember. She wasn't even sure how she did it. Fifi's mind flashed a warning as she finished. Tatiana pulled in the energy just as Bobby Sue returned, carrying her bag of dried herbs.

After wiping her shaky hands on a dishtowel, Tatiana took

the bag and rummaged for the right herb. For a moment, her eyes lost focus. The energy she had used to heal Jill had left her feeling light-headed. Finally, Tatiana found the correct herb and tossed a pinch of it into the bowl of hot water Bobby Sue handed her. Without speaking, she and Bobby Sue finished cleaning Jill's wounds and wrapped them in clean cloth.

Gareth burst into the room just as they finished, red-faced and breathing hard. He paled when he saw Jill and the pile of bloody rags. "Oh my God. Is she okay?"

"She's going to be fine."

"It's that blasted rooster!" Bobby Sue burst into tears. "That vicious beast attacked her. If Tatiana hadn't pulled her out of there, it would have killed her!"

Without another word, he picked up a large kitchen knife and stormed out the door.

Concern overcame Tatiana's fatigue. With an effort, she forced herself up and stumbled after Gareth. Life was too precious to waste, even a psychotic rooster's.

She caught up with Gareth as he opened the door to the coop. Old Henry raised his feathers and voiced a warning, but as soon as he spotted Fifi, he darted behind the hen house with a nervous squawk.

"Good," said the voice. *"Maybe he can learn some manners."*

"No, Gareth," she cried. "Please, don't kill him. I know he's nasty, but we need a rooster to make more chickens. I'll teach him, Fifi and I will. We'll look after him. See that he behaves... Please."

Gareth looked at the cowering bird and then over at Tatiana. She could see the surprise and indecision on his face. Finally, he took a deep breath, and as he let it out, she saw some of the anger seep out of him.

"That bastard so much as bumps anyone else again, or the other birds, and I'll have it spit and roasted for dinner. Is that understood?"

Tatiana threw her arms around Gareth without thinking, then jumped back and stared at the ground. "Thank you."

"Don't get too excited. This is just a stay of execution. As soon as we have a replacement, that beast is bound for the stew pot."

Tatiana nodded and headed back to the house.

"So when are you going to face your own fear?"

Tatiana shuddered as a sudden chill rippled up her spine.

Chapter Six

Five Years ADR – November

Cold wind whipped sheets of freezing rain into Tatiana's face, making it sting. She trudged on feet that felt like blocks of ice over the rock strewn ground. Fifi huddled in her sling, drenched and shivering. Finally, Tatiana noticed a dark shadow in the rock wall ahead. The cave opened a little farther in, the remnants of a campfire long abandoned sat in the center, and a pile of wood lay stacked against one wall. Tatiana built a small fire and stretched out her wet clothes to dry. Once wrapped in a woolen blanket, she nibbled on dried fruit and nuts while Fifi gnawed on a piece of jerky.

Fatigue and warmth made her eyelids grow heavy. A distant bark startled her awake. The fire had burned low and Fifi was nowhere in sight. Outside the storm still raged as Tatiana dressed. Lighting a candle she had scavenged from an abandoned home, Tatiana searched the cave. Almost hidden above a pile of rocks she found a narrow opening. A small yip echoed from the other side.

"Fifi?"

Another bark answered her. Tatiana scrambled up the debris pile and squeezed into the opening. Instead of the natural tunnel she had expected, the fissure opened into a concrete lined hallway large enough to admit a vehicle. At the bottom of the incline lay a pile of canvas bags, neatly stacked on a wheeled cart. Fifi sat on the pile wagging her tail. Each swish of her tail dislodged small metal disks that fell to the ground like raindrops. Candlelight glinted off gold coins. There wasn't much use for the things these days, but perhaps one would be enough to repay Gareth for his gift last year—if they survived long enough to make it back there.

Tatiana

"But we barely know anything about the girl, Gareth, except that she begged a can of food off you four years ago."

Tatiana didn't mean to overhear, but Sabrina's voice carried down the hall. So did the anger.

"I know something really bad happened that's had her running scared. She'll talk about it when she's ready."

"And what about that gold coin she gave you? If she had that what did she need a job for? It doesn't make sense."

"We've been through this, Sabrina."

"Business hasn't been good since Mako opened that market on the other side of town. What if she scares away the rest of our customers?

"Don't be ridiculous. You need help in here. We need help. "No we don't."

"Sabrina," said Gareth. "You're like a daughter to me. You may be a genius when it comes to business, but you have a lot to learn about being part of a family. There's no need to do everything yourself."

"But..."

"And," he continued, cutting her off. "As the eldest daughter, the others all look up to you."

"I don't want any more little sisters," said Sabrina.

Gareth laughed. "Spoken like a true older sibling. Just give her a chance.

"I'm just not comfortable around her."

"I don't understand why. What has she done to make you feel this way?"

"Nothing," said Sabrina.

"Just let her work in the store today. You need someone out here to help. Jill is in no shape to greet customers and everyone else is busy. Try her out and we'll talk again this evening."

A growing pit of fear burned in Tatiana's gut. Why hadn't Sabrina told Gareth about Fifi that first night? And why hadn't she said anything now when he asked her directly? That's what really made no sense. Tatiana knew damned well why Sabrina didn't want her around. But as far as she could tell, nothing had been done to ensure her dismissal.

During Old Henry's attack yesterday Sabrina had been out on an errand. Not uncommon in itself, but no one knew where she had gone. Her main concern upon return was more for the smashed eggs than Jill's welfare, although she did feign distress to Gareth. She may even have felt a little worried somewhere underneath the act. Even so, if Jill hadn't been sound asleep, Tatiana had the impression that Sabrina would have sent her back to work regardless of the bandages and blood loss. In addition, Gareth had insisted that Tatiana stay inside and care for the girl, so Sabrina had to help finish Jill's chores. Sabrina's anger and resentment had cast a pall on everyone's mood since then. She only acted pleasant near Gareth; although today she sounded more like a whiny child.

Walking quietly came naturally to Tatiana, but now she made an effort to make noise so Gareth and Sabrina would hear her. As she entered the store, Gareth smiled, but Sabrina stood with pursed lips, glaring in her direction.

"Bobby Sue said you wanted to see me."

"Yes," said Gareth. "I want you to help Sabrina in the store today."

"Yes, sir," she said, respectfully lowering her eyes.

"Well, then," said Gareth, "I'll be in the back doing some work. Call me if anything comes up."

They stood for several minutes after Gareth left the room.

"Grab those boxes by the front door and stack them neatly in the storeroom," Sabrina finally said. "Don't talk to any of the customers. And keep that thing of yours out of my way."

"Yes, Miss Sabrina."

Rows of shelves filled the store, all laden with odds and ends salvaged from before the Cataclysm as well as a variety of new merchandise. Most items were essentials, like dried food, salt, tools, and nails, but a few novelties nestled amongst them. Tatiana smiled when she saw a stack of Slinkys. Her papa had given her one year ago. The two of them had spent hours watching it walk down the stairs.

A steady stream of customers made purchases all morning while Tatiana lugged boxes. Some used metal coins, others bartered with salvage or homemade and homegrown items.

While she didn't talk to any of the townsfolk, Tatiana did get a pretty good idea of what Gareth had and where things were stored. One thing to say for Sabrina, she had a knack for organization. Every item had a place, a shelf label, and a line in the inventory book by the door of the storeroom. Tatiana doubted a toothpick could go missing without Sabrina knowing about it. And when it came to negotiating for bartered items, Sabrina was an ace at her game.

"You're really good at negotiating," said Tatiana, after their latest customer left. "How did you manage to get that man to pay double what they originally offered for that old pan?"

"Why thank you," said Sabrina. "I've had lots of practice. Maybe someday you'll learn how." Her voice dropped to a whispered growl. "When pigs fly, you little freak. Now shut up and move those barrels of nails back down the aisle. They're too far up."

Tatiana bit her cheek as she turned away. This was the fourth time Sabrina told her to move those barrels this morning. It wasn't the repeated task or Sabrina's harsh tone that made her eyes sting with suppressed tears. The reminder of how different she was hurt more.

"I am a freak."

"You're star-touched."

"Same thing. I'll never have a real home."

Lunch began to sound like a very good idea when Tatiana heard a noisy motor and smelled the strong odor of cooking oil. Fifi cocked her head to the side and sniffed at the curious smell. With one last bang, the motor stopped. She and Fifi poked their heads out of the storage room. Through the glass in the front window, they could just barely make out what looked like an old dirt-covered bus parked outside the store, along with several motorbikes and a truck.

People climbed off the roof, which had a large machine gun mounted on it, and tossed bags down.

A wiry man sporting rugged boots stepped out of the bus and shut the door behind him. He wore a red t-shirt and faded black jeans held up with a wide brown belt and a buckle almost as big as Tatiana's hand. Thick brown hair hung down his back, loosely tied at the nape of his neck with a leather thong, and a small earring dangled from his left ear. His beard was trimmed short. Several bikers dismounted and walked around the bus, eyeing the street and holding their automatic weapons with casual confidence. Two of them looked almost identical with cropped blond hair and leather pants. Their matching clothes were cut loose, yet still revealed their very feminine figures. Only the stones in their necklaces looked different. One had a purple stone and the other blue. On top of the bus, another guard remained at the gun.

"What do you think you're doing?"

Tatiana jumped and spun around. For a moment, she held her breath and her throat tightened. Sabrina walked toward her with Gareth, a pleasant smile plastered on her face. But Tatiana could feel the anger in her words, see it in her eyes.

"I heard the bus." Tatiana knew her voice sounded flustered, but couldn't do anything about it.

"Relax, Sabrina," said Gareth. "She's understandably curious about our friend Marty the Merchant. Not too many vehicles still running these days, and his does have a distinctive aroma."

Before Tatiana could protest, Gareth ushered her outside.

"Gareth! Good to see you," said the wiry man, "Ah, and Sabrina, you look as lovely as ever, but who's this new beauty?"

"Hi, Marty," said Gareth, taking Marty's hand while delivering a heartfelt hug. He motioned to Tatiana. "This is Tatiana. She just started last week."

To Tatiana's chagrin, Marty took her hand and kissed it. His earring, shaped like a small sword, swung back and forth as he spoke. "Ah, mademoiselle, your name is as exotic as your beauty."

Tatiana felt her face turning red while Sabrina bristled with resentment beside her. With a whispered thank you, she stepped back and kept her eyes on the ground. The crowd gathered around the bus was small, but Tatiana felt surrounded, as though everyone stared at her.

"I shouldn't have come out here."

"You have as much right to be out here as anyone else," said that other voice.

While Gareth, Sabrina, and Marty exchanged greetings,

Tatiana inched back toward the door. Not once did she look up, not even when Bobby Sue and the other women came out to greet Marty.

Nearly to the door, a sharp yip brought Tatiana up short. She looked around in alarm and saw that Fifi had leaped onto the step of the bus. Tatiana's gut froze. Why did that dog have to be so irresistibly curious? Sometimes it felt like having a five-year-old. Fifi stood there, wagging her tail frantically.

"Fifi, no. Come back here," she said, hurrying to get the dog before it drew any more attention.

"Well, I'll be," exclaimed Marty. He walked to Fifi and ruffled the fur on her head. "How in blazes did a teacup poodle like you survive all this chaos?"

"Ain't she the cutest little thing," said Bobby Sue.

"I'm sorry, Gareth," said Tatiana, scooping Fifi into her arms. "I'll take her back inside right away."

"Why? Why did you do that, Fifi?"

Tatiana rushed back toward the building, hoping no one would stop her with more questions. She hadn't gone three steps before an image flashed in her mind. Her feet froze and her heart raced again, this time with excitement. Tatiana turned around and returned to the bus. Rust and dirt obliterated any markings on it. Steel panels had replaced most of the windows, but a few glass panes remained. Tatiana lifted her hand and wiped some of the grime away from the glass, stretching onto her toes to peer inside.

"Books! You have books!" she said. A happy smile grew on her face, and Fifi leaped to the ground. It was as if someone had flipped a switch. Suddenly the crowd, which only moments earlier felt smothering, no longer mattered.

"Well ain't you chipper than a wren on a spring morning," said Bobby Sue. "Guess we know what makes you tweet a happy song. What kinda books you like to read?"

Tatiana's felt her face flush. "Everything: science fiction, drama, action and adventure, romance, mystery, science, history, poetry, biographies, fantasy. Whatever I can find."

Marty laughed and slapped Gareth on the back. "That's some reading list. Looks like you adopted a scholar this time."

"She's only been here a week," said Sabrina.

A lump formed in her stomach at Sabrina's sharp tone. Tatiana lowered her eyes so she wouldn't have to see the frown that creased the woman's brow or the way her whole posture stiffened.

"Tatiana's doing just fine," said Gareth. "Do you want a drink before we get started?"

"Maybe a little water." Marty smiled and rubbed his hands together. "Time to get down to business. Tatiana, since this is the first time we've met and you've shown such a keen interest in my books, why don't you go take a look."

Tatiana's head snapped up. Even Sabrina's sharp intake of breath couldn't dampen the excitement that raced through her. At a wave and nod from Gareth, she darted into the bus and eagerly sifted through the piles. There were textbooks, novels, cookbooks, and even a few old computer manuals. Nothing beyond that pile of bound paper mattered. She left Fifi by the door to watch while she searched.

Gareth and Marty chuckled as they entered the bus. After carefully climbing around Tatiana, they moved to the back. Tatiana tuned out their discussion of light bulbs and spare radio parts. She didn't even notice the people who waited outside the bus, chatting amicably under the watchful eyes of Marty's guards. For the next few minutes, breathing in the musty scent of old paper, Tatiana felt at peace. Books had always been a welcome escape from the real world for her, even before the Cataclysm. They also contained little nuggets of knowledge. The one she flipped through now was about chickens. With any luck, she'd learn something to help deal with Gareth's flock.

Chapter Seven

What can the star-touched do? We're still determining the extent of their abilities and some are better at certain skills than others. I'm a fact gatherer, not a scientist, so I'll make this short. All star-touched can heal, although the best healers I've seen are by far Winona, who has medical training, and Tatiana. The power they access stimulates the immune system, which can help the body regenerate damaged or missing body parts, a skill for which I am personally grateful. So, no immune system, and even they can't help you. Same goes for poisons. Wait it out and hope for the best.

William Darwinian
Official Chronicler for the League of the Stars

Bobby Sue

"I've really enjoyed chatting with you, Brother William," said Bobby Sue. "But I gotta get back to work now before the boss wears out her shoe tappin' it the way she is."

Brother William's smile went all the way up to his eyes. "It was a pleasure meeting you, Bobby Sue. Thanks for the warm welcome to Atherton and the tips. Is it okay if I visit some time?"

"Does the sun rise in the east? I'd love to hear more about you, your travels, and the League of the Stars."

"Then you enjoy the rest of your day," said Brother William, "I'll stop by once I'm settled in the League house."

"Maybe I'll come see you preachin' with the others."

"Hope you do."

Bobby Sue had to stop herself from staring at him as he walked away lugging a small suitcase. The League folks had been in Atherton for a year and a half, but this was the first time she'd talked to any of them. Of course the others weren't nearly as cute as Brother William Darwinian. She handed a cup of water to one of Marty's guards, still thinking about how sweet his smile was.

Only Gareth and Tatiana had entered Marty's bus so far, leaving Sabrina to chat with waiting customers. Every few minutes Bobby Sue saw her scowl at the vehicle. No doubt she'd find some way to make things difficult for Tatiana later.

"I don't know which is more incredible," said Gareth, as he and Marty exited the bus. "That you found someone with enough surplus fish for trade, or that they have a working cannery."

Marty laughed and sent a couple of his people in to get Gareth's purchases. "Knew you'd be appreciative. They only just got it running the week before I arrived and didn't have much stock yet, but that'll change in time. They've been buying up every scrap of sheet metal they can find. I think someone's hooked them up to trade with an old steel mill town a few hundred miles away. Industry is slowly growing as communication improves. It just needed facilitators to bring the towns together."

"You mean merchants like you," said Gareth.

"Of course. By the way, I bought every can they had and hid them for months, just for you."

"And I am most grateful," said Gareth, sweeping his hand in a welcoming gesture and bowing slightly.

"Care to wet your whistle?" said Bobby Sue.

"Absolutely." Marty then followed Sabrina into the bus.

Bobby Sue looked at the boxes and piles of books being unloaded and whistled. "That sure is a heap of books."

"Tatiana picked them out," said Gareth. "It's time we got Atherton's library opened again."

"Well ain't that a grand idea," said Bobby Sue. There was barely time to read anything these days, but with so many new choices she'd make time. "Tatiana still on the bus?"

"I sent her out a moment ago to help. You didn't see her?"

Bobby Sue shrugged. "She probably zipped in the door while I was looking the other way."

"Hope she gets back out soon. Sun's glaring right on all those people. I don't want anyone passing out from the heat. By the way, I have some errands I need you to take care of when you've finished delivering those drinks. Feel free to do some of your own shopping, but don't take too long. It's going to be a busy day."

"Sure thing," said Bobby Sue. "I won't be but a minute."

Bobby Sue waved as she left the vender in the town square, then clipped on her new barrette. The scissor-tailed flycatcher shaped clip held the hair off her sweat drenched neck, a welcome relief in this heat. Once she saw the Oklahoma state bird design she had to have it. Bobby Sue hadn't been back home since before the Cataclysm and missed her family. She wasn't even sure if any of them survived.

There were several bakeries in town, but the one she wanted was a little ways off of the regular market area. She paused for a moment to watch several League of the Stars disciples preaching about the star-touched before following a heavenly fragrance to her favorite baker. Her heart sank when she saw only a few paltry buns on the display. Dark circles hung under the baker's eyes and he gazed at the handful of passing people with a weary blank stare.

"You okay?" she asked, noting a recent scrape on his brow and a slight swelling on his left cheek.

"I'm just fine, Bobby Sue," he said, shoving a crumpled piece of paper in his apron pocket. There was a pinched tone to his voice. "What can I get for you today?"

"You sure nothing's wrong? 'Cause you look a bit ruffled up and I swear your hair's gone from black to gray in a week."

He brushed a hand across his kinky hair and smiled as a cloud of white puffed away. "Just some flour. Had a little, um, accident earlier."

"Well that's a relief," she said. "I was hoping for some of your famous meat pastries. You sell out already?"

The baker looked up and down the street before responding in a soft voice that she strained to hear. "Not at all. Just don't want those slovenly excuses for a militia to help themselves. I keep the good stuff hidden inside for my favorite customers. How many do you want?"

"Oh, thank heaven. Do you have a couple dozen or so?"

The baker raised his eyebrows. "That's a big order. Something special going on?"

"Sure is. Marty the merchant just got here. We need some sustenance to get us through the day."

"So I hear. Did you get a peek at his stock?" he asked as he ducked inside for the pastries.

"Not yet, but Gareth already bought a bunch of books and other stuff."

"Really?" He studied her a moment when he came out before wrapping her order. "That's not something he usually carries."

"Yeah, well, Tatiana, the new girl, completely lit up when she saw them books so he bought the lot. Gareth's gonna try to get the library reopened."

"That would be great. There hasn't been one since the librarian died six years ago. This Tatiana must be something special."

"She's real sweet, but kinda shy. Loves readin' somethin' awful."

"Good luck getting council approval for the library. That means hiring a new librarian and fixing up a building. I bet that Hugh Hafley fellow raises a stink. Not sure how that miser managed to get a merchant position on the council."

"Hugh gives me the creeps," said Bobby Sue, suppressing a shudder. "I've seen the way he looks at young girls. Neil isn't a big fan of Gareth's either and he's head of the carpentry guild."

The baker nodded and handed Bobby Sue the pastries. "Those two have been at each other since high school, but Neil is a decent guy. He'll do what's right. Enjoy the pastries."

Her mouth started watering. "I swear you have the best pastries in all of Atherton. They're better than my grams used to make."

The baker grinned. "You're just saying that."

"It's the truth and don't you ever let anyone tell you otherwise."

"Thank you, Bobby Sue. You have a blessed day and say hi to Gareth for me."

"Will do. See you soon."

Carrying such tasty treats made Bobby Sue's four block walk seem like a mile. At least she had Brother William to think about. Halfway back she lifted the basket to her nose and inhaled deeply. She'd have to tell him about this bakery. All her taste buds screamed for her to sink her teeth into a pie, but she managed to resist the urge. Instead, she sighed and partially closed her eyes.

A sweaty hand covered her face and yanked her backward. The basket was ripped from her hand. Bobby Sue could barely breathe let alone scream. The heels of her shoes dug gouges in the gravel as she was dragged between two buildings. Her last glimpse of the main street showed no reaction from anyone.

Still struggling to regain her balance, she clawed at her attacker. A few cusses were her only reward. She couldn't dislodge the hand. Finally, she got her feet under her and kicked back hard. He cussed again and loosened his grip. Bobby Sue clamped her teeth on the fleshy part of his filthy palm and jabbed behind her with her elbows.

"Enough of this," he hissed, slamming her onto the ground. Air rushed out of her lungs as he put his knee on her chest and pressed a knife against her throat. "You move or scream and I'll cut you apart piece by piece. It'd be a shame to damage such a pretty face. Got it? Now keep those daggers to yourself and your feet still."

Tears burned Bobby Sue's eyes and her head throbbed from hitting the ground. Somehow she kept herself from flailing despite the instinct to fight. Gareth wasn't there to help her get away from this thug. No one was.

"That's better," said the man. He smiled at her with a mouth full of half-rotted teeth. Needle marks covered his arms, many of them puffy and red with infection. "Maybe we can have some fun before I turn you over to my client."

"Get your grubby hands off her." Joe's voice echoed down the dark alley.

"Buzz off. This one's mine."

"Like hell she is," said Joe as he charged.

The knife clattered to the ground as Joe's fist landed on the thug's chin. Bobby Sue heard a bone crack, but she wasn't sure if it was from the thug's chin or Joe's hand. Blood dripped down the man's face as he jumped up and drove Joe into a wall. She rolled out of the way as the two men exchanged blows. What Joe lacked in strength, he made up for in speed and ferocity. The other guy staggered back from the onslaught and tripped over some trash. Joe slammed a steady rain of blows with no sign of slowing the attack.

Bobby Sue struggled to her feet and grabbed his arm. "Enough."

Joe looked up, his eyes seemed battle glazed for a moment before they focused on her. The concern on his face took her by surprise. "He didn't hurt you, none, did he, Bobby Sue?"

She touched her neck, remembering the feel of cold steel against it and shook her head. "I'm okay. If you hadn't been here…"

"Ain't no one gonna hurt you while I'm around," said Joe. He cupped her trembling hands in his. "I know I ain't much, but I care about you. I always have."

"I know you do, Joe."

Bloody gashes covered his knuckles, but it was nothing compared to her attacker's face. Joe wasn't her favorite person, but he had just saved her life. She had no doubt he would look after her. At least until he got drunk again. She'd seen enough mean drunks to know she didn't want to get involved with one.

"How's about we get you home."

"Yeah, we should do that," said Bobby Sue, still shaken.

As they exited the alley, a figure blocked their path. "Is there a problem here?"

"No sir, Mr. Mayor," said Joe, holding his head up high. "Not since I stopped that man back there from hurting my friend. She's safe now."

"Is that true, miss?"

Bobby Sue bit back the bile that rose in her throat at Mako's sudden appearance. Joe held her closer than she would have preferred, but she trusted him more than Mako. Something about that man just didn't sit well and it had nothing to do with his wearing a fancy black suit in the middle of summer. Several guards stood beside him. None of them seemed concerned or surprised at a blood drenched man in the alley.

"Yes," she said, once she was sure she could speak without sounding ill.

"Good thing you were nearby," said Mako. He glanced down the alley at the unconscious man and nodded. "Looks like you made short work of the problem. Perhaps you should consider joining the militia."

"Thank you, Mr. Mayor, sir," said Joe. "I'll think on that. Sure glad you happened by."

"Just doing my part to keep Atherton running smoothly."

"Right now I best get Bobby Sue home safely."

"You do that," said Mako. His grin look about as real as a singing pig to her. "We wouldn't want anything else to happen to her. There's been a rash of muggings today. I'll make sure that miscreant gets locked up properly."

Bobby Sue shivered as he flagged a couple of guards and sent them down the alley. Thinking about what almost happened made her heart race again. She hurried away with Joe still clinging to her arm. For once, she didn't mind.

"You saved my life," Bobby Sue said as they neared Gareth's place. "Why don't you come on in? I'm sure Gareth would love for you to stay for supper. Then you'll already be here for Marty's travel news."

He looked at Marty's bus and wrinkled his nose. There was a long line of people waiting to go in. "Nah. I got stuff I need to take care of. Maybe we could go for a walk tomorrow."

Bobby Sue sighed. She wondered how long it would take before he asked her out again. "Joe. I'm real grateful for what you did for me. Really, I am, but I'm not interested in dating. Not now, not ever. I'm sorry."

A scowl creased Joe's face and his shoulders grew taut. "Yeah, well, don't say never. You don't know what the future will hold. Or when the next firestorm is gonna flatten the world. Just sayin'. I'm here. And there don't seem to be anyone else knockin'."

"Thanks for walking me home, Joe," said Bobby Sue, through a tightening throat. Brother William sure seemed interested, but she didn't mention that. "You sure you won't come in?"

He kicked some of the loose gravel on the road and shoved his hand in his pockets. "No thanks. Just tell Gareth what happened. That I'm not a total screw up."

"I will," said Bobby Sue. "And thanks again."

Chapter Eight

While only winged animals can actually fly, a few star-touched have jumped so high that they gave the illusion of flight. Others have managed to increase their speed where they appear but a blur. It's not something all of them can do. As I've mentioned, while all the star-touched can heal and start fires, they also have specialties, certain abilities that they are more adept at than others. Like the telepathic link most have, but it's usually with one specific individual that they've bonded to.
William Darwinian
Official Chronicler for the League of the Stars

Gareth

In exchange for first pick of his goods, Gareth let Marty and his entourage use the tavern as headquarters, an arrangement that benefited them both. The day's wheeling and dealing had ended for Marty, but business boomed in the tavern. Not a seat could be found, and dozens of people stood at the bar or leaned against the walls. Gareth couldn't remember the last time the place had been so packed.

More customers continued to enter, among them a good friend. Alan Burns Senior was over six feet, making him stand out in most crowds. He and his wife ran a garment shop a few blocks away. There was a smile on his face as he worked his way over to Gareth, but his eyes didn't look as cheerful.

"Gareth," he said, clasping his hand in a tight grip. "Seems Jessica and I have you to thank for Junior's shift in mood."

The only child his age to survive the cholera epidemic that hit Atherton after the Cataclysm, Alan Junior had remained a dower and taciturn ten-year-old. Gareth hadn't seen him smile since he was a toddler.

"How so?"

"That little white dog of yours. It's been coming by the shop every afternoon for the past three days. Junior's been smiling, laughing, and talking of nothing else. I had no idea where it came from until this afternoon when I saw it on your doorstep."

"Oh, you mean Fifi," said Gareth. "She belongs to the new girl, Tatiana. I didn't realize the thing ever left Tatiana's side."

"I'm eternally grateful that it does. I'd like to thank her sometime." His dark brown eyes narrowed and he leaned in close, his voice barely audible. "We need to talk later. More shops were hit this afternoon, including Odessa's and the baker Bobby Sue always raves about. The attackers wore masks and destroyed everything they didn't take."

Gareth felt his gut clench. Odessa was a friend and a former town council member who resigned shortly after the election. He'd been so wrapped up in work that he hadn't spoken to her or any of the other council members in months. "So, no way to identify them, just like the others. Is she okay?"

"Nothing broken, but they roughed her up pretty bad. Gareth, she's selling her place to Mako. Same deal as all the others. She stays as his employee." Burns pulled a piece of paper from his pocket just enough for Gareth to see the seal. "I got this buyout offer from Mako two weeks ago. Odessa got one of these a couple months ago."

"Damn," he said through gritted teeth. "Bobby Sue mentioned the baker looked a bit ruffed up this morning and some druggy jumped her on her way home. Joe spotted the snatch and beat the heck out of the guy."

"Damn is right. She okay?"

"Yeah, but Mako happened by around the same time."

"Coincidence my ass," said Burns. A deep frown furrowed his brow. "He doesn't happen to be anywhere without a reason."

Anger churned in Gareth's heart. He had heard of shops being strong armed into selling, but no one could prove Mako or the militia had anything to do with it. All anyone saw were masked intruders or drunken brawlers. The drunks were always picked up, but the militia had been unable to identify any of the masked men. At least that's what they said. These attacks on Odessa and Bobby Sue hit Gareth harder than any of the others.

How long before thugs started showing up his door?

"There's more," said Burns. "People have been disappearing. Newcomers, mostly women. The guards at the gate say they just left town, but I'm not so sure. Two of the missing vanished right after the weaving hall hired them."

"We'll talk later," said Gareth. "After Marty's report."

He looked around the room, noting for the first time some of the hushed tones and worried expressions. Conversations ended abruptly when Gareth raised his hand for attention. The sooner he got things started here, the sooner he and Burns could talk more in depth.

"Okay everyone. I know you're all here for the national news report, so let's ask Marty to get started."

A few chuckles erupted around the room, but everyone soon quieted down to listen. Visitors from out of town were more common than they'd been four or five years earlier, but not an everyday occurrence, and radio communication remained unreliable. Marty was well-liked and one of the few repeat visitors. He took a drink, put his mug on the table, and rubbed his hands eagerly, basking in the attention.

"Ladies and gentlemen, children of all ages, it's always a pleasure to visit this fine town of Atherton," he said, with a flourish. Marty's booming voice echoed around the silent room. A big grin filled his face and he winked at a woman to his right. "Where shall I start this evening?"

"Hey, Marty. How far did you get this time?"

"What's new out east?"

"Forget east, what's going on in the south?"

Gareth held his hand up again. Some people were just too damn impatient. "You're not going to hear anything if you don't let him talk."

"Thanks, Gareth," said Marty. "I'll start with that first question. As you know, I try to reach at least one new town every trip. I usually hear about them from other places I visit. Last year I didn't hear about any new ones on my trek. Even if I had, not everyone has been kind enough to manufacture things I can use as fuel. My thanks to your excellent distillers for the alcohol, and the butchers for the rendered fat." Marty raised his mug in salute to a group of men in the back corner and received a hearty round of applause in response.

"This time I found a cluster of small villages and independent hamlets in southern Wisconsin. For the most part they were doing okay with the exception of perhaps one little place called Winocca. It's very far away from the other villages and extremely cautious of strangers. They almost didn't let me into town. Finally, the doors opened, permitting me to pass through into their stupendous stone fortress." Marty stopped for a moment to suppress a chuckle and roll his eyes. "Unfortunately, there wasn't a stonemason or bricklayer in the bunch. It had to be the most crooked, wobbliest wall I've ever seen. I swear I was afraid to breathe too hard for fear of blowing it over."

"Sounds like they would have been better off working in wood," someone called out through the laughter.

"Definitely," said Marty, nodding to the man in the back who had commented. "Your security barrier, even with its patchwork material, is far superior to that pile of rubble."

"It isn't exactly pretty."

"Or tall," said another patron.

"Can't argue with that," said Marty. "But at least it offers some protection and you have a decent government system in place. In their case, the wall became more of a liability. Shortly before I left, part of it collapsed, killing a young boy and injuring two men. That wasn't the only problem they had. Their 'president', and I use that word lightly, lived in his own little paranoid world. I doubt he'll be in charge next time I make it back there."

Murmurs rippled through the room. Gareth frowned and wondered what Marty would find next time he came back to Atherton. He'd seen changes here lately that he didn't like. Mako was buying the place up and Snider, well, Snider made him uneasy. That man was in charge of the militia, the same militia that was hassling small businesses, taking whatever they wanted. Not too long ago Gareth had had the ear of every council member. Now he felt disconnected from all the council's decisions. Would Marty be telling stories of his demise to some strangers soon?

"After I left that bunch I followed my usual route through Illinois, into Indiana," continued Marty. "And then back here to

Kentucky. Story's the same in most places. Hard times, roving bandits that strike without warning, and mini dictators popping up all over the place."

Frowns and worried looks appeared on faces. "Hey, cheer up," he said, "It's not all bad. The Penn-York Republic became official last October. In the past eight months, all of New York, Pennsylvania, and parts of New England have joined. Heck, even two or three towns in Ohio have agreed to join the Republic."

A bald man in the back spoke up first. "That's all well and good, Marty, but what do all those towns get out of it? It's not like this Penn-York of yours has an army big enough to protect all that land. Hell, even if everyone stood hand-in-hand you couldn't have enough people to make a line around the size territory you're talking about. What's to stop organized bandits from nibbling away one town at a time? Some of those groups hit and vanish before people even know what happened."

"Penn-York has more defenses than you think."

"Like what?"

"I'm not at liberty to share that information, but rest assured, our borders are watched very closely."

"Our borders?" questioned Gareth.

"Everyone needs a home base," Marty said with a grin. "We also have a fast communication system."

"How fast? You got phones or something? Radios?"

Marty shook his head. "No movement on that front. The science community is still trying to get the old technology to work. What we do have are several reliable power sources, including a nuclear power plant. We're lucky so many power plant technicians survived and were able to get it on line. Having enough juice to power lights, heat, and most importantly, refrigeration, has been a key benefit for our residents. Almost every town has been wired into the grid and the few that aren't will be before the year's out. We're even repaving and creating new roads to connect towns and repairing some bridges. If you come to visit don't expect perfection, but it's far better than dirt. Since the end of October we've also been minting our own coins. You'll probably start seeing them with travelers before too long if you haven't already. None of that would have been attainable if it hadn't been for those wonderful farmers and scientists. Without their cooperation none of this would have been possible."

Marty paused and reached for his mug while the crowd digested all the information. Gareth smiled, noting that Marty had managed to avoid answering questions about Penn-York's defenses or communication system. The man had a knack for diverting attention, and news of improved roads worked well. Better roads meant more travelers would eventually head toward Atherton. Perhaps in time phones could be repaired. It almost reminded Gareth of the old days.

"Any news from the south yet?" asked Bobby Sue.

The cheery smile that Marty had been wearing all day vanished. He put the mug down reluctantly, swirling the liquid a bit and watching the ale slosh as he did so. These were sure signs of bad news. Worse, Gareth knew, for Bobby Sue. She still held out hope that some of her family had survived in southern Oklahoma.

"Don't have a lot of information from the south. Most of its still in chaos, with disorganized, every-man-for-himself domains. The rest have divided into mini-dictatorships. The warlords take what they want and to hell with anyone else. I'm not going there and most of my fellow merchants feel the same."

"It can't be that bad, can it?" a man asked, a nervous twitter in his voice.

Marty gave the crowd a stern look and raised his eyebrows. "Can't it? The warlords and dictators all condone slavery. They don't recognize the rights of anyone who isn't able to fight. If you're not in the select circle, you sure as hell better be trying to get in it. Everyone else is property to be used, sold, starved, beaten, or just plain killed. Most farmers struggle to get food staples to grow, but the only things that are thriving in their fields are poppies. Apparently it's a good trade crop and the warlords are good at using the drugs to exploit and control people."

A somber mood hung over the room, and when Marty didn't volunteer any more news, small conversations started up again. It took several minutes before isolated sounds of laughter sprung up. Gareth gave Marty a pat on the back and went to see to the other patrons' needs, noticing for the first time that Tatiana wasn't anywhere in sight. He had given her the evening off and thought she would have joined the others to hear Marty.

"Hey, Bobby Sue," he said, as she hustled by with a tray of mugs. "You sure you're okay?"

"Don't you worry about me none. We Oklahoma gals are made of some tough stuff."

"Tougher than nails apparently," he said with a smile. "Have you seen Tatiana?"

Bobby Sue shook her head. "Not since just before comin' down. Last I looked, she had her head down in one of those books you bought this afternoon. Bet she's still curled up 'round one now."

"Thanks."

The door swung open abruptly, knocking into the wall and almost crushing a man, who slipped out of the way just in time. Snider stood scowling in the doorway, flanked by a couple of militiamen. The two men, newcomers to Atherton, made Gareth's skin crawl, especially the stocky, dark-eyed one. Built like a linebacker, Diddler always had an odd, semi-psychotic look about him. Even now, his mouth twisted into a thin smile and his eyes seemed to leer at every woman in the room. He was also one of the creeps who had tried to drag Bobby Sue into the brothel last year. Duval, also stocky and muscular, looked bored as he surveyed the room. His neatly trimmed hair and beard made him look more refined, but Gareth wasn't fooled. The two men were a matched set of no good.

"Looks like business is decent this evening, Gareth. Good to see you," said Snider. His voice dripped with contempt and sarcasm, booming in the now silent room. "Where's Marty the Merchant?"

"Right here." Marty stood. "Who's asking?"

Marty's movements seemed as casual and indifferent as a cat, but Gareth noticed the balanced placement of his feet and the way he was poised to easily shift his weight, ready to counter an aggressive act. To most, Marty didn't look like much, but anyone who knew about fighters could tell from his stance that he wasn't someone to trifle with. Gareth knew this, and from Snider's expression, Snider noticed as well.

"Mayor wants to see you."

"It's a bit late for administrative meetings, don't you think?"

"The safety of Atherton is always a high priority for Mayor Mako Scaffeld," said Snider with a smile that looked anything but friendly. "He wants a report of your travels."

"What's this about, Snider?" asked Gareth.

"Nothing that concerns you. The Mayor just wants to talk."

Gareth pointed at Duval and Diddler, barely keeping the anger out of his voice. "If talk is all that's on his mind, then why the extra thugs?"

"Can't be too careful, now can we? Especially with a special guest in town," said Snider, nodding toward Marty. "Wouldn't want anything to happen to him walking through town at night, would you?"

"There's nothing urgent to worry about," said Marty. "I'll come see him first thing in the morning."

"Mayor wants to see you now," said Snider.

"It's late. There's no reason why this can't wait until—"

"It's okay," said Marty, cutting Gareth off. "I think I'd like to meet this mayor of yours."

Gareth fumed silently as Marty left the tavern with Snider and his two goons, followed closely by Marty's twin guards, Thelma and Louise. He didn't like this one bit. Why in God's name did Mako need to see Marty now? More and more, Gareth wished he hadn't distanced himself from the council after Mako won the election.

Chapter Nine

Ten Months Four Days ADR – June Tenth

Tatiana sipped the thin vegetable stew, their main meal for the day. It wasn't much, but now that the skies had cleared, food would be easier to find. After only four days it already felt warmer. She and Auntie had been the last to be served, as usual, even though they had found most of the ingredients. The men always ate first so they could guard the camp, then the women, then Tatiana and Auntie, who had more trouble with her stiff joints every day. It was only a matter of time before the older woman became unable to contribute. Tatiana worried about that day. She'd already seen them abandon others.

This little ragtag group of seven survivors had been her only companions for the last nine months, drawn together out of necessity, not out of any kind of affection or inclination to enjoy each other's company. Only Auntie seemed to care about Tatiana, but Tatiana wondered whether Auntie saw another young girl when she looked at her.

Arguing often took the place of conversation, especially when the group stumbled on new stragglers. Tatiana's knowledge of plants had ensured her a place in the band even though she was only a child. She could find food the others missed or didn't recognize. If not for that, they would have left her months ago.

Cold fingers grasped Tatiana's wrist and yanked her to her feet, sending her bowl crashing to the ground. Beside her, Auntie screamed as a strange scruffy man accosted her. Two limp bodies, the men who had been guarding the camp, were dragged in and dropped next to the fire a moment later. The leader of Tatiana's group was marched in at gunpoint. Blood dripped from a nasty slice across his cheek and his hands were bound behind him. The two women, both able fighters as Tatiana had seen on previous encounters with marauders, were similarly bound.

Tatiana looked up into the face of her captor. His eyes, sunken in sallow sockets, were as cold as his hands. Months of beard growth covered his face, and despite his gaunt appearance, his fingers held firmly. All the men had a similar hungry look. Her band wasn't the ideal family, but these newcomers seemed far worse.

"Look what we have here, John. Three breeders, an old cow, and fresh meat. Good haul, don't you think?"

One of the strangers looked at them and laughed. "Hell, Carl, you can have the kid if you want. She's a little too young for my taste. I prefer my women well built, and these two are strong." He emphasized his words by slapping one of the women on the buttocks.

Snickers from the other five men echoed around camp as they searched for valuables and tied her and Auntie. Carl ran his finger down Tatiana's cheek before joining them. The lustful longing in his eyes made her tremble with fear. Tatiana was only ten, but she'd seen enough in recent months to know what that look meant. Tears streamed down her face. More than ever she missed Mama, Papa, and the happy life they'd had.

"This stew of theirs ain't bad, but it could use some meat. Toss me a haunch."

"Oh, my God!" moaned Auntie, as the strangers began to butcher the dead men.

Tatiana shuddered in shock and horror. Nausea churned in her gut. Carl's earlier words began to sink in. Fresh meat. The strangers viewed the men as food, and Auntie wouldn't be far behind them. Is this how these men survived, by eating people?

Revulsion eroded away the terror holding her in place and a strange feeling started to build inside of her. It began in her chest, and spread a tingling sensation all the way to her toes and fingers. Energy poured into her body. She felt swollen, as if her skin was stretched like a balloon. Tatiana's heart pounded as the energy burst out of her. She knew exactly what she needed to do. With a strength she hadn't had before, she broke her bonds and sprang to her feet. The strangers, focused on their grisly task, were caught completely off guard. It was their last mistake *before fire enveloped them.*

Tatiana

Stacks of books surrounded Tatiana. Eventually they would go to the town library, but until then Gareth said she was free to read them. A creak outside the door made her jump, nearly dropping the mystery novel she was reading. The sudden movement woke Fifi who gave a startled yip. Tatiana froze as the door swung open.

"Hi, Tatiana," said Bobby Sue, as she slipped into the room.

Air hissed out of Tatiana's mouth. She hadn't even realized she'd held her breath. "Bobby Sue. You startled me. I didn't expect anyone to be up this early. Is everything okay? Are you feeling ill?"

"I'm just fine," said Bobby Sue. "But, Snider came into the tavern a little bit ago and took Marty off to see Mako. Place cleared out pretty quick after he left so Gareth insisted I get some extra rest on account of what happened today."

"Probably a good idea," said Tatiana. "You have a big lump on your head where it hit the ground. Concussions are nothing to sneeze about."

"I suppose." Bobby Sue sat on the edge of Tatiana's bed and gingerly touched the back of her head. "I can't believe how stupid I was walkin' with my head in the clouds. Didn't think anyone saw that crazy man grab me. Sure was lucky that Joe did. To think of what might have happened just gives me shivers somethin' awful."

Tatiana moved next to Bobby Sue and hugged her. A lot could have happened today, things that Tatiana didn't want to think about. She closed her eyes and swallowed, thankful that Bobby Sue didn't have to face that nightmare. "You're safe now."

"So are you," said the voice.

Tears stung Tatiana's eyes. *"No, I'll never be safe."*

"Thanks to Joe. I sure wish he'd be happy with us just bein' friends. He's real scary when he's riled up. If I hadn't a stopped him he would have killed that guy. One of my neighbors had a husband like that when I was a kid. It didn't end well." Bobby

Sue paused and fiddled with her hair. "That guy that grabbed me was creepy, but thinkin' back, he said somethin' real odd. I could a sworn he mentioned somethin' about givin' me to a client."

"Maybe you misunderstood," said Tatiana, praying that was true.

"You're probably right," said Bobby Sue. I was so rattled at that point I must have heard wrong. I know I'm rattling along now. Sure glad you're here to listen to me ramble. You're real easy to talk to. How's the chicken book comin'?"

"Actually, I finished that one a few hours ago. This mystery is great, but a little intense. You want to read it when I'm done?"

Bobby Sue's eyes grew wide. "Finished a whole book? Already?"

"Yes," said Tatiana. "It's amazing how many different varieties of chickens there are. The smallest breed, Malaysian serama bantam, is only fifteen centimeters high and as little as five ounces. That's smaller than Fifi. A bit different from the Jersey Giant which can grow to thirteen and in one case, twenty pounds! Did you know that chickens have been domesticated since before 6000 B.C.? The first were..."

"Wait," said Bobby Sue, waving her hands and laughing. "How'd you do that?"

"Do what?"

"Remember all them little details?"

Tatiana shrugged and felt her face flush. "I just do. I remember everything I read. Always have."

"That's amazin'," said Bobby Sue. "You must have a photographic memory."

"Only with words. Pictures don't stick."

"It's still pretty awesome. Speaking of which, I love the way Fifi ran up that man's leg and hopped on his shoulder this afternoon. I've seen dogs do all sorts of jumps, flips, and fancy walkin', but never that one. How'd you get her to learn it?"

Tatiana bit her lip and stared at her hands. The tricks had been all Fifi's idea, but she couldn't tell Bobby Sue that.

"Now don't you go getting' shy on me now," said Bobby Sue. "You should be proud of the way you trained up that little pup of yours. You know what? I'm really not tired yet and it'll be a while before anyone else comes up. How about you tell me more about yourself? Where you from? Before the Cataclysm, I mean."

A lasting friendship was something Tatiana had always dreamed of, but her dreams seemed to clash with reality on a frequent basis. Maybe for a little while, at least, she could pretend.

"Things could be different."

"I hope they are."

Chapter Ten

The League of the Stars was founded a year after the Day of Reckoning. While we do believe that the star-touched are a gift from our creator, our main goal is to educate people about them so they aren't afraid. Too many star-touched have been killed because of fear and ignorance.

We also try to teach the star-touched and help them understand and control their amazing gifts. To that end, we have formed a school for the star-touched in Penn-York, a safe haven free from persecution. At last count the League has identified almost a hundred and fifty star-touched. Most are at the school, but several travel around in search of those still in hiding, using birds to keep in touch with us.

For people who are uneasy about so many star-touched gathered in one location, there is nothing to fear. All of the star-touched I've met are very peaceful people who only wish to live their lives like everyone else.

William Darwinian
Official Chronicler for the League of the Stars

Gareth

A knock at the tavern door halted Gareth's pacing, a task he'd been doing in earnest since Marty left two hours ago.

"It's me," said Marty.

Gareth breathed a sigh of relief and yanked the door open. Marty filed in with his two guards. The twins headed to their room, but Marty planted himself at one of the tables.

"So what did that bastard want?" asked Gareth, as he placed two large mugs of ale on the table.

"If you don't sit down, I'm not telling you anything," said Marty.

Gareth sat heavily in a chair and took a long pull on his ale.

"Sorry, a lot on my mind right now."

"No kidding. Anything you care to share?"

"I'd rather not talk about it. So what did Mako want?"

Marty's eyes narrowed and he took a sip of ale. "He wanted to know what I knew about Penn-York. I was both sufficiently informative to satisfy him it wasn't a threat to Atherton, and vague enough to keep my pledge to the Republic."

Gareth put his mug down and raised his eyebrows. "Damn, Marty. You're working for them, aren't you?"

Marty had the kind of teasing smile a child would give to another, an 'I know something you don't know' smile.

"How long?"

"Since the beginning."

"And the extra hands and fire power that's joined your little caravan, Penn-York supplying them?"

"I can't answer that."

"You just did," laughed Gareth.

Marty raised his mug in salute. "How did things go after I left?"

Gareth gave him a sour look. "How do you think they went?"

"Sorry about that. I'm sure they'll all be back tomorrow. Besides, it saved me the trouble of trying to get in to see Mako on my own. It's best he not know who I work for. Today wasn't all bad for you. At least you got some good bargains. I know I did."

That brought a real grin to Gareth's face. It had certainly been an interesting day. The way Tatiana had jumped out of her shy shell when she spotted those books amazed him. It was nice to see how well she interacted with the people in line and she even got Fifi to do some tricks. Marty's special delivery proved a pleasant surprise as well.

"Here's to travel, connections, and fair trade," said Marty, raising his mug.

"I'll drink to that." Gareth waited until they'd both had a good long drink. "Now, tell what you didn't say earlier."

Marty stared at his ale, swirling it around in the mug. "Didn't want to panic the folks here too much, but some of the warlords down south are ending their squabbling and fighting. They're organizing. Divided, they're not much more than a local menace, but together…I really don't want to think about what they could do."

"That bad?"

Marty nodded. "Not everyone is interested in voting and fair play. Thank goodness the northeast got it right. Penn-York is probably the closest thing to pre-Cataclysmic America there is."

Gareth shifted in his chair, trying to ignore the gnawing concerns of Atherton and his conversation with Burns. He could feel Marty's eyes burning into him, as if Marty were trying to incite some reaction out of him. Changing the subject seemed more prudent. "Isn't the northeast where that League of the Stars started?"

"Yeah," said Marty, drumming his fingers on the edge of the table. "They're into everything up there, but in a good way. They've gotten people to work together. Procured resources we couldn't find elsewhere. That kind of stuff. Now don't get me wrong, I don't believe in all of their ideology. Heck, I don't think the star-touched believe all the things those League folk say, but we'll take all the help we can get. One of them traveled here with me. Spent most of the trip talking about the star-touched. Nice man. You should talk to him."

"No thanks. I've already seen them preaching in the market square. They seem harmless enough."

Marty shrugged and sipped his ale. "League of the Stars disciples have a reputation for reliability and honesty. If they promise you something, you can be sure they'll follow through or die trying. They also always seem to have just the right amount of coins or valuable metals to trade. They're the only folks I let buy on credit."

"Credit for drifters? Are you nuts?"

Marty just smiled. "They're good for it. Remember, they've set up a home base in the northeast. A few months back I got into a disagreement and had to move on before one of them could pay me. Two days later I woke to find a bag of Penn-York coins and a note apologizing for the delay. I'm not the only merchant with stories like that."

"That's just weird for these times." Inside, Gareth cheered. If enough people of integrity stood up for the right thing, maybe they could oust some of the dictators and hoodlums wreaking havoc on society. Gareth slipped his hand into his pocket and held the gold coin Tatiana had given him. Could she be connected to the League of the Stars?

Marty drummed his fingers on the table. "Did you know your border patrols are charging merchants to enter town?"

Gareth stared at his mug moodily, shoulders drooping. "I heard. Council's decision. What did you have to pay?"

"It doesn't matter. What's important is that they demanded to know my business destination. They were very clear that Mako ruled the town and doubled the toll when I told them. I remember the first time I came here after the Cataclysm. This wasn't much more than a ghost town, but you were getting it together. It's grown quite a bit, in part because of the east-west route that runs near here gets traveled often. I know several merchants who frequent this town. You've had a significant influx of people."

"Yeah." Gareth stared somberly at his empty mug. "Atherton has grown quite a bit."

"Not all of the changes have been good, Gareth," said Marty, looking him in the eye.

Gareth sighed. "I know. Commerce is up, but drugs are becoming more prevalent. I mean it's not like Atherton didn't have its share of drug problems, but not to this extent, and certainly not opium. That all started after Mako came here."

Marty nodded. "I have intel that says they're being shipped up from a warlord down south." He paused for a moment before continuing. "What's happened to you, Gareth? I thought you were head of council. Heck, weren't you running for mayor? What do you know about this Mako?"

Gareth shifted uneasily. "I don't know much about him. He swung in here a couple years ago and sweet-talked half the town. I guess they wanted change. He won the election by a landslide."

"And Snider?"

Gareth shrugged. "Mako's right hand man and sometime delivery boy? Chief thug of Mako's imported border guards? I know even less about him. He stays in the background most of the time."

Marty's brow furrowed deeply. "Snider isn't as slick as Mako, but in my opinion he's far more dangerous, especially in his role as militia chief. He's following Mako's orders now, but I get the feeling Snider is just waiting for a chance to seize control. I'm surprised you didn't spot that. Gareth, Mako has ties to the southern warlords and I'd bet anything Snider does as well. Watch your back around both of them, Gareth, especially Snider. Mako didn't just ask about Penn-York tonight. He had a lot of questions about you as well and how we met. I told him we were casual business associates but I'm not sure he bought that.

"I'm pretty sure Mako's afraid of you, that you'll try to challenge him. And you probably should, sooner rather than later. I didn't like the look of the people hanging around his house or the businesses plastered with his name. What the hell happened to you after the election?"

Gareth's mouth felt suddenly dry, but he just stared at his empty mug. "Town liked Mako better than me," he shrugged.

"And you just rolled over, ran away with your tail between your legs?"

Marty's voice was flat, and his disappointment felt like a slap in the face. A tight knot formed in Gareth's gut. He'd thought he had the townspeople's confidence until the election results came in. Darren Smead, a weaver who was a well-respected accountant before the Cataclysm, tallied the vote. Losing had shaken Gareth and he reacted the same way as when Margaret died. This time instead of booze, he had lost himself in his business. The result remained the same: he'd withdrawn into himself and away from the world.

"Gareth?"

"I guess losing the election got the better of me," he said with a sigh.

It was impossible to miss the anger in Marty's voice or the way his eyes narrowed to slits of near fury. "Well, get over it, damn it. This town needs you. I need you. There've been at least three other towns I know of that have been overrun in the last few years. All of them after Mako Scaffeld paid a visit. I don't want Atherton to be the next."

"We're a bit far from Penn-York," said Gareth. A sour edge slipped into his voice. He knew Marty was right, but the scolding still made him bristle.

"You're closer than you think, but that doesn't matter."

"Listen, Gareth, we've know each other a long time. I picked up some special merchandise recently. I want you to have it."

"I don't want handouts, Marty."

"Then just store it for me. I don't want to be carrying all this stuff around. In fact, I'll even pay you a storage fee if it'll make you feel better."

He and Marty were friends, but merchants didn't just give things away. "What is it?"

"A few AR-15s and ammunition to go with them."

"Semi-automatics?"

"Modified."

"When did you start dealing in arms?"

"Since I needed to use them to keep bandits at bay. I don't want to come back here next time to find you dead. You're good with a shotgun, but it's not going to do you any good, or your little family here, if Mako comes at you directly. Just promise that if the need arises, you'll use them."

Marty was right. Denial couldn't last forever. He needed to be ready when Mako became insistent with his buyout offers. He looked at Marty and nodded, wishing his mug still held some liquid to clear the dry knot in his throat.

"I'll take them."

"Good. Now let's hope you never have to use them."

Chapter Eleven

Five Years BDR- April

Tiny toddler-sized fingers pushed into the mass of spidery roots, trying to separate them without snapping the delicate fibers. The spicy odor of rosemary wafted through the air from the jostled plant. Bits of loosened soil fell to the ground. At last, the roots hung loose and free.

"Very good, now place it in the hole and cover the roots with soil."

Soft, moist soil slipped through her fingers as she sprinkled dirt over the roots like she had seen her mama do earlier. When she finished, the little twig of rosemary stood lopsided, like a tiny pine sapling that had been trod upon. The child's lower lip curled down in disappointment. Her mama's plants all stood up straight.

"Don't fret, dear. It just needs a little more soil to hold it up."

With utmost care, the girl pushed a handful of soil under the lower side of the plant, pushing it into an upright position. Her heart beat happily, and a smile filled her face. She reached for the small yellow watering can her mama and papa had given her for her birthday, and gave the plant a nice long drink. The pride she saw on her mama's face made her glow.

"How's my little Tat doing in the garden today?" said a dark-haired man.

The little girl jumped up and leaped into his arms, heedless of the dirt and mud covering her hands. "I pant wosmawy, Papa. See my wosmawy?"

With a big grin, he kissed her dirt-smudged nose. "What a super job you did, Tat. It looks beautiful and smells wonderful. Pretty soon it will grow and bloom just like you."

The child giggled and buried her face in the man's shoulder. Her little hands rubbed his back, leaving dirty smears on his light blue t-shirt. A moment later, her mama wrapped her arms around both father and child, leaving her own handprints on papa's shirt.

Tatiana

Tatiana studied the red-feathered chickens as they milled around the enclosure and occasionally pecked at the food left over from the morning meal. For the past five days, she had spent all her free time observing Gareth's little flock, trying to decide how best to proceed.

Fifi, who had been sitting at her side, jumped up with her ears perked and her tail swishing. A moment later, Tatiana heard what Fifi had picked up: footsteps, wide and heavyset. She stood and turned around.

"Good morning, Gareth."

Gareth wore his usual dark blue slacks and light blue button down shirt. A wide belt held his pants in place on his waist, which had thickened with age. His hazel eyes held a cheerful twinkle when he greeted her, although it dimmed somewhat when he looked at Old Henry.

"Good morning to you, Tatiana. Still trying to save the rooster, I see. That bird has been nothing but trouble since I bought him four months ago. Whoever said chicken farming was easy didn't know chickens."

Tatiana glanced at the milling fowl. After her observations this past week, she agreed with his evaluation. "Where did you get them?"

"Some traveling salesman. He swore they were the best layers around." Gareth shook his head. "I should have known better, but thoughts of fresh omelets got the better of me. Should have listened to Sabrina and roasted them months ago. I guess I miss the old days."

"We all do. According to that book you purchased, these are Rhode Island Reds. They're supposed to be good egg layers. They could be past their laying days, but I think they're just out of sorts because of Old Henry's behavior. The book mentioned that the males tend to be a bit aggressive, although they don't usually attack people. Old Henry is a little over the top with the aggression, but Fifi and I are working on that."

Gareth smiled. "You sure didn't waste any time reading those books. I've never seen anyone get so excited over bound paper."

Tatiana felt her face flush and lowered her gaze. Storybooks made anything seem possible. When she read, she could leave her real self behind and be whoever or whatever she wanted.

"What else did you learn about these feathered fiends?" asked Gareth, half in jest.

Tatiana bit at her lip for a moment. "Well, it seems that the brooding instinct has been almost completely bred out of them..."

Deep furrows creased his brow. "Meaning?"

"Unless I can train one of them to sit on the eggs, we're going to need to build an incubator."

Gareth rubbed a thick hand across his face, massaging his temples a moment before shaking his head in disgust. "You mean none of these blasted birds know how to hatch an egg?"

Tatiana shook her head. "Only one of them has shown any interest in the nesting box, but she'll need work to keep her there. It takes three weeks for the chicks to hatch and the hens usually turn them every fifteen minutes. I read about some behavior modification techniques. If Pavlov can make a dog salivate at the sound of a bell, I'm sure..."

Gareth put a hand on her shoulder, shaking his head from side to side. "Did that book mention how to build an incubator?"

"Yes."

"Then build one."

"We'll have to bring it inside," she said. "And once they hatch we'll need someplace warm and safe for the chicks. They'll get trampled in the regular pen. And we'll need to make sure the eggs we try to hatch are actually fertile."

"Tat," said Gareth, taking her head in his hands gently. "Whatever you need to do is fine, just do it. Something tells me that if you can't do this, no one can."

Tatiana's heart leaped, and a happy warmth flowed through her veins. She felt her face flush again. Only her father had called her Tat. His death shortly before the Cataclysm had been hard on her and her mama. "I'll do my best," she whispered, unable to keep the slight tremor out of her voice.

"Is something wrong?" asked Gareth.

Tatiana shook her head. Tears began to pool in her eyes. "My papa used to call me Tat."

"I'm sorry," said Gareth. "I didn't mean…"

"It's okay," she whispered. "I like it. It reminds me of happier days."

Gareth brushed the tears from Tatiana's face and wrapped his arms around her. She let his caring emotions swath her, driving away some of the bitter memories of the past eight years. He was so like her papa.

"Gareth?"

Tatiana pulled back from Gareth as soon as Sabrina spoke, lowering her head. The shock and confusion in Sabrina's voice was nothing compared to the jealous emotions that lashed in Tatiana's direction. It was substantial enough to make Tatiana flinch as if she'd been slapped. If only she could block what everyone else felt. Alone, different, isolated; the weight of the past few years crashed around her. Gareth didn't seem to notice anything amiss, and greeted Sabrina with a warm smile.

"Everything okay, Sabrina?"

"Of course it is," said Sabrina, giving Gareth a peck on the cheek. She made a point of insinuating herself between Tatiana and Gareth. "One of those League of the Stars disciples is here. Says he wants to talk to you."

"Well, I'd better go see what he wants."

Tatiana's head began to spin and she struggled to keep from shaking. What could a League disciple want with Gareth? Did they know what she was? Had Sabrina finally broken her silence? Was it him? She looked around frantically for Fifi, wondering where the dog had disappeared to. Would she come back with ribbons in her ears again? It felt as if cold hands compressed Tatiana's chest. Memories of pain and cruel laughter surrounded her. Finally, she sensed Fifi's mind, soothing, comforting. A moment later the little dog snuggled into her arms. Tatiana clutched the soft white fur, burying her face until the panic fled.

Chapter Twelve

I remember the day I came to the Abuda Institute Orphanage in Sacquanico, Tennessee. It was only four years past the Day of Reckoning. The entire campus churned with as much chaos as that fateful day.
    William Darwinian
    Official Chronicler for the League of the Stars

Bobby Sue

Bobby Sue swallowed the last bite of meat pie, savoring the spices. All that remained of their meal were a few scattered crumbs. It took every bit of willpower to keep from licking her fingers as she studied Brother William Darwinian's face Every time the wind blew, sunlight filtered through the leaves, creating a shifting dappled pattern on the picnic blanket where they sat. Even the yellow and orange star painted on William's forehead seemed to twinkle as the foliage moved. His cheeks rounded every time he smiled, like a pair of sun-kissed peaches. Dark brown wisps covered his chin; trimmed short, just shy of a shave.

"You've been in Atherton for less than a week and already found the best bake shop in town. How'd you manage that?"

Brother William smiled with a playful sparkle in his hazel eyes. "I have a knack, especially when I'm trying to impress a pretty lady."

A soft giggle escaped Bobby Sue's lips. "I bet you do. You made some points with Gareth as well. I thought he was going to drop down in a dead faint when you asked permission to take me out. Not many fellas ask these days."

"I got the impression that Gareth is a bit more protective of his employees than most people."

"He's more like a mama bear the way he looks out for us."

Brother William smiled. "Well I'm glad I passed inspection."

"Me too. The last fella to come sniffin' was some drunken relation of his who don't seem to know what no means. That melon was pickled and fried before he took one step. I mean he may be sweet on me now, but he's got a vicious temper, especially when he drinks, which is always. I don't want nothin' to do with that."

"And me?"

"You a nice sort. I like that."

"For a moment there I thought Gareth would say no. I don't think he's too keen on the League of the Stars. I was half afraid you'd say no as well."

"But I didn't," she said.

A sudden gust made her hair flutter over her eyes. William brushed the stray strands off her face, fingertips just barely touching her skin. Tingles ran up and down Bobby Sue and she leaned in closer, hoping for the caress of his lips. She barely knew him, yet it felt like they had known each other forever. His eyes looked warm and inviting, but he didn't try to kiss her. Finally, she met someone that she didn't want to beat off and all he did was smile. Bobby Sue wound some of her hair around her finger, not sure what to make of this stranger with the cropped, dark-brown hair. Gentlemen suitors just didn't exist anymore, but he sure acted like one.

"So where you from, William?" she asked.

"Western Pennsylvania originally. I was off at college studying journalism when the Day of Reckoning began."

"Wish there were still colleges to go to now," she said, twisting her mouth into a sour pout. "I always wanted to go to school like my parents did. That's where they met, you know, my folks. Met in psychology one-oh-one."

"And what would you study?"

"People and how's they communicate, how's they think. What makes them do what they do. That kinda' thing. I guess I like makin' people smile is all. Silly idea anyway. We barely got school for kids let alone adults."

"Learning is never silly, Bobby Sue. It's what keeps us moving forward. The day you stop trying to learn is the day you stagnate. That's why I started traveling after the Day of Reckoning, to learn about what was going on and record it.

Someday, someone will want to know."

"Okay, mister learns-a-lot, tell me about that mark on your head and the star-touched. What can they do? How many are there? Where they come from? What..."

"Whoa there," he said, waving her off in mock defense. "That's not a single lesson. That's a whole year's work load."

"Well, now you have an excuse to ask me out again, don't you?

William laughed. "Bobby Sue, I don't need that kind of excuse to see you, do I?"

"Really? What else you got on your mind?"

William's face turned brighter than Bobby Sue's hair and he scrubbed at his close trimmed head. A slight shadow fell across his eyes, and the smile faded from his face. Bobby Sue glanced away, not sure why William suddenly looked upset. When she looked back, he was studying the river that flowed near their tree, still rubbing his head.

"Careful or you'll smudge that purty paint of yours," she said, purposely exaggerating her southern accent. That earned a weak smile.

"Don't think I haven't before. I only started painting my head six months ago. It's still new."

"But what does it all mean? Do the star-touched wear painted stars too? Is that how you know who they are?"

"Heck no," laughed William. "I don't think there's a star-touched in existence who would mark themselves like this. They want to blend in. Most don't want anyone to know they're star-touched."

"Then why in blazes do you and your League folk do it?"

"To make us stand out. We're the educators. Our job is to teach other people about the star-touched so they're not scared of them. Too many people died during the riots four years ago. They died because people didn't know the facts. They didn't understand, and still don't."

"Well, you may as well have painted a target on your head. Even I know there are parts of this country where you're liable to be tarred and feathered if you go preaching 'bout something other than Jesus."

William turned his head, examining a robin as it chattered in the tree above them. His voice sounded distant, almost painful. "I've run across my share of closed-minded people, Bobby Sue. I'm well aware of the risks. Believe me, it wasn't a move I made without careful thought."

"Sorry, I didn't mean to upset you, William. It's just I know so little. I mean I read and all, but not like Tatiana. I swear that woman eats, breathes, and sleeps books. She already read most of the books Gareth bought, and get this. She remembers them. Word for word. I've never seen anything like it."

"She sounds like a pretty amazing person. I'd like to meet her. But that's not why I asked you out for lunch. Right now, Bobby Sue, I'm more interested in you."

"Are you now?" said Bobby Sue scooting closer to William. "Well, we'll have to do something about that, now won't we?"

Chapter Thirteen

Ten Months Eleven Days ADR – June Seventeenth

Still traumatized from the encounter with the cannibals the week before, Tatiana shivered and rocked back and forth. They were dead, nothing more than ashes. She squeezed her eyes shut but memories of their screams made her nauseous. Never, she could never let that happen again.

Her group was safe, but for how long? Two women, a man, a kid, and one old lady were no match for the gangs they had encountered. They would need to merge with another band if they wanted to survive.

She opened her eyes and looked up in time to see one of the women quickly look away. They all reacted to her that way. Even Auntie acted distant. They're afraid, she realized with dismay. They're afraid of me. I'm afraid of me.

Tatiana

It took three days to gather the materials needed to build the incubator. Scraps of wood, some light fixtures, and an old glass window lay scattered around Tatiana. Yesterday Tatiana had caged off Old Henry and one of the hens with chicken wire to be sure the eggs she picked were fertilized. Old Henry looked happy, but the hen less than thrilled. Tatiana hadn't the heart to leave the poor thing locked up like that for long. The hen needed to be isolated until her eggs were collected, but she would shoo the rooster out of there at night.

Several hours past noon, Bobby Sue skipped in and plopped on the grass next to Tatiana, a great big smile plastered across her freckled face. It was impossible not to feel the happiness that poured from the woman and swirled around Tatiana. Blocking any emotions had become increasingly difficult, especially with Sabrina's sour mood constantly bombarding her. The brief hug from Gareth the other day had accentuated the problem. It didn't help that Tatiana spent so much time fussing with the chickens instead of scrubbing floors and dishes. It was a good thing Gareth had made his wishes clear on the matter. But that didn't help Tatiana's situation, or that of any of the other women.

"Looks like you enjoyed your time off," said Tatiana, smiling at Bobby Sue.

Bobby Sue hugged her knees. "Did I ever! I can't remember being this happy in a long time. I feel like I'm floatin' on a cloud."

Tatiana put her tools down, curious as to what had made her friend so bubbly. If only she could bottle some of that joy and feed it to Sabrina. "You going to share or just sit there like the Cheshire cat?"

Bobby Sue's grin only grew wider. She looked from side to side, as if she were checking for hidden spies. Leaning in close, she whispered with mock secrecy, "I spent the day with a wonderful man, a perfect gentleman. I think Gareth likes him, too. At least he passed inspection enough for Gareth to give me the time off. Sorry I didn't say anything before, but I was afraid I'd jinx things. I've been practically burstin' the past three days since he asked me."

"So tell me about Mister Wonderful."

"Remember the day Marty the Merchant came? Well, a young man traveled with his caravan. I had a great chat with him that day. Anyway, he came here to live with the other League of the Stars disciples. I told you about the buildin' they rent on the southeast edge of town.

"We went to the river near the northern gate for a little picnic. It felt so peaceful and quiet there, nothing but fields and a few trees. There's a beautiful willow tree a short walk from the main road. You can hear birds chirp and there's nothin' as soothin' as a gurglin' stream. It seemed like the past eight years never happened. Tatiana, I've met so many fellas that want nothin' other than to paw their way all over me, but this one is different. We spent the entire time just talkin'. Oh, my gosh, I forgot to mention his name. I must sound like such an airhead. Anyway, his name is William Darwinian, Brother William when he's preachin', and he is the sweetest guy I've ever met. Did you know..."

A crushing pressure built around Tatiana, trapping the breath in her lungs. Shivers ran down her spine. Not here. Not now. How could she not have noticed his arrival? How could she have missed something like that? No matter where she went or how far, Brother William soon followed. A ghost, always over her shoulder.

"Too close for his own good."

Tatiana placed her hand on Fifi's head, caressing the soft fur.

"I don't want these powers," she thought.

"You need them to help people."

"I want to be normal."

"But you're not."

"Hey, Tatiana. You okay?"

"Sorry," said Tatiana. "I think I'm a little tired."

"Well that's no surprise," said Bobby Sue. "Gareth gave you time off yesterday afternoon and you spent it all workin' on that bachelor pad for Old Henry. You need to go off property every now and then. Take a look at the rest of the town. It's not all creepy like the west side. Some parts are quite nice."

Tatiana forced a smile. She'd seen enough of the town the day she had arrived. Well-tended crops and herds of cattle flourished in the fields and pastures within the protective walls. The few buildings and fields that stood outside could be seen from several watchtowers around the town, but those towers were manned by men with cold eyes. Tatiana had no desire to run into those people. She also didn't want to risk bumping into one of the League disciples again, especially Brother William. If one of them were to recognize her...

"I'll think about it," she said softly, wondering how long she'd be able to stay in Atherton.

"No you won't. You'll keep hiding from them."

Chapter Fourteen

One Year BDR – August

The young girl looked longingly at her papa, her deep blue eyes pleading. "Read to me again about Karana left alone on the island, Papa, please."

The tall man tucked the sheets under the seven-and-a-half-year-old girl's chin and smiled. "Why don't you tell me the story, Tat? Mama and I must have read this book to you a thousand times. I bet you memorized every word."

Tatiana giggled. "Of course I know the story, Papa. But it's so much better when you read it to me."

"Well tonight you're going to have to run through the story yourself while you sleep."

Tatiana stuck her lip out in a pout. Dreaming wasn't the same as reading. Her eyes brightened as an idea formed. "Could we go to Karana's island someday, Papa? She lived on La Isla de San Nicolas. It's near Los Angeles."

"My little Tat," said Papa, smiling. "I'll look into it, but no promises."

With a yawn, Tatiana stretched and slid her hand under her pillow, searching for the small book she kept there. Tatiana had found a copy of *Island of the Blue Dolphins* by chance in an abandoned library several years ago and had slept with it ever since. Asking her papa to visit the island in her favorite book felt like a lifetime ago. It had been such a disappointment to learn a military base stood on the island, making it off limits to visitors. The sea had begun to reclaim the island even before the Cataclysm. Tatiana doubted it existed anymore with the rise in sea levels. She gave the paperback a loving caress before climbing out of bed and dressing.

Too bad there wasn't another copy for the Atherton library. After a month of negotiations Gareth had finally convinced the town council to reopen it. The books he had purchased from Marty the Merchant helped jump start the project. In fact, since Marty's visit, Gareth spent a lot of time talking to the council. In some ways he seemed more alive, but Tatiana noticed a definite undercurrent of growing concern in him.

A few splashes of cold water on Tatiana's face from the basin and pitcher in the corner of the room brought her fully awake. Pre-dawn remained her favorite time of day. The other girls were still asleep in the small dormitory, located in the attic of the main building, but they would rouse soon. Three cots lined opposite sides of the room, each with a small cabinet or box beside it for personal items. Tatiana slept in the back, next to Bobby Sue and across from Jill who slept curled up in a ball under her covers.

Each of the girls had added personal touches to their area. Bobby Sue had been able to save some photographs of her family. Jill didn't have any pictures, but tucked under the blankets, where no one could see, she snuggled a small stuffed octopus. Cook had a blue porcelain bowl that belonged to her grandmother, and the other two girls had posters and old magazine clippings pinned to the wall. Sabrina had a small, private room across the hall.

Tatiana and Fifi slipped out of the room and down the narrow stairs that led to the ground floor. The kitchen stood beside the rental rooms and behind the tavern. Neat and organized, the space had a sink with a long Formica counter on one side and a large fireplace with a built-in oven on the other. The oven, a heavy makeshift steel contraption, filled half of the fireplace. It looked like someone had stuffed an old Franklin stove in a box. A metal plate on top was used for warming and low temperature cooking. Boiling large amounts of liquid required swinging a pot over the fire using the steel arm mounted to the wall. Tatiana filled the pot with water after adding fuel to the carefully banked coals. By the time the rest of the house was awake, it would be ready to brew tea.

With the water set, Tatiana began her next morning task, checking and turning the eggs in the incubator to the left of the oven and fireplace. Gareth had let her use one of his few batteries to electrify the incubator. So far, she hadn't had any success with the dozen or so eggs she had chosen. Tatiana sighed as she removed another rotten egg. Sabrina, already annoyed by the whole incubator concept, became even more irritated every time Tatiana had to dispose of one.

"I don't understand, Fifi, I know these were fertilized, but they just don't seem to mature. What am I doing wrong? I can feel the life in them; feel the growth for a few days. Then it just withers and dies."

Fifi sniffed the egg in Tatiana's hand, then wrinkled her nose and sneezed.

"We'd better get rid of it before Sabrina finds out."

Fifi growled softly, her usual reaction to any mention of Sabrina. Tatiana shook her head and unbolted the door that led into the backyard. A sturdy six-foot wooden fence surrounded Gareth's backyard property, but nothing could be foolproof, hence the multiple dead bolts on all the outer doors.

Dim gray shadows gradually lightened as Tatiana exited the building. She drew in a deep breath of the sweet July air. It was warm, not too humid, and filled with the smells of growing things, like the sweet chamomile flowers outside the door and the crisp beans climbing the poles in the garden. She tossed the egg into the compost heap and headed to the chicken coop.

Old Henry squawked from his private enclosure, feathers lifting into an aggressive posture. Ignoring the rooster, she gathered up the eggs hidden in the coop. The last one she picked up was from the hen that spent the previous day with Old Henry. Tatiana had placed her in a separate pen overnight.

The smooth brown egg felt warm to the touch, like it had only just been laid, but cooler than the incubator had felt that morning. Could excess heat be the problem? Tatiana cupped it gently in her hands and reached for the bubbly energy always at her fingertips. With a slight twist of disorientation, her mind and senses sank into the fragile shell. She felt more than saw the cells pulse with life. A surge of excitement flashed through her as the cells split and throbbed with energy. No matter how many times she did this, the wonders of life always amazed her. Tatiana withdrew from the egg after committing the temperature to memory. Now she just needed to match it in the incubator.

"I have a good feeling about this one, Fifi. What do you think?"

Fifi's tail thumped rapidly and a joyful sparkle glinted in her eyes. Cradling the fertilized egg in one hand and carrying the others carefully wrapped in the edge of her skirt, Tatiana headed inside. Cook, already busy preparing the day's meals, greeted her. The woman had a knack for rolling out of bed and getting straight to work without missing a beat. On the counter sat a basket filled with a ceramic water jug and several meat pies Cook had made last evening. Tatiana marked the egg with a piece of charcoal and placed it in the incubator just as Bobby Sue entered the kitchen.

"Good mornin', y'all," said Bobby Sue. "How're the eggs today, Tatiana?"

Tatiana sighed and shook her head as she reached for the dimmer switch controlling the incubator lights. "Nothing yet. I'm going to lower the temperature. I think it might be too warm."

Cook clucked her tongue and shook her head. "Better not tell Sabrina. That woman sees lost revenue in every broken shell."

"I won't talk if y'all don't," laughed Bobby Sue. "The last thing anyone wants to do is give her bad news. Jill should be down in a minute. I got the bag you packed last night. You ready for your first day in the fields?"

"Yes," said Tatiana. "But I don't have a hat."

"Not a problem. I got one for each of you. It's Jill's first time, too. 'Fraid we don't have gloves, though."

Tatiana took the straw hat Bobby Sue offered. Yesterday, Gareth had informed her that his turn to send workers to tend the cooperative farm had arrived. The arrangements had been in place since shortly after Clear Sky Day seven years ago. Depending on the size of their house, every household helped to tend the crops in the fields a minimum of three weeks during the growing season. In return they received a portion of the harvest. As the town grew, so did the farms. Dozens of people now spent most of their time working the fields. Tatiana, Bobby Sue, and Jill would be doing Gareth's shift this year, and everyone would be back for the fall harvest.

"Thanks, but I'll be fine without gloves." Tatiana helped

Bobby Sue pack the rest of their lunch basket, her mind buzzing with questions. "I was wondering. Big cash crop farmers didn't survive after the Cataclysm. They didn't know what to do without fancy machinery and most people couldn't tell a jam from a jelly, never mind a jerky. How'd Atherton make out so well?"

Bobby Sue brushed a stray hair from her face and winked. "That's 'cause our farmers have special skills. A fair sized Amish community lived here before the Day of Reckoning. They had all the old fashioned farming and food preservation know how. Weren't too keen on mingling in the beginning, but they changed their minds when bandits almost burned them to the ground. Now they take care of running the farms and the rest of the town takes care of keeping them safe."

Tatiana's heart skipped a beat as Bobby Sue mentioned the Day of Reckoning. She'd been using that term more often since she began dating Brother William last month. Most people still referred to that day as the Cataclysm. The Day of Reckoning was a League of the Stars term.

"Enough talk," said Cook, handing them each a thick slice of bread with cheese. "And don't worry about the incubator or the chickens. The rest of us will keep this place running just fine."

Jill stumbled into the kitchen, rubbing her eyes, a small bag slung over one shoulder. Bobby Sue shoved a piece of bread and cheese into her hand and turned her around, nudging Jill back through the doorway. "Come on, sleepy head. Mr. Zook will be here in a minute to pick us up. If we miss him we'll have to walk all the way to the fields and we don't know which one."

Jill plopped her hat on her head and took a huge bite of the bread as she walked. They left the tavern as a large flatbed wagon pulled up. Two stocky brown horses stood still as the women climbed aboard, bringing the passenger count up to a dozen men and women. Fifi, who had followed them out, darted into Tatiana's lap, startling a few people.

"Hey! What's with the rat?" said the driver.

A large, weathered felt hat, which at one point might have been black, perched on the man's head. As he stared at Fifi, his brow wrinkled, accentuating his dry, sun-splotched skin. His look was stern, but Tatiana sensed a mixture of curiosity and amusement. Offended at being called a rat, Fifi began to growl. Tatiana sent a silent reprimand then picked her up so the driver could see her more clearly.

"Fifi isn't a rat, Sir," said Tatiana. "But she can chase them out of the fields for you."

The driver raised his eyebrows and squinted his brown eyes, clearly unconvinced the dog could chase anything away. "Well, it's on you then, but if she gets in the way she's liable to get stepped on."

"Yes, Sir."

With a sigh, the man clucked his tongue and snapped the reins. The horses jumped into a fast walk, their thick hooves making a loud clopping sound on the otherwise quiet street. Occasionally a pebble, dislodged by their passage, skidded across the packed stone road.

"That's John Zook," whispered Bobby Sue. "He's the owner and manager of one of the bigger farms. We'll be stayin' at his house till our shift is done. It's not far, but Mrs. Zook, Magdalena, likes to make sure everyone has a nice meal in their belly after a hard day's work and a good night's rest for the next day. He's also on the council. Gareth told me the other day that Mr. Zook and Mr. Herr, the owner of the biggest cattle farm, have missed a bunch of meetings lately. Mako doesn't send word about emergency council meetings until after they've happened."

"That's not fair."

"No, it's not," said Bobby Sue. "Gareth wasn't happy when he found out."

They continued along the road, heading north for several minutes. Just over the river that meandered through the northern section of town, they passed a smithy and stable. Turning left, the wagon headed down a small dirt track through a large field of wheat. Tall grasses rippled in the gentle breeze. They were still green, the seeds just forming. The wagon stopped at the edge of another field. These three-foot high plants were laden with fuzzy little pods.

"Leave your bags in the wagon," said Mr. Zook. "Everybody out and grab a basket. We're harvesting soybeans today. Snap the pods off with a twist and put them in the baskets. The stems will be harvested for feed next week. Each of you pick a row on the left and work your way to the end. I'll meet you on the other side after I drop your bags off at the house."

Mr. Zook rode off as the workers spread out across the field with the baskets that had been piled on the ground. Tatiana scanned the field they were in. It looked huge. With a little sneeze, Fifi ducked under the first plant she came to and nuzzled away the large brown leaves to make a nest.

"You're a big help," laughed Tatiana.

Fifi wiggled her tail and closed her eyes, leaving Tatiana to shake her head as she secured her hat and grabbed a pair of gloves. Before long the sun would be beating down on them in earnest.

"Y'all ever harvest before?" asked Bobby Sue, as she grasped a bunch of the finger length fuzzy pods and twisted them off.

"Yes," said Tatiana. "My parents were avid gardeners."

Jill, however, stood next to the brown plants with a perplexed look on her face. The small white scar over her eye stood out sharply on her chocolate skin. "I never done it. My parents worked at an aquarium. Dad sold souvenirs in the gift shop and mom fed the fish."

"That's a pretty important job," said Tatiana. "Was your mom a marine biologist?"

"I dunno," she shrugged. "I just remember hangin' out there a bunch. The sharks were cool, especially at feedin' time. Watching her feed the giant octopus is still the best. He was kinda shy. Mom used to wiggle a squid on the end of a long stick to coax him out. That creature would wait until the bait got real close, and then snatch it before Mom could pull it back."

"You're lucky," said Bobby Sue. "I only got to go to an aquarium once, when I was eight."

Jill reached a tentative hand down and yanked at a soybean pod. Her plant took an extra beating for her to get the pod off, but she dropped it into her basket with pride. They spent the rest of the day filling the new baskets Mr. Zook supplied at the end of every row. Each of them fell into the rhythm of grab, twist, drop as they harvested the pods.

By the end of the day, Jill's complaints about all the bending, squatting, and cuts on her hands had gotten old. Tatiana wasn't exactly comfortable herself, but at least she had been smart enough to use the gloves. She had learned early on that complaints did nothing to ease discomfort. If anything they made it worse. When they stopped for the day, she allowed herself to stretch and rub her sore muscles.

"Thank goodness," said Bobby Sue, as she rubbed her own back. "I was beginnin' to wonder if you were human the way you kept going. You're like a machine."

Tatiana smiled, but inside her heart jumped. It wasn't the first time she had received that comment. Nor was it the first time she had asked herself that same question.

The voice echoed in her mind. *"Of course you're human."*

"But I'm different."

"You're still human."

"I'm as sore as you are," she said out loud. "I just distracted myself while I worked."

"How'd you do that?" asked Jill, wincing as she sucked the latest cut on her thumb.

"Sometimes I hum or sing a song in my mind. Other times I imagine myself somewhere else."

"Like in the stories you read?"

"Yes, or in a happy memory. It helps make the time go faster."

Despite the hat, Bobby Sue's cheeks and the tip of her nose were red. "Well, I'll be sure to try that trick tomorrow."

"Me too," said Jill.

Chapter Fifteen

Three Years BDR

She bit into the baby beet, letting the sweet juice roll over her tongue. Mama had roasted them with a hint of fresh rosemary, the same rosemary that Tatiana had helped plant just two years ago. Almost everything on the table had been grown in their garden. But even foods they hadn't grown were freshly made, like the tender strips of pasta coated in browned butter. Each bite melted in Tatiana's mouth. Mama's food was made with more than mere ingredients; it was made with love.

Tatiana

Tatiana struggled to keep her eyes open as the wagon wound its way out of the fields and onto the road. Talk dwindled, fatigue and food being foremost on everyone's mind. The horses increased their pace as a large white farmhouse came into view. Two thick chimneys, the kind built in the interior of a house, protruded through the roof of the simple bi-level, one on either side of the building. Behind it loomed a barn and a fenced in chicken coop. Tatiana wondered if one of the Zooks could shed light on Gareth's chicken problems.

As they drew closer, details became evident. A covered porch spanned the entire front of the house with several chairs and benches spaced along its length. It wrapped around the left side and disappeared from view. Three large windows were visible on the ground floor with the door. Several smaller windows dotted the second level. Wood was stacked to the right of the door with a much larger pile on the side of the house.

Mr. Zook drove past the house and stopped just outside the barn near a hand pump. Four men, all wearing the same kind of clothing and dark hat as Mr. Zook, greeted them. More than their attire was similar. They had the same facial features, some less aged than others, but all in their mid to late thirties. Even their beards were identical. Each covered only their chins and rose up into sideburns. None had mustaches and the space just below the lips was clean shaven as well. Two of the men were busy unhitching horses from another wagon.

"These are my sons," said Mr. Zook. "They'll show you where to put the baskets. Once that's taken care of, wash up at the pump and go on down to the house. I'm sure Magdalene has supper just about ready to serve."

With the last of the soybeans carefully stowed, everyone gathered around the pump. Tatiana waited until last, then washed Fifi before she stuck her head under the cool, crisp water. It felt good to wash the sweat and grime away. She gave her head a shake, then raked her hands through her long dark hair.

With Fifi perched on her shoulder, Tatiana followed Bobby Sue and Jill to the house, entering as the sun sank. The room bustled with activity, everyone moving with purpose as though in a well-rehearsed dance. Even the children carried plates and utensils to the long wooden tables. One voice loomed above all the casual conversations, handing out directions with confident authority. Over two dozen people filled the space, but it was easy to tell the Zook family from the house guests by their attire. All the Zook women wore simple calf-length dresses with white aprons, their hair neatly pulled back and covered with a small white bonnet. Men sported dark pants, suspenders and light-colored shirts. Tatiana scanned the room, noting the age gap between the two teens, a girl and boy, and most of the other children who ranged in age from one to five.

Unsure where to go, Tatiana moved to the side and bumped into a small sideboard under the window to the right of the door. There were many strangers in the room and several stared in her direction. Tightness spread across her chest and she lowered her eyes. Could they see what she was? Did they know?

"Sorry, dear, but dogs aren't permitted at the table." The firm but caring voice that had been directing the chaos cut through Tatiana's panic.

Standing at the other end of the large, thick oak table that ran perpendicular to the front of the house, stood a woman with her hands on her hips. Despite the stern stance, the woman's blue eyes sparkled as she studied Tatiana. The emotions she exuded were as soothing as a balm. If John Zook was the patriarch of the Zook family, this had to be the matriarch, Magdalena.

Fifi yipped once, then leaped off Tatiana's shoulder, disappearing through a throng of feet. A moment later, Tatiana spotted her across the room with a group of toddlers. Magdalena smiled at the youngsters. Gray-streaked black hair adorned her head, parted down the middle and rolled back into one neat bun under her bonnet.

"Hi, Mrs. Zook," said Bobby Sue. She nudged Tatiana and Jill forward. "Thanks for having us. I see you already met Tatiana. This here's Jill and the cute little ball of fur is Fifi."

"Welcome to our home, ladies. Supper is almost ready." Magdalena looked at Jill's blistered and cut hands and frowned. "See me after supper, Jill. I have some salve for those hands of yours.

"Thank you, Mrs. Zook. Them beans are fiercer than an alley cat."

The smile returned to Magdalena's face. "Indeed they are."

"Is there anythin' we can do to help?" asked Bobby Sue.

"There are some bowls and platters ready in the kitchen. Alma can show you which ones. Please put them on the tables."

The three of them hustled off to the kitchen where Alma, a cheerful thirteen-year-old with brown hair, sent them right back out laden with dishes. A moment later, Mr. Zook came in and everyone found a seat around the tables. It seemed as though someone had flipped a switch. All conversation ended, leaving the room silent. Around the table, heads bowed, the entire Zook family prayed in silence. A few of the guests looked around perplexed, but no one made a sound. Then just as abruptly, talking resumed and everyone reached for the food.

Tatiana dug into her meal with zeal. Memories churned inside at each bite of the sweet and tangy pickled beets and bread slathered in apple butter. Meals of her childhood had been mostly home grown. There was always enough, enough to share with a stranger passing by, and enough to bring to the local shelter when needed. Chicken, meat, and fish were on the menu infrequently, but with all of the herbs Mama used, they weren't missed.

Tears blurred Tatiana's vision. Every taste and smell of Magdalena's cooking reminded her of home. Mama had cooked mostly from memory and intuition. If only she had written some of her recipes down, Tatiana would have remembered them.

"You ok?" asked Alma.

Tatiana jumped, quickly drying her eyes with her sleeve. She had forgotten that Alma sat next to her. "I'm fine, just thinking about my parents."

Alma bit her lip and Tatiana could sense the uncertainty that flashed through the girl's mind. "Bobby Sue said you love reading as much as I do," she said after a short pause.

"Yes," said Tatiana. "Stories take me places I can only dream of." She bit at her lip a moment and glanced across the table at Jill. "I've been reading a lot about chickens lately, but it isn't helping much. I can't get any of our eggs to grow. Do you know much about them?"

"Chickens?" Alma laughed, the sound sweet and light. "I can tell you all you need to know about them."

Jill looked up mid-chew. Fear flickered in her eyes before she resumed eating, pointedly ignoring both Tatiana and Alma. The indifferent attitude Jill displayed didn't fool Tatiana. She'd have to talk chickens with Alma later.

"Hey, Alma," said Bobby Sue, "who are those men over there talkin' to your dad and grandpa? They're dressed too nice for field work."

Leave it to Bobby Sue to change topics. Across the table Jill looked up, relief evident on her face. Tatiana looked down the table to the men who were deep in conversation. They weren't exactly dressed formally, but not for hard labor either. They looked more like salesmen.

"They came down from Ohio, about a week's travel time north of here," said Alma. We get all sorts of merchants this time of year. Some are looking for produce or preserves, but most want our surplus grain. That's what those men want to buy."

"Why not put the extra in the surplus grain storage Atherton built three years ago?" asked Bobby Sue.

"They're nearly full. Better we sell it to those who need it than let it rot. Besides, the merchants take care of all the pick-up, delivery, and security arrangements on the road."

Once everyone had eaten their fill, the makeshift tables were cleared and disassembled as quickly as they'd been erected. Within moments, all the benches were lined up against the wall. Tatiana and Alma were deep in conversation when an exasperated voice shouted across the room.

"Russell! You put that dog down, now."

A cluster of youngsters chased after a four-year-old boy. Clutched in his arms was a familiar white fur ball. Alma intercepted the child as he ran past and scooped him into her arms. A small tickle under his arms elicited a squeal of laughter and loosened his grip. Fifi leaped from his arms, shook herself out, then led the remaining children on another circuit of the room.

"I have him, Aunt Fannie."

"Thank you, Alma," said Fannie, as she took the wriggling boy with a heavy sigh. "I don't know where that dog came from, but it's got the children all riled up."

Tatiana lowered her gaze again. It felt as though a cold, wet blanket had landed on her head. Would they make them leave? Her words jumbled out in a panic. "I'm sorry, Ma'am. Fifi didn't mean any harm. Really she didn't. I'll take her outside."

"That won't be necessary," said Fannie. A smile filled the woman's face and the beginnings of laugh lines creased the corners of her eyes. "There's no need to worry, unless you call me Ma'am again. Fannie will be fine. Just settle her down is all."

The fear that had chilled her lifted. After a quick word of thanks, Tatiana spun around, tracking the little dog by the children's laughter as they darted around the room.

Fifi paused as Tatiana mentally told her to calm down, but the dog's eyes filled with the same mischievous glint the children had. In a second she took off again—and landed in a large calloused hand as big as she was. Fifi scurried up the man's arm and flopped on his shoulder, panting heavily. Below, the children jumped up and down. One wrapped his arms around the man's tree-trunk sized thighs and tried to climb.

"That will be enough of that," said Magdalena. She stood in the center of the room. Her voice wasn't loud or harsh, but did carry a clear authoritative tone. "Leave Mr. Minto alone. Now, off to bed."

When the children had left, Magdalena's gaze fell on Tatiana. With leaden feet she walked toward them, fully expecting to be scolded. Fifi whimpered an apology, her ears flat against her head. Tatiana just stared at the floor.

"Tatiana, dear."

"Yes, Ma'am?"

"In the future, kindly keep a tighter eye on your dog. It's not good for the children to get so excited before bed."

"Yes, Ma'am. I understand."

"Good. Now kindly relieve Mr. Minto of his shoulder ornamentation."

Wordlessly, Tatiana retrieved Fifi, noting the burn scars that dotted the man's arms and face, a sign of someone who worked around dangerous fire. Still, there was gentleness around his eyes that offset the brusqueness of his physique. He was far from a giant, but there was no doubting the strength in those broad shoulders or the bulging muscles on his arms and neck.

"You must be Gareth's new girl," he said, holding out one of his mammoth hands. "You can call me Ted. I run the blacksmith shop by the river. Stopped by to deliver a new plough blade and they wouldn't let me leave without a meal."

The good humor in Ted's voice eased Tatiana's heart and she smiled back. "Thank you for catching Fifi."

"My pleasure," he said, gently patting Fifi's head. "I grew up with poodles, although ours were a bit bigger. Peaches was a standard poodle and when she tried to jump into my arms, she almost knocked me over."

Tatiana giggled, having a hard time picturing anything knocking the blacksmith down. After a round of goodbyes, Ted and the visiting merchants left. The remaining guests spread their bedrolls on the floor. Tatiana, Bobby Sue, and Jill made their camp under the big oak table with a couple of other women. The sturdy wood created a pseudo cave, giving some sense of privacy in the packed room. Even surrounded by so many strangers, Tatiana felt more at home than she had in a long time. The evening's events played in her mind as she drifted off to sleep.

Chapter Sixteen

Two Years Eight Months ADR – April

Silence hung over the woods as Tatiana shrunk into the damp hollow. Alone—again—cast out by yet another group because of what she could do. Chills ran down her spine as she heard the hunters prowl closer to her hiding place. She'd seen people like them before; wild, empty of humanity, the kind who would kill almost anything for food. Tatiana was nearly twelve now, almost ripe for their other appetites. She squeezed her eyes shut, praying the scouts wouldn't spot her. She didn't want to hurt them, not like the others. No one deserved that kind of death, not even these savages.

Tatiana

As she climbed into the wagon on the last day of their work in the fields, Tatiana looked longingly at the remaining plants, wondering who would be harvesting them. Bobby Sue and Jill were already seated amongst the baskets of sweet corn they had picked today. This time, another wagon would be waiting by the blacksmith's shop to take the baskets to the farm. Tatiana, Jill, and Bobby Sue would return to Gareth's, as they had at the end of each week. Even during harvest the Zooks didn't work during Sabbath.

"Today I imagined I waded in the creek behind my grandparent's house catchin' crayfish," said Bobby Sue. She wiped sweat from her face. "What about you, Tatiana?"

"I helped Mama and Papa with their garden. Papa had a grape arbor that he used to trim and fuss with."

"How were the grapes?"

"Super sweet inside and ultra-tart on the outside," laughed

Tatiana. "They weren't much good for eating, but they made the best jam I've ever had."

"Okay," said Jill. "Now you're making my mouth water. I can't remember the last time I had grape jam, let alone a fresh grape."

"Me neither," said Bobby Sue. "There aren't any vines in Atherton or any of the near-by towns. Got some great peach trees, though."

"There's gotta be grapes somewhere," said Jill. "Maybe Marty will find some."

"He found canned fish," said Bobby Sue. "Who knows what he'll bring next."

A dun-colored dog charged around the corner from the main road and rushed at the horses, snarling ferociously. The short but stout dog had a rounded head and a strong square jaw, perfectly designed for fighting. Many scars covered the animal's hide, a testament to previous battles. Eyes wide with terror, the horses reared and lunged in opposite directions. Dust billowed as they squealed and bucked. Everyone held on as the wagon lurched, spilling several baskets of corn onto the ground. One of the horses stumbled and Tatiana felt its surge of pain run down her spine. She bit her lip to keep from crying out as Mr. Zook tried to bring the horses under control. All the while, the vicious dog darted around the wagon nipping at the horse's feet.

"I told you to keep that cur away from my animals," yelled Mr. Zook, as two men sauntered into view. Both wore stained militia jackets and teetered as though they had been drinking heavily.

"Aw, relax, Zook. Bucky's just having some fun." The men laughed.

"Get it away from my horses!"

One of the men gave a halfhearted whistle and called Bucky. The horses continued to jerk, lifting the wagon with a twist. Corn and bodies were caught in mid-air for a moment as the wagon shifted.

A small surprised yelp warned Tatiana that something else was amiss. She looked around in alarm and saw Fifi on the ground amidst a dozen cobs of corn. A small shake sent dust billowing up from her fur. Bucky stopped dancing around the wagon. Saliva dripped from his jowls as he snarled at Fifi. Without thinking, Tatiana leaped out of the wagon. She landed between the little dog and Bucky. It wasn't until she alighted on the ground that she remembered Fifi was completely capable of protecting herself.

Most animals Tatiana had met took to her right away, but only madness and bloodlust shone in Bucky's eyes. She stood rooted, too stunned to react as the snarling dog leaped for her throat.

A white blur intercepted the beast, leaving streaks of blood along the animal's neck. Startled, Bucky stepped back, trying to focus on this new, bounding target. Fifi darted around, under, and over the larger animal, which snapped vainly at empty air. Tatiana's heart raced faster. She could feel Fifi gathering energy. The last thing either of them needed was for Fifi to transform in public.

"Fifi! NO!"

A few feet from the vicious dog, Fifi froze. Her anger twirled recklessly and Tatiana prayed the little dog would listen. Fifi hesitated for only a moment, and then darted into the wheat field followed closely by the crazed beast.

"What the hell was that thing?" said the man who had whistled to Bucky earlier. His slack-jawed expression accentuated his booze glazed eyes.

"I think it's supposed to be a dog," laughed his friend, as he started to stagger toward the field. "Come on. This should be fun."

Mr. Zook's booming voice halted them before they reached the first row. "YOU TWO WILL STAY OUT OF MY FIELDS!"

"Oh my God!" said Bobby Sue, as she started to climb out of the pitching wagon. "That monster will tear Fifi to pieces."

"Stay where you are," Mr. Zook shouted above the screaming horses.

Bobby Sue halted at the command and cast a worried glance at Tatiana before looking back toward the fields. Everyone in the wagon strained their necks to catch a glimpse of the dogs.

No one moved as Mr. Zook tried to calm the panicked horses. The two men stood rooted to the ground just outside the field, their eyes trained on the stalks of wheat. Tatiana eased herself closer to the horses and whispered soothing words. The others were worried about Fifi, but she knew who really faced danger. The two horses, still wide-eyed with fear, were of more concern to her. The one on the left side of the wagon held its left foreleg off the ground. With difficulty, Tatiana tuned out the snarling chaos now audible in the fields. Energy tickled Tatiana's fingertips as she opened her mind. She reached out until the horses stood with only a slight quiver.

Thankful for the distraction in the field, she ran her hand down the leg of the injured horse, letting her mind follow the pain. The sprain shimmered in her mind like a softly glowing red light, a very different feel from a break and much easier to heal. Energy radiated from her hands into the joint above the hoof, knitting the stretched and partially torn ligaments.

By the time she finished, the snarling had stopped and the horses stood quietly. Everyone stared at the wheat, which showed no movement, but Tatiana already knew the outcome of the dogfight. Gasps of surprise burst from the crowd as Fifi stepped onto the road. She shook once to remove the last vestiges of debris from her fur and then wagged her tail. There wasn't a spot of dirt on her snowy white coat.

"What the..." exclaimed the whistler. He looked suddenly more sober.

"Where the hell is Bucky? Bucky! Here, boy. Bucky, come. What did that rat do to my Bucky?" yelled the other man.

Just then Bucky slunk out of the field, his tail tightly curled between his legs. Fresh wounds streaked his fur. Even over the men's cussing, Tatiana could hear the dog's pathetic whimpers. One look at Fifi and Bucky tried to bolt, infuriating the two men.

"Maybe that will teach you to keep your animal under control and out of the fields," said Mr. Zook, as he jumped from the wagon to check the horses. "Someone could have been killed. I don't care where you came from or who you think you work for. Guards are supposed to protect people in this town, not terrorize them and their livestock."

It felt as though a storm had gathered around the men and Tatiana flinched as one of them reached for the pistol on his belt. She held her breath, waiting as Mr. Zook glared at them. One of the men grabbed Bucky and slung a coarse rope lead around his neck. A sharp jerk on the lead made him whine in pain. Without another word, the two men spat on the ground and disappeared down the road.

Tatiana heard Mr. Zook breathe a sigh of relief, but she felt the tension that still permeated his body.

"Is everyone okay?" he asked, and then turned toward Tatiana. "That was a dangerous thing you did, jumping in front of that beast. Are you all right?"

Tatiana gathered Fifi in her arms and snuggled her close. "I'm fine," she whispered.

"I'm going to have to have a talk with that so-called General Snider. Putting our militia in the hands of that war worshiper was a bad idea," said Mr. Zook, as he ran his hand down the leg of the horse Tatiana had healed. A flicker of surprise crossed his face.

"I could have sworn I saw him limp a moment ago."

Mr. Zook looked at Tatiana then studied Fifi for an inordinate amount of time, making her chest tighten with that familiar heavy weight.

"Oh, God. He suspects."

"Probably."

"They all must suspect something."

"Don't jump to conclusions. Most people see only what they want to see, but they will think twice if they see anything else amiss."

"You're good with horses," Mr. Zook said, after a few moments.

"I like animals. Most know I mean them no harm."

Mr. Zook's eyebrow went up, as if he were waiting for a different explanation. Tatiana bit her lip and buried her face in Fifi's fur, trying to quell her building panic.

When she said nothing more, he nodded, a hint of a smile grazing his face. He lay his big calloused hand on Fifi's head ruffling her fur. "And you are definitely more than you seem."

Tatiana smiled, but inside her heart trembled.

"You don't know how true that is, Mr. Zook."

"Or does he?"

Chapter Seventeen

Bobby Sue

Bobby Sue twirled a strand of red hair around her finger. Tears stung her eyes as she surveyed the damage from the pre-dawn break-in. Glass shards covered the floor and flour dusted the room. Merchandise lay scattered about and one of the shelves wobbled on a broken leg. Most disturbing was the man who moaned near the door and the blood splattered around him.

Beside her, Jill and Cook shifted nervously. Gareth held his shotgun as steady as ever, but his jaw muscles twitched. Even Sabrina had lost her stiff composure and clung to Gareth like a frightened child. No one spoke as they watched Doc Johnson patch up the would-be thief.

"You should have sent for me sooner," said the doctor, as she tied off the last bandage.

"Couldn't risk it. Not with his buddies running about," said Gareth. He readjusted the grip on his shotgun. "Tatiana stopped the bleeding well enough. Besides, I have faith in your abilities."

Doc Johnson's neat rows of braids swayed as she turned. Her dark-brown eyes scrutinized him. "I'm a veterinarian, Gareth. Not a blasted surgeon. I should be birthing cows and treating cats and dogs, not people."

"You're also the only doctor this town has, Edna. Beside, none of us are living the life we thought we would." A deep breath escaped his lips. "Why don't you go wash up and eat before you leave."

Doc Johnson shook her head as she headed to the back. She paused at the door. Her skin almost blended in with the dark wood. "Get some sleep, Gareth. Doctor's orders. You look like crap."

"Mr. Burns said the same thing."

"Smart man."

Gareth rubbed a hand across his face. "I'll rest when it's safe."

"Always were a stubborn son of a bee."

"Yeah."

The strands of hair Bobby Sue held pulled even tauter. She worried about Gareth as well. Dark circles hung under his eyes and worry lines creased his face. Doc Johnson was right. He needed sleep. Then again, it was Gareth's insomnia that caught the thief in the act. Too bad he didn't catch the others.

"Gareth," she said, when no one moved. "Can we go back to cleanin' now? Or do you still want us to wait?"

"May as well start, Bobby Sue, but keep away from him," said Gareth, as he leaned over to check the man's bonds.

They set to cleaning and picking up fallen items while Gareth kept his gun trained on the prisoner. More creases grew on Gareth's forehead as the sun continued to rise. People began to fill the street. Frightened faces glanced their way then hurried off.

"Bit of a mess," said Snider as he sauntered into the store as if out for a stroll.

Gareth's scowl increased. He stood stiff, like a fully wound spring. "It's about damned time you got here, Snider. I sent for you hours ago."

"Sorry, busy morning. Lots of rabble-rousers out last night." He nudged the prisoner with his foot, looking completely board and disinterested. "So what happened?"

"Four masked men tore the grate off and broke the glass. Started smashing things as soon as they came in. I shouted a warning, fired. This one fell. The rest scattered."

Snider looked at Gareth. The eyebrow on the scared side of his face twisted up. "Lucky you heard them and got here before they did too much damage. You must be an awful light sleeper."

"Yeah, real lucky." There was an edge to Gareth's voice. "I was in the office, working."

Snider pressed his foot on top of the injured man eliciting a deep moan. "Tsk, really messy, Gareth."

"Serves him right for breaking in. Now, get him out of here. I have a business to run."

"And I have my job," said Snider. "Need to do some investigating. You said there was another attacker?"

"I told you there were three others." Gareth's eyes narrowed. "They ran off when I fired. Heard some snarling and yelling not long after they left."

"That so?" said Snider. "Interesting. I'll take a look outside. Someone will be around to pick this one up."

"And when will that be?"

Snider smirked. "Hard to tell. As I said, it was a busy night."

Bobby Sue saw Gareth draw in a deep breath as Snider left. He wasn't the only one on edge. That man made her skin crawl like curdled milk, especially when he looked at her.

"He'll find the other men, won't he, Gareth?" said Cook. Her voice shook and she had half her apron twisted into a wad. "If they come back…"

"They won't. We'll be fine." said Gareth. Then he looked at Sabrina, who had fussed with the same boxes behind the counter for the past hour. "It'll be all right, Sabrina. You just worry about getting the store ready. Let me take care of those hoodlums."

It was another hour before Snider's men took the prisoner away. They were barely out the door when William burst in, flush faced and out of breath. Gareth's gun swung toward William's chest. Bobby Sue felt her heart began to race. For a second no one moved, then Gareth lowered the gun.

"Are you trying to get yourself killed?" said Gareth. "What are you doing here?"

William moved to Bobby Sue's side. His hand cupped her cheek and she leaned into it. "I was worried. One of the brothers heard talk in the town square. They said the doctor was here. I came as soon as I could."

"Only one hurt was the crook," said Bobby Sue. "But I'm glad you're here."

Some of her tension melted away as she looked into his hazel eyes. There was something there, she was sure of it. Why else would he rush here to check on her? His breath caressed her face as he leaned in closer. A kiss, all she wanted was one sweet kiss.

"Great. The whole town knows," said Gareth.

William's hand dropped to his side and he stepped away from Bobby Sue. "It wasn't just your place, Gareth. There were a dozen break-ins last night."

"Let me guess," said Gareth, "None of them were owned by Mako."

"I don't know." William took the broom from Bobby Sue and moved to the other side of the room. "But I can find out for you."

Bobby Sue bit her tongue. Gareth had lousy timing. She watched William sweep, hoping for another glance, a smile, anything. Even after Gareth and Sabrina ducked into the office and Jill went to help with the other choirs he didn't peek at her. In fact, he seemed to look everywhere but her direction.

Bobby Sue marched over to him. "What do you think you're doin'?" Her tone was harsher than she intended.

William's Adam's apple bobbed up and down. "Helping."

"You wanna help," she said, snatching the broom back. "Fix that wobbly shelf for Gareth. The tools and stuff are already there. I can handle the sweepin' myself."

He looked at the shelf across the room, then back at Bobby Sue. With a small nod he hurried over there and started to work. Silence settled across the room until Bobby Sue felt like she was going to burst.

"Can I ask you a question, William?"

"Bobby Sue, you can ask me anything you want," he said with one of his charming smiles.

"You folks don't do anything ridiculous like vows of celibacy, do you?"

William's face turned red and his eyes widened slightly. "We're ah...more the fruitful and multiply type."

"Well, you coulda fooled me," she muttered and went back to cleaning.

Chapter Eighteen

Day Of Reckoning – August Twelfth

Water roared and rushed around the woman and child as they held onto the soggy mattress. Fiery balls of rock soared across the sky before plunging into the churning mass of water and debris. Steam and scalding water shot up after each impact, scorching anything it touched. The surging water carried their wayward bed across town, smashing it into cars, trees, and buildings. Luck kept the mattress from flipping or being crushed and sheer will kept them both on top of it.

Tears streamed from the young girl's eyes, partially from the mist and smoke, but mostly from terror. Her mind reeled in confusion, trying to make sense of the chaos around her. Over the roaring water and explosive impacts, she heard an occasional scream or cry for help, but those voices were becoming scarcer. She clung desperately to the one stable thing that remained—her mother hanging onto the other side of the mattress. The mother whispered words of encouragement to the nine-year-old girl.

A fiery ball of debris landed only feet away, spewing scalding water over half the mattress. The woman cried out in pain, her face a mask of horror and agony. Trees ripped up by their roots careened toward them. Their wake tilted the mattress dangerously and forced the woman and child to claw for purchase.

Minutes passed, which seemed an eternity, while boulders bounced in the surf like pebbles on a beach. All the girl heard now was the roar of the water mixed with the crash and snap of objects not easily broken.

Out of nowhere a tree surged up from beneath the dark swirling waters beside the floundering raft. Branches clawed

*out, grasping like a mythical sea monster. The girl saw one
monstrous arm, dark and stripped of foliage. "Mama!" she cried
in alarm, her voice raw and raspy from overuse. A deep gouge
in the mattress marked where her mother had clung only seconds
before. "Mama!" she cried again.*

*Alone and numb with shock, she rode the waves, determined
to heed her mama's last words: "Hold tight, Tatiana. Don't give
up hope."*

Tatiana

Tatiana woke shivering and drenched with sweat. Some
things weren't easily forgotten or left in the past. The Cataclysm,
the so-called Day of Reckoning, was one of them. Her heart still
galloped erratically with the memory of the surging waters and
her mama's final words. She had held on that day and most of
the next until the sea deposited her raft high in the hills. Days
later, after subsisting on wild berries, she stumbled onto other
survivors. If it hadn't been for her parents' love of camping, the
knowledge of plants she had learned from her mama, and her
passion for reading everything, including survival stories, she
doubted she would have lived. Some of what she ate had still
been guesswork. Except for sporadic untouched pockets, much
of the identifying foliage she would have used had been
destroyed. Farther west, she found food less scarce.

Soft nuzzling and a warm, wet tongue brought Tatiana back
to the present. She snuggled against Fifi's fur.

"I don't know what I'd do without you," she whispered. Fifi
wagged her tail and gave Tatiana another gentle kiss.

After a few minutes, Tatiana drifted off to sleep again,
untroubled by nightmares. She stirred as the first rays of sun
snuck past the partially shuttered window. The movement
earned her another kiss from Fifi before the dog jumped off the
bed. Animals on the furniture were a definite 'no no' with
Sabrina, but no one in the little dorm was going to tattle. As far
as Tatiana could tell, Sabrina had also remained silent about
what had happened that first night. Their relationship had settled
into an unspoken truce over the past two months, though Sabrina
still assigned Tatiana the most strenuous and disliked tasks.

Tatiana started her usual routine with putting a pot of water up to boil for the herbal tea she brewed every morning. Her familiarity with plants, each with its own healthful properties, seemed to help improve everyone's mood, even Sabrina's.

This morning's chores began in the small stable, actually a converted storage shed. Gareth didn't often board horses, but the travelers staying with them had been willing to pay to keep the animals close. They weren't the first travelers Mr. Zook had sent their way since the incident in the fields, three weeks ago.

As Tatiana approached the stable, a hazy golden glow filled the sky, granting the promise of another beautiful day. Quiet nickering from the cream-colored mare and brown and white pinto gelding greeted her. She rubbed the soft velvety fur on the animals' noses, then slipped through the fence into their corral. They had only been there a couple of days, but already welcomed her like an old friend. The horses followed her into the stable like a pair of dogs eager for attention, nosing and jostling her as she filled the water trough and feed bin.

Although Bobby Sue had mentioned the Zooks had at least one gas powered harvesting machine, which thanks to Marty's assistance ran on oil and alcohol, the people of Atherton relied almost exclusively on horses. Tatiana had seen the occasional solar-powered, wind-powered, or steam-powered vehicle, but most people weren't as inventive. Horse travel had become the norm. It certainly beat walking.

After cleaning the stable, Tatiana dumped the wheelbarrow full of old straw and manure into the compost heap and did a quick survey of the grounds. Several weeds poked up through the rich soil of the garden. The annoying little vines were difficult to control, and would take over without constant vigilance.

Tatiana sighed and gave Fifi's head a pat. "Come on. We'd better see about Old Henry before anyone else gets up."

Old Henry's behavior hadn't improved much since the attack, and Jill remained too terrified to go near the coop. Even the incubator freaked her out. Her wounds had healed, but not her mind. None of the other girls wanted anything to do with the rooster either. Tatiana planned on starting with Jill's problem.

"Deal with your own problems first."

Shivers ran up her spine at the voice's blunt statement. After all she'd been through, was she finally going insane? Old Henry's crowing broke that train of thought. It was time for their daily dance. She slipped into the coop with Fifi to gather the brownish eggs and feed the chickens. With plume fully erect, the rooster charged. The creature didn't make it two feet before Fifi transformed and pinned it to the ground with one giant paw.

Once released, Old Henry squawked and ran to the opposite side of the coop. There he remained, preening his feathers as if nothing unusual had happened. Tatiana winked at Fifi, now back to her normal form and licking her dainty paws clean.

"I don't know how y'all do that without gettin' your skin pecked off."

Tatiana looked up, surprised. She hadn't noticed anyone approach, but Bobby Sue stood just outside the chicken coop with her arms folded across her chest. Tatiana bit at her lower lip, wondering if Bobby Sue had seen Fifi change.

"That demon attacks everyone else that goes near it," continued Bobby Sue.

"What, Old Henry?" said Tatiana. She smiled, but a nervous flutter twisted in her gut. "You just have to show him who's boss."

Bobby Sue raised an eyebrow. "Oh, really? And having a guard dog doesn't hurt either, I bet."

Tatiana continued to smile, but her heartbeat quickened. Bobby Sue showed no sign of alarm, just her usual friendly attitude. The woman had an honesty about her that shone in sharp contrast to Sabrina. They'd talked often. Or at least Bobby Sue talked. Tatiana mostly listened.

"Some things are just better left unsaid."

"And some things need to be talked about."

"You'd better get washed up. Sabrina's in a mood this morning."

"Well, perhaps this will put her in a better one," said Tatiana, handing Bobby Sue a basket full of eggs.

"Wow. That's a dozen eggs. Those chickens didn't lay half as many before you came here. What have you been feedin' them?"

"The same as always. They're just a lot less stressed."

A frown creased Bobby Sue's pretty face. "Glad to hear someone's less stressed. Jill won't come near this place and I think Gareth is still planning on rooster stew for Thanksgiving."

Tatiana shook her head. "Not until we have some little roosters to replace him. It'll be at least a year before the chicks are old enough, assuming they survive the winter. I hope Sabrina lets us keep them inside when it gets cold or they might freeze to death."

"Fat chance of that," said Bobby Sue with a laugh. "The only reason she lets Fifi and that incubator full of eggs you rigged in the house is because Gareth said so. Any chance some of them things might actually hatch?"

Tatiana held Fifi close, soothing the growl that rumbled at the mention of Sabrina, and praying Bobby Sue wouldn't notice. "I think one or two might hatch today."

By the way," said Bobby Sue, as they walked to the house, "William stopped by the store yesterday afternoon, but I couldn't find you. I wanted you to meet him."

An icy chill radiated through Tatiana's body. Bobby Sue really liked Brother William. She talked about him constantly, but each time she mentioned his name, Tatiana's heart jumped.

"What are you afraid of? He's not going to hurt you."

"Then why won't he leave me alone?"

Tatiana brushed some loose hairs out of her eyes, trying to ignore her annoying inner voice. She argued with herself more every day. Yesterday she had busied herself in the garden when Brother William visited. She didn't want to run into him. She didn't want any reminder of what happened four years ago.

"Why not? Let him help you like you helped him."

"Tatiana?" Furrows creased Bobby Sue's face, and Tatiana could feel her concern.

"Sorry. My mind drifted."

"Where were you yesterday? I looked everywhere for you."

Guilt tugged at her conscience again, making her throat feel tight. "I was doing chores all day. With that crazy floor plan, we must have missed each other in the halls."

"Liar. You were avoiding her."

"Anyway, he told me Bucky's owners got flogged in the town square early yesterday morning for what happened with

Mr. Zook last week. Snider did it himself. I guess Mako and Snider are afraid to upset the farm owners. They know this town can't survive without them."

"That's reassuring," said Tatiana, but she worried what would happen if Bucky's owners or Mako and Snider got over that fear.

Bobby Sue seemed ill at ease as well. The strand of hair she had wrapped around her finger was pulled taut. "William promised to stop by again in a few days if he can. He's real busy 'cause of the upcoming Day of Reckoning. You can meet him then."

Tatiana's heart dropped.

"What if he knows who I am?"

"Of course he does."

Shivers continued to race up and down her spine.

"I don't want everyone to know."

"Eventually you'll need to face what you are."

Chapter Nineteen

Three Weeks ADR – September

Water thundered in Tatiana's ears, drowning out the meager birdsong. It wasn't anything like the raging flood she had survived only a few weeks ago, but the sound made her chest constrict, leaving her gasping for air. On the other side of the river stood the remains of an orchard. "Hold tight, Tatiana. Don't give up." Mama's words helped calm her panic, but words wouldn't get her to the food that stood twenty feet away. The only way across was a partially rotted tree that had fallen across the banks. Below raced the water, chilled by the rapidly dropping temperatures. One step, she just needed to take one step at a time. Mama's mantra played over in her mind, each repetition drawing her further across the river until she stood on the other side. Behind her raged the swollen river and some of her fear.

Tatiana

Tatiana gave the wrench another twist before placing it back in the toolbox. The generator had stopped working that morning and Gareth had asked Tatiana to fix it while he patched the roof. For the past few hours she had poked, cleaned, twisted, and tweaked the old contraption. Thankfully, Sabrina had left on an errand as soon as Gareth handed out the assignment, so Tatiana had been able to work in peace. She had even enlisted Jill's aid for the final stage of repairs, explaining what she was doing as she worked so the girl could learn how to do future maintenance. After one final check, she crossed her fingers and gave Jill a nod. The young girl pedaled with a steady rhythm and the generator hummed. Holding her breath, Tatiana watched the amperage needle rise then checked the bank of old car batteries along the wall.

"Well?" asked Jill.

"It worked," she said. A feeling of triumph washed over her. It felt good to fix things. "The generator is putting out more amperage and the batteries seem to be taking the charge. The real test will be when you stop pedaling."

Jill hopped off the bike. The needle wavered for a second, but remained steady. Tatiana smiled at Jill. Once all the batteries she had tweaked were fully charged, they should work for days longer than they had.

"How long do you think it'll take to get them fully charged?"

"Several hours," said Tatiana. "After that, we'll only need to ride this thing a few hours a day if we don't waste electricity."

"Yay!" Jill did a little victory dance and for a moment seemed like her old self.

"What's all this yelling about?" demanded Sabrina, as she marched into the room.

"The work is complete, Miss Sabrina. We need only to charge the batteries. Your dining hall will be fully lit anytime you wish from now on." Although she didn't look directly at her, Tatiana could sense Sabrina's revulsion. It was strong enough to send shivers down Tatiana's spine.

"She knows about Fifi. She knows about me. Why hasn't she told anyone?"

"Is there anything you can't do, Tatiana?" said Sabrina. Her voice dripped with sarcasm. "You're a mechanic, herb expert, cook, healer, master animal handler; it's a wonder we survived without you. And you," she said, turning her wrath on Jill, "you've had enough time to laze about. Get to work. Now!"

Two small eyes glimmered in the dark behind Sabrina. Anger bubbled just below the surface of the growing energy. Tatiana held her breath, willing Fifi to calm down. As soon as Sabrina marched out of the room, Tatiana scooped the fuzzy canine into her arms and held her close.

"So what's next on the agenda?" asked Jill, as she finished cleaning up from their repair job. "I really don't want to scrub the bathrooms just yet."

"I have just the thing," said Tatiana. She placed Fifi on the ground, brushed off her dress, and held her hand out to Jill. "There's something I want to show you."

"Sure," said Jill. "Wanna hear something real interesting?" Jill didn't even pause for an answer. "I was talking to Brother William yesterday. He came for a visit, mostly to see Bobby Sue, but Cook and I got to chat for a while."

Every breath seemed to take more effort as panic squeezed Tatiana's chest. She had to force her feet forward as they moved toward the kitchen. Everywhere she moved, Brother William closed in. First Bobby Sue, and now Jill.

"He's getting too close. I should go."

"No, you shouldn't."

"Anyway," continued Jill, oblivious to Tatiana's discomfort, "he said the star-touched can do all sorts of cool things like go real fast or get super strong. For a little while anyway. They can't hold that power long. And each of them is good at a specific thing. They're not all great at everything. I guess that makes sense. Everyone has their specialty. He told me about a couple of guys that are super good at talking long distance, mental like. Can't remember the word he used. I think he said their names were Eric, Gavin, Shea, and Ia...Eye...dang. I can't remember the fourth. It was kinda strange.

"Iolana," said Cook as they entered the kitchen. "Some kind of bird if I recall."

"Yeah, that's it. Thanks, Cook."

All the excitement fled Jill when she saw where Tatiana was headed. Tatiana felt the girl's anxiety grow, but there was no time to waste. Life surged in the incubator, ready to emerge. Tatiana pulled Jill close enough to peer into the glass-topped incubator just as the first chick fought its way out of its shell. The small damp form flopped beside its broken shell.

"It looks so helpless," Jill whispered. Emotions swirled around her, a mixture of delight and wonder, gradually overlaid the fear and pushed it away.

"That's because it is. It can't survive without someone to look out for it, to care for it. We can't put it in with the big birds. The clumsy oafs would trample it."

"So where we gonna put it?"

"In that small pen," said Tatiana, pointing to a three foot

square of wood and mesh next to the incubator. "When the chick is dry, move it to the pen. I've already set up a small dish of food and water."

Panic began to fill Jill's face. "What? You want me to touch it?"

"It's only a helpless little chick. You said so yourself. It can't hurt you or anyone else. Someday this chick will grow and if you care for it properly, it will see you as its family."

"But..."

"If it'll make you feel more comfortable, Fifi will stay with you."

Jill looked at Fifi who wagged her tail, all previous anger at Sabrina long forgotten. The little dog gave a happy yip. Confident that Fifi and Jill had things under control, Tatiana slipped out of the kitchen, leaving them to watch over the new chick. If all went as planned, she would have Jill walking through that chicken coop by late Fall.

Chapter Twenty

Word has been sent for any star-touched to come as quickly as possible, but I don't know how long it will take. I only pray they will arrive before it's too late.
William Darwinian
Official Chronicler for the League of the Stars

Bobby Sue

"You ready to go?" asked William.

He looked so handsome in the full length white tunic he wore that Bobby Sue couldn't help but smile. A plain white robe finished the outfit. The only ornamentation was the orange and yellow star painted on his forehead. She nodded then looked up at the darkening sky nervously. The smile slipped from her face. A date with William was always exciting, but the anniversary of the Day of Reckoning made her uneasy. She, like many other, usually spent the evening inside trying to put that horror out of her mind. Even now, the thought made her shiver. William's arm slipped around her.

"If you're not comfortable you can stay in. I'll understand."

Bobby Sue took a deep breath. "No. I ain't cowerin' inside tonight. If Jill can get over her fear of them chickens, I can watch a few meteors fall. Besides, we ain't ever had a Day of Reckoning remembrance ceremony in Atherton. I can't miss the very first, now, can I?

"Good."

His smile as he held out his arm made her heart flutter. "Now you're sure none of them rocks is big enough to hit the ground?"

"Well if one does, we'll face it together."

"That's not very reassurin'," she said. "Or funny."

He gave her a squeeze as they walked. "Don't worry. It'll be fine."

Several dozen people stood in the town square when they arrived. Not a lot considering Atherton had at least two thousand residents. A few vendors still wandered about with trays of food, but most had already packed up. A lot of people didn't want to be out tonight. Three league disciples stood near a small platform handing out tapered candles. All of them wore the same garb as William. He nodded to the other disciples then picked up a basket of candles.

"May the stars watch over you," said William, handing her one of the slender candles.

"And may the stars watch over you too," she said. He'd only told her a few things about this ceremony, and the blessing was one of them.

William continued to pass out candles as people arrived, leaving Bobby Sue time to study the platform. In the center was an oil lantern on a three-foot-high tripod and large thick pillar candles sat at each corner. Like the disciple's outfits, nothing had any ornamentation.

Gazing around the square she noticed a few guards watching from a distance. Mako's dark suit stood out from his perch on the steps of the white council building. A cluster of guards and a few council members joined him, including Hugh Hafley and Darren Smead. Bobby Sue shifted closer to William and twisted a lock of hair around her finger. Hopefully they were there to prevent trouble, not cause it. A familiar figure shuffled past the building and looked in her direction. Joe's eyes met hers for a moment before a group of people blocked her view. Her heart began to pound. By the time they passed, there was no sign of him.

"What's wrong?" asked William.

Bobby Sue forced a weak smile. "Nothin'. Just saw someone for a second, but he's gone now."

"Wasn't the guy who attacked you two months ago, was it?"

"No, the one who saved me."

"Ah," said William, with a nod. "Think he'll be a problem?"

Bobby Sue sighed. "I sure hope not. Depends on how smashed he is."

"I'll keep an eye out."

Conversations remained hushed as the crowd grew. By the

time the sun set, about a hundred people had gathered. At a nod from one of the disciples, William put his basket down.

"You'll have a good view from here."

There was a slight quiver to William's voice and his face looked pale. She grabbed his hand as he started to step onto the platform. It felt cool and damp."

"What's wrong?" she whispered. "Why do you look like you've just seen a ghost?"

He licked his lips for a moment and swallowed. "This is the first time I've been part of this ceremony. I've only observed in the past."

"Never thought you'd get stage fright," she said with a smile. "You'll do just fine. And I'll be right here waitin' for you."

William smiled and stood with the other three disciples. As one, they raised their arms to get everyone's attention. The smattering of conversations stopped immediately.

"Eight years ago today, the creator's wrath rained down on us," said a blond-haired disciple. "Fire and rock battered the land. The oceans rose to wash away our sins. All the earth convulsed and spewed its molten innards to cleanse itself of the hurt and poisons we inflicted on it. In the end only a few of us survived. Today we remember those lost in the Day of Reckoning."

The disciples circled the oil lantern, spiraling closer until they were close enough to touch it. Flames shot up above their heads and a gasp rippled through the crowd. Bobby Sue saw William flinch back from the flames. His posture looked tense. When the flames died back, the disciples turned. Each held a small lamp on a chain. They walked to the four corners and began swinging the lamps until they spun over their heads. The lamps moved so fast, that the light seemed to form a circle and Bobby Sue could feel the heat from the flames. Finally, the disciples stopped spinning the lamps and used them to light the large pillar candles.

"To all who've left this life, may the stars watch over you."

"May the stars watch over you," said Bobby Sue and a few others.

"To all who yet live, may the stars watch over you."

This time, more people responded. "May the stars watch over

you."

"Step forward now and add your light to this day of darkness," said the blond disciple. "Then we will continue the ceremony with a silent vigil."

No one spoke as they filed up to light their candles. Bobby Sue gave William a questioning look, but he just shook his head. Sweat dripped down his face. Even after he joined her, his hands still shook. She slipped her arm around him and squeezed until the trembling stopped. There was definitely something wrong, but she'd have to wait for answers until after the vigil.

Minutes began to stretch. The entire time, William kept his eyes fixed on his candle, without even a momentary glance her way. She was pretty sure that wasn't part of the ceremony since the other disciples stared at the sky. Everyone was waiting for the first meteor to streak across the sky. Bobby Sue swallowed past a knot in her throat. She couldn't help thinking that another large one could kill them all.

"Bloody crackpots," someone shouted.

"You want to see rocks fly, try this one."

With a loud clang, the lamp fell over and a rock tumbled across the platform trailing burning oil. William dropped his candle and yanked her back from the growing flames then shielded her from a sudden rain of stones. With her head pressed against his chest, she felt his heart pound as heavy as hers. Voices continued to spew ridicule from multiple directions. The crowd began to panic.

"That's enough," said Mako over all the yelling. He waited until everyone quieted and stopped moving. "Snider."

"Yes, sir."

"Make sure these people are not disturbed further."

"You heard the Mayor," said Snider. "Let these folks continue their observances."

Several people hurried away, but a few retrieved fallen candles to continue the vigil. The other disciples began to lead people away from the burning platform. William grabbed her hand and started walking away.

"I'm taking you home where it's safe," he whispered.

"You need to stay. You're part of the ceremony."

"Not anymore."

"No." Bobby Sue dug her heels in and pulled out of his grip.

He stared at her for a moment and his jaw twitched. "It's too dangerous. I...I don't want anything to happen to you."

Bobby Sue put her hand on his cheek and studied his eyes. He looked like a hare ready to bolt. Something told her this was more than just afraid for her. "It'll be fine, William. I want to stay. I want to be here with you."

"You sure?"

"Sure as pie," she said. "Now grab some of them dropped candles and let's show our respect for the dead."

His eyes closed for a moment and she saw him take a deep breath.

"You are one special lady, Bobby Sue."

Chapter Twenty-One

Three Years ADR – August

Heads down, children rushed about the campus. Was this really the haven she hoped for? The traveler who'd sent her here had described a bustling town, untouched by the ravages of the Cataclysm with plenty of food and electricity. The reality was far from impressive, but the gates had opened willingly enough. There had been warmth and caring in the voices of the men and women who had greeted her, but beneath all loomed a feeling of hopelessness.

As they led her past rows of warehouses, Tatiana had seen the beginnings of disrepair. Even so, the town of Sacquanico was far better off than others she had passed through. The grounds of the Abuda Institute Orphanage once belonged to Abuda University and the campus library was magnificent. Tatiana clutched the scrap of paper that listed her afternoon classes. She'd already memorized it. Only one of her morning teachers had been an adult. The rest were teens, some not much older than she. Discipline in those classes seemed overly quick and harsh. She only hoped that the afternoon would show a better side of the school.

Fear, pain, confusion. They smashed into Tatiana's mind like a hammer. The schedule fell from her fingers as she ran toward the source. It called to her. There was no need to ask for directions. A small child cowered in the corner of the room. Over her stood a tall teen with a stick. Tears streaked the child's dirty face, half hidden by a curtain of blond hair. Her mind tumbled and churned with thoughts that made no sense and behind it all energy surged, pulsed, ready to explode. Tatiana knew that energy and what it could do. She didn't think about the boy, or the stick as it swung toward the child.

Pain lanced Tatiana's back as the stick landed across it, a human shield protecting the child. Their eyes met and Tatiana felt herself drawn into their depths, sifting through a jumble of thoughts until she at last reached the core. A voice, timid and soft, echoed one word in her mind. Fiona. All the loneliness that had haunted Tatiana these past three years vanished in an instant as Fiona's love poured into her.

Tatiana

Loud laughter and talk filled the tavern as Tatiana bustled around serving customers. A pair of traveling musicians were entertaining, the ones who boarded their horses in Gareth's shed. One played guitar and the other sang. There were too few performers these days and it felt good to hear music again. The men set up near the fireplace, with a couple of stools and a pitcher of ale. Microphones and electric guitars were things of the past. Tatiana didn't recognize any of the songs, but she still enjoyed the melodies and lyrics.

The added entertainment brought in more revenue than ever, but Sabrina insisted that expenses were greater than income. No matter how well they did on a given day, the costs were always more. It just didn't add up in Tatiana's mind. Something had to be wrong with their calculations. Even last evening's somber Cataclysm anniversary had packed the room with thirsty customers. Many had been intent on drowning their memories. Others had toasted lost loved ones.

For her part, Tatiana was glad of the distraction. There was a time she would have relished standing out under the stars and watching the annual meteor shower. Those days were long gone. Now the thought brought only chills and nightmares.

"Tatiana."

Gareth held up a few mugs and nodded toward a table in the back corner. Three people, including a young boy, waved at her. Tatiana smiled and hurried to empty her tray. This was the fun time of the evening, before any of the customers had too much to drink and needed to be escorted out.

"Good evening, Mr. Burns, Mrs. Burns, Mr. Junior Burns." She winked at the ten-year-old and placed the mugs on the table.

"Good evening yourself, Tatiana," said Mr. Burns. "How's that pooch of yours? Alan here has done nothing but talk about her all day."

As if on cue, Fifi scampered up Alan's leg, leaped onto his shoulder, and began bathing him in a flurry of tiny licks. The boy rolled off the chair onto the floor, giggling hysterically. Sheer joy emanated from both his parents.

"How's business?" asked Tatiana.

A dark cloud seemed to flash in Mr. Burns' eyes and his brow creased. His smile looked strained. "Things are going just fine. Thanks for asking."

The room suddenly grew silent and the musicians stopped. Alarmed, Tatiana turned toward the door where a handsome man in his mid-thirties stood with two stocky bodyguards. Short jet-black hair covered his head and a thick tuft of whiskers hung above his upper lip. The rest of his face was clean-shaven, a sharp contrast to the mostly bearded men in the room. His well-fitting black suit could not completely hide the rippling muscles it covered. Like a cougar studying its prey, the man scanned the room with deep-set brown eyes.

Though they had never met, Tatiana knew, by the reactions in the room, that he had to be Mako Scaffeld. An icy chill ran through her, and Fifi backed cautiously into the shadows under the table. They'd met Mako's type before; proud, boastful, conniving, and predatory.

"Mayor Scaffeld," said Sabrina. The words slid from her mouth like silk. "Welcome to Gareth's Tavern. What brings you to our fine establishment this evening? How may I serve you?"

Tatiana saw Gareth grimace as Sabrina sidled up to Mako like an old friend and ran her hand across his striking yet harshly angular face. He took her hand and smoothly planted a lingering kiss on it. Sabrina's eyes darted toward Gareth and her emotions vacillated between excitement and guilt, like a child reaching for an extra cookie. She pulled back from Mako, but he held her hand firmly. No one needed empathic abilities to sense the desire that churned in him.

"Had I known such beauties as you were hiding in this place, I would have come sooner. Please, call me Mako."

"What do you want, Mako?" said Gareth.

"Why, Gareth," Mako answered, with a hurt tone that didn't fool Tatiana. He released Sabrina, then moved closer to Gareth and smiled. "I'm merely checking to see that my people are being well cared for. I am the mayor of this fine town, after all, am I not? Besides, I heard you had some interesting entertainment of late. Quite a boon to your profits from what I understand. I'm sure you'll send in your share of taxes at the end of the month."

"We've already paid our taxes."

"Oh, didn't your hear?" Mako moved to a nearby table and shooed away the customers with a wave of his hand. He sat not quite facing Gareth. "The council just approved a new sales tax which is to be paid at the end of each month. The power plant isn't going to re-build itself. Neither is that library you insisted on. We need funds for construction."

"What happened to the funds put aside in April? It's only August."

"I'm afraid they were used up, cost overruns and things. You know how it goes."

Sabrina, who had disappeared into the back room for a moment, returned with a glass and a bottle of bourbon from before the Cataclysm. Mako looked appreciatively at the bottle, and then let his eyes linger on Sabrina's curvaceous body as she poured some of the amber liquid into the glass. She handed him the glass, then moved away, spacing herself equally between Mako and Gareth, easily within sight of both. Tensions eased as he sipped casually at the drink and whispered conversations began to echo through the tavern once more. The musicians continued, this time with a ballad about lost love. A few people left, but most tried their best to ignore the two heavyset men who loomed around Mako like a couple of lineman guarding a quarterback.

Apprehension gnawed at Tatiana and she bit nervously at her lip. Sabrina had been known to be overly friendly with some of the customers, but never around Gareth. She seemed almost too familiar with Mako. And if she told him about what had happened...

"She's said nothing yet. There's no reason to think she will."

"She's ambitious. He's powerful. It's a dangerous

combination."

"New taxes, my ass," muttered Mr. Burns.

His chair scraped across the floor as he stood, making Tatiana jump. Deep creases furrowed his forehead and she could feel the cold fury he held in check. He handed her a quarter-sized copper Penn-York coin.

"This is the fourth tax hike since that guy took office. His supposed tax collectors are more like extortionists. The money's being spent on his pleasures. I'm not staying in the same room with him."

Tatiana nodded her understanding as Mrs. Burns tried to quietly usher Alan toward the door.

"I don't wanna go! I wanna stay with Fifi and Tatiana." The boy's complaints rose in pitch and volume.

"We'll come back another time, Alan. I promise," said Mr. Burns.

Nothing worked. The noise began to draw attention, and Tatiana saw Mako cast a curious eye at the stubborn boy. She placed her hands on Alan's shoulders and crouched down so that their eyes were level.

"Listen to your parents, Alan. I know you don't understand, but this is not a good time."

"But..."

She shushed him with a raised finger. "They're trying to keep you safe. Now do as they say or Fifi won't play with you."

The young boy stuck his lip out, disappointment shining in his eyes, but he stopped yelling. With one last mournful look, he followed his parents out the door. Tatiana busied herself by wiping the table and gathering their barely touched mugs. When she was halfway to the kitchen door, a booming voice halted her steps.

"You," called Mako. "Come here."

Tatiana felt a shiver run up her spine and slowly turned toward the voice. She could feel her heart racing.

"No, not me. Let me be."

But Mako was indeed pointing at her. Sabrina's eyes darted from Tatiana to Mako and her emotions churned in a confusing jumble. She was happy, sad, fearful, bold, and angry all at the same time. A leering half smile cracked Mako's face. Tatiana could feel his eyes scan her body, mentally removing the dress she wore. The chill in her spine spread to her limbs as she desperately placed a non-expressive mask over her face.

"You're the one called Tatiana, aren't you?" he asked. "The one with the dancing dog I've heard so much about."

"Yes, sir," she said. Her voice, although barely above a whisper, had no difficulty in carrying through the silent room.

"You're quite the looker. Come here, girl, so I can see you more clearly, and put your pooch through its paces."

Gareth glowered. "She doesn't take orders from you."

"I said come here!" Mako ordered, ignoring Gareth. His smile felt as false as his heart.

"Get out of my tavern, Mako. You're not welcome here."

Mako looked at Gareth as if he were an annoying bug interrupting a pleasant picnic. "I'm not leaving until I see the girl and her dog perform. And I suggest you stay out of this, Gareth. It would be a real shame if Duval and Diddler here were forced to arrest you or if the health inspector had to shut you down."

It was an empty threat. There was no health inspector. The two bodyguards sneered at Gareth. Diddler cracked his knuckles for emphasis and grinned. The semi-psychotic smile he gave her twisted her gut. Duval, the more reserved of the two, merely shifted, making his gun clearly visible.

Tatiana's throat tightened until she could barely swallow. Images flashed through her mind—memories, a nightmare of something that happened a long time ago. Mako's face looked different, but to her he seemed the same as that other one. Years had passed, but the memory hadn't lost its sharpness. Part of her wanted to flee, but another more stubborn part, that always seemed to get her in trouble, refused.

"Well?" said Mako.

"Fifi," said Tatiana, with only a slight tremble to her voice, "does not feel like performing any more this evening. Perhaps another time."

With that, she turned and left the room. Fifi dashed through the door behind her so quickly that no one even saw her slip through. Tatiana's heart pounded as she ran through the halls. She was safe, but would Gareth and the other girls be okay? The thought brought her up sharply. While indecision froze Tatiana in place, Fifi's spontaneous nature kicked in and the dog zipped back to the tavern door. Like an echo, sound rippled in Tatiana's mind. She held her breath. Through a crack in the door, in strange blue-gray tones, Tatiana saw a bemused Mako let loose a hearty laugh.

Chapter Twenty-Two

Bobby Sue

"Joe! Joe stop it!" Bobby Sue yelled in a futile effort to end the fight. "Get off him."

The two men grappled in the dirt, heedless of Bobby Sue and anyone else who came too close to their melee. Her basket of carefully chosen produce lay forgotten in a tumbled pile on the ground.

"Demon worshiping blasphemer!" Joe took another wild swing at William. "You should be stoned with the rest of your devils."

William dodged the blow easily and delivered a sharp left hook into the other man's face. Tears streamed from Bobby Sue's eyes. They had been having a pleasant conversation before Joe interrupted them. William had just finished his daily discussion of the star-touched in the town square. There hadn't been any warning before Joe charged.

Worry mixed with anger over the unprovoked attack. What if William got hurt? Joe was crazy enough to kill him. Bobby Sue continued to call for help, but most of the people in the town square had hurried away or moved to a safe distance to watch. A few merchants were craning their necks to see from their vending carts, but none came near. No one wanted to get involved. She glanced frantically around the square in hope of finding someone to help. The militia seemed to be everywhere these days, poking their noses into everyone's business, but when real trouble started, they were never around. Their sudden absence from the town square added to her aggravation.

"Gareth," she cried, when his head popped out of the council building, probably drawn by the noise. "Gareth! For God's sake, stop them. Please."

Muttering curses, Gareth raced across the gravel strewn lawn that served as the town square, right into the jumble of flailing limbs. "What the hell do you think you're doing, Joe?"

As if possessed, Joe continued to swing and curse as Gareth pulled him off the League of the Stars disciple. Bobby Sue grimaced at the smell of liquor on Joe's breath as Gareth dragged him past her.

One of Joe's flailing feet caught on her skirt, nearly yanking her over. She teetered for a moment before William caught her hand as he stood. A half smile greeted her, heedless of the blood from his nose and split lip. It did little to improve her mood. Bobby Sue pulled a handkerchief from her pocket and attempted to staunch the flow, keeping a wary eye on Joe, who still struggled in Gareth's grip. Purple welts ballooned on the drunk's face and blood dripped from a cut over one eye, but Bobby Sue was more worried about William. She couldn't help but notice how the crimson running down the disciple's face made the yellow and orange star painted on his forehead stand out even more brightly.

"Let go of me you freak-loving son of a..."

"Shut up," said Gareth, shaking Joe, as one would discipline a wayward pup. "You can't just attack people you don't agree with."

"Lies! The bastard preaches lies. He wants everyone to think those wacko star-touched are good, but they're evil. They're demons. They'll burn us alive, cut our throats in our sleep!"

Gareth delivered a sharp smack to the side of Joe's head, temporarily stunning him. "Sorry," he said to William. "You okay?"

"I'll be fine," William said, as he pinched his nose with Bobby Sue's handkerchief. His other hand was encased in her grip. "I can take care of myself fairly well. Are you going to be able to control him?"

"Don't worry. I know how to handle him." Gareth gave a nod and began half leading, half dragging Joe down the street. After a few halting steps he stopped. "Bobby Sue, looks like I'm going to need your help after all. You can visit another time."

After a moment's hesitation, Bobby Sue pulled away, letting her fingers linger for one extra second on his hand. The smile on William's face said more to her than words. His eyes seemed to sparkle. As she turned to help Gareth, she saw Snider, leaning casually against the council building. A smirk twisted across his face, leaving her feeling cold despite the hot August weather. It wiped away the joy William's smile had created.

It didn't take long to cover the two blocks from the square to Gareth's place, even with Joe dragging his feet. Frustration clearly showed in Gareth's expression as they walked, but Bobby Sue doubted it had much to do with the fight. This morning he had gone to complain about the new tax. As of this afternoon, he still hadn't been admitted into the council meeting. Closed sessions weren't unheard of, but the timing of this one seemed suspicious, especially after Mako's visit last night.

"I'm beginning to wonder why I bother helping you, Joe," said Gareth, as he threw him onto a stool at one of the small round tables and sat next to him. "What if you had killed him? There's no getting out of jail for good behavior anymore. Those days are gone. You beat a man to death and you'll hang."

"He's a follower of Satan, a devil worshiper. He deserves to die."

Bobby Sue returned to the table with a bowl of water, a rag, and a couple of mugs. "You were falling for that guy's crap, weren't you?" He pushed her hand aside when she tried to mop at his bloodied face and took a swallow from the mug. With a cough and a gag, he spat out the liquid, showering both Gareth and Bobby Sue.

"What the hell is this?"

"It's called water, Joe," said Bobby Sue. Her hands scoured vigorously as she mopped up the mess. "Most normal people drink this instead of booze."

"Damn tramp."

"That's enough, both of you," said Gareth. He rubbed at his temples until the creases in his forehead diminished. "So where've you been, Joe? You haven't been by in weeks."

"Traveling." Joe hunched over and his eyes darted everywhere but Gareth's face. "No place in particular."

"Run into any other League disciples in your travels?"

"None of your damned business," said Joe.

He wiped a glob of blood from his face with the back of his hand. Old scars and ripped open scabs covered his knuckles.

More old scabs decorated his face.

"Joe," said Gareth, in a softer tone. "You're family. That makes it my business. What made you hate the star-touched so much?"

"Thou shall not suffer a witch to live! You are to stone them; their blood will be on their own heads!"

"Cut the religious shit," said Gareth. The command burst from his lips like a growl. "Just tell us what the hell happened. I know you've never wanted to, but it's time. Now spill."

Bobby Sue blinked in surprise. Gareth rarely used profanity, but the harsh words seemed to have the desired effect on Joe. The man's eyes glazed over. When he finally spoke, his voice sounded more like a frog's than a human's and a tremor rippled across his body. "That creepy, freaky little girl and her girlfriend."

"What girls?"

"At Abuda."

"You were at Abuda?" said Bobby Sue. "I thought it was for kids."

"I was born in Sacquanico, you dimwitted idiot," grumbled Joe. "Lived just outside town before the Cataclysm. When Abuda opened, I worked in maintenance from the day it opened until they shut it down. Too many blasted kids poured in. Things were all whacked out in the early years but it wasn't too bad. They finally got someone to keep order in the place."

He sat there staring at his mug for a while, until Gareth gave him a nudge.

"One girl," Joe continued, "Some snot-nosed eight-year-old, complained all the time about kids pickin' on her. We didn't pay her any mind. She made no sense, just blurted weird nonsense. Her girlfriend, some older wacko who showed up a couple of years after Abuda opened, kept her out of trouble. One night the little brat woke up screamin' bloody murder 'cause she couldn't find her girlfriend. She just stood there clingin' to a lamppost all night long, screechin' at the top of her lungs. Nothing anyone did could get the bitch to shut up. She woke the whole god-damn town. Near about dawn those lights showed up again."

"It was probably a meteor shower, Joe," Gareth said calmly.

Joe's face scrunched up in anger and turned bright red. For a moment Bobby Sue thought he would start throwing punches again. "Meteors don't fly in circles or hover overhead. These did." Blood-speckled spittle sprayed across the table. After a moment, Joe got his anger under control and continued. "Anyway, the next mornin' everyone is standin' around her tryin' to figure out what she was sayin', and she starts accusin' half the kids of attackin' her friend."

"Where was her friend?" asked Bobby Sue.

"Who the hell cares? Shut up and listen," snapped Joe. He took a drink of water and grimaced. "Three of the older boys, the ones who kept order, came to try to calm her. She took one look at them and fire shot out of her fingers. Before anyone could stop her, they were burnin'. The screams." He squeezed his eyes shut and covered his ears. A sickly pale cast fell on his face and his shoulders shook. "It was awful. When she finished with them, the little bitch burst into flames and killed herself."

Gareth shook his head. "I heard rumors about that, just before the riots started. Didn't realize it was at Abuda."

"My God," said Bobby Sue. "She was star-touched. William said that them fires are a last-ditch defense mechanism and he knew of only one star-touched who could control them."

Joe's face twisted into a sneer as Bobby Sue spoke, and she saw his fists clench. The look made her heart freeze.

"What about the friend?" asked Gareth, drawing Joe's attention away from Bobby Sue.

"Huh?"

"What about the girl's friend? Where was she during all this?"

"Don't know. Don't care. I left town that day before anyone could cook me and haven't looked back."

Bobby Sue's mind reeled with questions. If there was a star-touched at Abuda, the League had to know about it. Everyone knew they kept accurate records of everything even remotely connected to the star-touched. And William was one of the recorders. Yet in all their chats about star-touched, William had never mentioned it. Why not?

A jumble of contradictory rumors had surfaced about Abuda, but nothing that could be substantiated. Some called it a well-disciplined school, while others talked about terrible abuses and cruelties committed against the students. No one could agree whether the perpetrators of those crimes were teachers or other students. About the only thing that anyone agreed upon was that Abuda represented a failed experiment that ended in disaster after only three years. Joe's was the only firsthand account she had heard, but she wondered what he wasn't saying. Not to mention what William had failed to say as well.

"Gareth."

He looked up as she moved to the door. "What is it, Bobby Sue?"

Bobby Sue's throat felt tight, especially with Joe still scowling at her. "You need me anymore? In all the commotion I left my basket in the town square. I'm gonna go look for it."

Gareth's eyes narrowed. "Make it quick. It's getting late."

Bobby Sue slipped out the door and hurried to the town square. There was no sign of her basket or William. Snider was gone as well, but a couple of unkempt militia men loitered at the edge of the square pestering a food stand. The late afternoon sun cast long shadows on the ground. It wouldn't be long before merchants began to close up shop for the night. She twisted a strand of hair around her finger and bit her lip. The smart thing to do would be to go home, but too many nagging questions ate at her common sense. At the top of the list was William's health, immediately followed by why the hell he hadn't mentioned something as important as Abuda.

Chapter Twenty-Three

Four Years ADR – August

The eight-year-old girl clung to the lamppost screaming for Tatiana, the one person who made her whole crazy world make sense. Tears streamed down her face. Dozens of grownups tried to calm her, reassure her that they'd find her friend, but nothing they said helped. How could it? They didn't understand. She didn't even understand. Confusing images filled her mind and unimaginable pain ripped through her. Lights zoomed across the sky like they did every year since the Cataclysm, making even the grownups afraid.

By morning her tears were spent, but she wouldn't let go of the pole, wouldn't talk. She just sat there, slumped at the bottom, too exhausted to move. Children finally ventured out with the rising sun to gawk at her blank stare. A jolt of recognition shot through her when a fourteen-year-old boy came near.

"I know what you did." The words hissed from between her parched lips.

His eyes widened, then the boy crumpled to the ground shaking and crying, begging forgiveness. As more of the older boys came near she repeated the same words until each had confessed their part in Tatiana's disappearance. One by one, they lay bits of raven hair and scraps of clothing at her feet until a small mound formed.

Then the three who tormented her sauntered by; the ones who hurt her friend. One look at her and they smiled. This time she didn't cringe with fear. Energy flowed through her and she struggled to her feet. With balled fists she spat out the same five words, emphasizing each one.

Laughter filled her ears, the same laughter they used when they hurt Tatiana. Blind rage took over. Uncontrolled energy blazed across her entire body. Fire shot from her hands and eyes, engulfing the three boys. Their screams rent the air. Within seconds the power overwhelmed her as well, and she followed them to an ashen grave.

Tatiana

Tatiana chewed at her lip as she studied the sales ledger. Yesterday she had traded a pound of nails for ten pairs of mittens, but the book only listed four pair. She continued to scan Sabrina's neat handwriting for more errors. The mitten mystery was the tenth discrepancy she'd spotted since opening the book. Even some of this morning's sales were wrong. It wasn't like Sabrina to make mistakes. It also wasn't like her to leave Tatiana in charge of the store. With both Gareth and Bobby Sue downtown and everyone else busy with other tasks, Sabrina had little choice when a sudden and important errand came up. The opportunity thrilled Tatiana. At least until she noticed the discrepancies.

Other than a flurry of customers earlier in the day, things had calmed down, leaving Tatiana time to peruse the ledger. Keeping a sharp ear out for the bell over the door, she stepped into the storage room. Cross referencing items in the records with the actual stock revealed similar inconsistencies. None of it made sense. Neither did Sabrina's assertions that income had been dwindling. Tatiana began to pace the floor. Should she tell Gareth? Did he already know? He really loved Sabrina. The last thing Tatiana wanted to do was hurt him or drive more of a wedge between them.

Fifi growled and flashed an image of Sabrina returning to the store. Tatiana quickly closed both the ledger and inventory.

"Welcome back," said Tatiana. "Did you have any trouble with your errands?"

"Not that it concerns you, but no. Hope you didn't mess anything up," she said, flipping through the ledger. Sabrina slapped her hand down on the last page. "Didn't you sell anything?"

"No one came in while you were gone."

"Good. Then I don't have to go apologizing to our customers about your pathetic sales abilities. Go inside and help Jill."

"Yes, Miss Sabrina."

Tatiana struggled to keep her face neutral. Just once, she'd love a single kind word from that woman. Even one good morning or good day would suffice. As soon as she reached the common room she leaned against the door to compose herself. Maybe Bobby Sue could help shed some light on Sabrina's behavior.

Chapter Twenty-Four

Bobby Sue

After a careful look around the nearly empty street, Bobby Sue knocked on the door of a small building at the edge of town. The block seemed too quiet, even for late afternoon. Across the street a pair of eyes peered at her through a filthy window. Bobby Sue turned away and knocked on the door a bit harder. She had never ventured out here and began to wonder if it had been a good idea. Maybe there was a reason William had always met her in the town square or at Gareth's. Most of their outings had been walks along the Atherton river or just outside the town gates where most of the farms were. This part of town looked run down compared to Gareth's neatly kept neighborhood. The ramshackle buildings were dirty, little more than single story shacks packed with unwashed bodies. A few houses had small gardens, unlike those further west which were squished together like beans in a can. She shivered thinking about the drug addicts and drunks that hung out in those areas and near Mako's brothel.

Footsteps approached and a shadow hovered behind the quarter-sized peephole. The door swung open and William's arms enveloped her, pulling her inside. After a cautious glance, around he closed the door. An involuntary gasp left Bobby Sue when she saw his swollen, split lip and blackened eye.

"Are you okay?" she asked.

"I'll be fine," he said as he brushed hair off her face. His playful smile ended in a grimace of pain. "It isn't the first time I've been jumped. A year ago I almost got burned alive by some fanatical witch hunters."

That revelation surprised Bobby Sue. It also explained his reaction at the ceremony the other night. She studied the bruises that covered his face, now cleaned of both blood and paints, and wondered what else about his history he hadn't mentioned. His slender, wiry body seemed to flow as he led her to the living room.

William's hand caressed her cheek. "I'm really glad to see you, but you shouldn't have come here alone. This area isn't safe for unescorted women, especially so late in the afternoon."

"I kind of figured that out a bit too late to turn back," she said with a weak smile. "Besides, I had other things on my mind."

"I didn't think Joe had hurt me that bad."

His hazel eyes twinkled and drew her in like a moth. At least the one that wasn't swollen shut. She wanted nothing more than to press her lips to his and leaned in close enough to feel his breath on her face. There was such longing in his eyes—then with a flicker, it was gone and he stepped away, just like he always did. Was she reading his signals wrong?

Doubt gnawed at her and she turned to hide her disappointment, studying the living room, which was really only three steps from the front door. A small threadbare couch, a couple of homemade benches and an old beat up coffee table were all that decorated the space. The simplicity of the décor didn't surprise her. None of the League of the Stars followers she had seen flaunted any wealth. Most dressed in simple, everyday work clothes, though they never seemed to be short of cash for food and necessary supplies. More mysteries.

"You shouldn't have come here," he repeated, after a moment.

Bobby Sue turned back to him and planted her hands on her hips. "Well, forgive me for worryin' about you."

"I didn't mean it like that, Bobby Sue."

"How come you never mentioned Abuda? There was a star-touched there." The words shot out more harshly than she had planned.

A shadow crossed William's eyes and he rubbed a hand over his short brown hair. None of the other League disciples shaved their heads, and his seemed unusually short for a simple haircut. She immediately dismissed the idea of it burning off. If he had been burned that badly there would have been scarring. Not a single blemish marred William's skin. Then again, maybe he just liked short hair.

A deep sigh left his lips. It sounded sad and resigned. When he spoke, it was with the teaching voice he used in the town square, not the personal tone he usually used with her. "I'd be delighted to share all I know with you. Please sit. I have some water boiling. Would you like some tea?"

"That would be nice," she said. Her throat tightened and she struggled to keep her voice from wavering. If he was going to act all formal, then so would she. "Thank you."

He disappeared behind a curtain strung across the back of the room and reappeared a few moments later with two steaming mugs. She took a sniff of the fragrant drink, trying to identify the herbs. It smelled sweet but was too hot to drink yet, so she set it on the table to cool.

"Why don't we start with what you already know, Bobby Sue?" he said. "Then I can fill in the gaps."

"Other than general rumors about gangs of kids running rampant at the school, all I know is what Joe told me today. He lived there."

"He did?" said Brother William, with a raised eyebrow. He gave his lip a ginger touch, as if deep in thought, before continuing. "Curious, I don't remember seeing him there."

Bobby Sue twisted at her hair and frowned. "So you were there. You didn't have anything to do with what happened, did you?"

"No," he said, spilling hot tea in his lap. "Well, maybe a little bit, but not until after."

"After what?" she said. "After the three boys and girl burned? Joe said he left right after that."

William nodded and tried to brush away the tea that had soaked into his pants. "I'd only been in town for a day and didn't really know anyone. When the burning happened, I was on the mountain with the search party. Joe must have left before I started interviewing people. Please, tell me what he said."

Bobby Sue related Joe's story as well as she could. All the while, William listened carefully, giving no clue as to his reaction. When she finished, he placed his cup on the table and leaned back on the couch with a sigh.

"And people wonder why the riots happened. Much of what Joe said is correct, but he either wasn't aware or chose to turn a blind eye to everything else. The little girl was star-touched."

"I kinda figured that one out. The whole fire thing tipped it off." She regretted her sarcastic tone as soon as she said it. The hurt look in his eyes made her stomach twist, but she was tired of being in the dark.

"So was her friend. They were a mentally bonded pair."

"Bonded?" she said, leaning in with curiosity.

"Most star-touched are. As a whole there is some kind of mental connection between all the star-touched, but it's different with a bonded pair. The pairs have a special more intimate relationship, like sisters and brothers. They can communicate and share more easily. It seems to help keep them in balance, more emotionally stable. The two are so connected, that the loss of one can be utterly devastating to the other. A lot of star-touched lost their bonded pairs in the riots and some never recovered. Others re-bonded with another person, or more commonly, an animal, such as a bird, a cat, a dog, that sort of thing. Several are still searching for that special someone that makes them complete. Fiona, that was her name by the way, couldn't control her abilities. Without her bonded to help she became overwhelmed."

Hungry for information, Bobby Sue leaned even closer. There was so much to learn. "What happened to her friend? Who was she? Was she killed? Is that why Fiona lost control?"

"Slow down," he said, holding up his hand. A small smile crooked across his swollen face and his educator facade slipped away. "I can only answer one question at a time. Let me explain what preceded the incident. Most of the children at Abuda liked the Lost One, who was about fourteen at the time."

"Lost One? What's that supposed to mean?"

"That's what we call Fiona's bonded," he said, returning to his town square teaching tone. "From the day she arrived, the upperclassmen that had taken control of the school lost their stranglehold on the other students. She stood up to them and wouldn't allow them to harass the other children. She was especially protective of Fiona.

"On the night in question..." Brother William grew silent and wrinkles creased his brow. She could see the unease in his eyes. He squirmed as though he'd sat on an ant hill. Finally, he took a deep breath and let it out slowly. "When Fiona wouldn't stop screaming, several search parties were sent out to find the Lost One. I was with one of the groups looking in the surrounding hills. It was the anniversary of the Day of Reckoning, so everyone was already on edge. Lights shooting across the sky didn't help."

"I remember that night," gasped Bobby Sue. "Everyone said it was another meteor shower."

"Those weren't meteors," said Brother William, shaking his head. "We're not sure what they were."

"That's what Joe said."

William pressed his lips together and nodded. "I didn't find out the details until the next day, but a gang of kids had ambushed her friend. It was a vicious attack. Each of the boys took trophies. Hair, scraps of clothing. Whatever those animals could grab before they left her. They were spurred on by the three boys who'd been terrorizing the other students and half of the town. Once everyone who'd hid inside for the night came out, Fiona confronted the attackers. All but those three confessed and begged forgiveness.

"And those three?"

"They laughed. Fiona was only eight-years-old. She broke down, lost control of her powers; killed all three before she died."

"There are a lot more details, but I wasn't there at the time, but I do have some firsthand accounts if you want to read them yourself."

Bobby Sue nodded. "I think I'd like that."

"Wait here."

Sounds of shuffled papers and books drifted out of the room he disappeared into. After a moment he returned with a leather-bound journal. He sat on the couch and began to leaf through the thick book, finally pointing at a passage. "Here, I must have interviewed over a hundred people in the week following the incident. This accounting is the most detailed and accurate. It's from one of the first adults to reach Fiona that night. She wrote it out herself and gave it to me to copy down."

Tears burned Bobby Sue's eyes as she read. She opened her mouth to speak several times, but for once, couldn't find the words. Shock, anger, outrage, all churned inside her. The killings that had sparked the riots hadn't been a vicious and premeditated murder like so many people were led to believe. They were the acts of a confused and terrified child.

"Star-touched pairs can see through each other's eyes," said William, his tone sad, almost defeated. He squeezed her hands which had started to tremble. "Even while asleep. Once Fiona awoke, the visions probably became even more vivid. Another star-touched once told me that at times, seeing through their partner's eyes felt like they were actually there. Pain and emotion could be transferred. The attack was bad enough, but Fiona was much too young to comprehend the rest of what happened."

A tight knot formed in Bobby Sue's gut. She knew, but needed to hear it. "The rest of what?"

A slight tremor shook his body. He gripped her hands so tight they hurt. "After the younger kids left, the three older boys took the Lost One into the hills and raped her."

So much had happened since the Day of Reckoning, so many evil things. "And Fiona saw it all?" she said, through gritted teeth.

"We believe she felt it as well. It would have been as if it were her," he said. "Seeing those three saunter over so arrogantly...Fiona lost control. Without her friend to help contain her powers, she was overcome by anguish."

With what had happened to that little girl, burning those three boys didn't seem so deplorable. Guilt clawed at Bobby Sue a second after the thought hit her mind. Life was so fragile. So was humanity. One misstep could send the entire human race into extinction.

"Did you ever find her friend?" she asked, her voice barely audible.

William remained silent, his eyes moist and pain filled. "My search party found her in the mountains. Her physical wounds were healed, but without Fiona, she was lost, drifting, withdrawn. I tried, but I couldn't reach her. By then the riots had begun."

Helpless. Powerless. Bobby Sue was all too familiar with those feelings. They all were. "It must have been awful, watching her die."

"Oh, she didn't die," said William. "You have to understand, we were surrounded by chaos. Abuda stood at the very center of the riots. In all the confusion, she disappeared."

"She's probably dead."

"No," he said with conviction. "She's alive, but still in pain, still living with that nightmare. One of these days, I'm going to reach her. One of these days I'm going to help her put what happened behind her so she can live again. I have to."

Those last words came out more like a whisper. Their implied pleading piqued her curiosity. "Why you?"

William closed his eyes and took a deep breath. "I had sworn to protect her until another star-touched could arrive. I was supposed to watch, keep her safe. When the mob came to the front door I stepped out of the room for a minute, just to look. I didn't think anything could happen in so short a time. When I returned to the room, she was gone. Not a sign of her anywhere. She simply vanished." William stopped to massage his head. "This all happened just after I joined the League. I saw those lights swirling and hovering in the sky that night. It made my blood feel like ice. We believe they were angry spirits. Other star-touched have been killed and tortured, but those lights have only appeared once.

"Maybe the spirits took her back?" The words seemed stupid as she said them.

William gave a half sigh, half laugh. "If only it were that simple. No, I know she's near. I've tracked her for years. Every now and then I hear a story or find a tiny clue that points toward her, but each time I get close, she slips away. She's afraid to face her past and who she is, so she's constantly moving. I failed my duty that day. I have to help her, if only to redeem my honor." He looked at her with a strained longing. Tears glistened in his eyes. "Until I complete my quest..."

His words faded away and the look on his face made Bobby Sue's heart ache. It wasn't hard to fill in the blank. Until he completed his task, the two of them were stuck in romantic limbo. She looked away and twisted her hair, unsure of what to say. It wasn't fair. Leave it to her to find the one knight in shining armor that had a real quest.

"There's somethin' I still don't understand," she said after a moment, her throat tight with emotion. "Why call her the Lost One? Wouldn't it be easier to find her with a danged name?"

"Again, not that simple." The frustration in his voice was obvious. "Right now, the Lost One is hiding. Using her name would be like a spotlight pointing her way. It would make her a target to any seeking to harm the star-touched. And what about others with similar names? They'd be caught in the crossfire, more senseless deaths. There are enough of us that know her real name. When she's ready to face her past, we'll be waiting, ready to help."

"Waiting? Ready to help!" Bobby Sue's hands clenched into tight balls and she felt her face flush. "YOU – ARE – AN – IDIOT, William Darwinian! It's been four years. You're so busy watchin' and waitin', your missin' the whole point. She's hurtin' and may never be 'ready' to move on. Some folks need an extra nudge in that department." She poked a finger in his chest, emphasizing each word. "Enough a' your stalkin'. Next time you get near that girl, you talk to her, damnit. Do you have any idea where she is now?"

He winced at the sharp words, and his eyes grew wide. When he didn't answer right away, she scowled, arms crossed. Finally, he spoke, his voice wavering slightly. "I know exactly where she is, Bobby Sue. I've known for a while now."

Chapter Twenty-Five

Gareth

"I'm sorry, Gareth. Really I am. I just can't supply you anymore."

"Damn it, Denny. Why not? I've been buying your ale since you started that brewery. Is it Mako? Snider? They putting pressure on you?"

Denny looked away and his Adam's apple bobbed. "Sorry, Gareth,"

He slipped out the door before Gareth could respond and hurried off into the night, head bent down. Gareth slammed the lock on the door and ground his teeth. Business had been slow that evening, probably due to last night's dramatics and the new tax. Now this. With a frustrated sigh, he poured himself a drink, grabbed the ledger book, and sat down at the same table he and Joe had used earlier. Thank goodness the man had been long gone when those two League disciples brought Bobby Sue home. Gareth didn't need another scene at the tavern.

Leaving the drink untouched, Gareth rubbed his head. He had enough ale for a while with what he made himself, but it wouldn't last forever, and a tavern without drink couldn't survive. It had to be Mako's meddling. Would brigands break in next? He'd had two offers now from Mako, offers he would never accept. On top of that, the new tax was going to take a chunk out of their already dwindling income. He couldn't figure out where their profits were going, but something had to change soon. The thought of having to lay off anyone made him sick. It simply wasn't an option.

Gareth fingered the gold coin Tatiana had given him while he entered the day's income from the Tavern and reviewed the week's earnings. Handling the coin seemed to relax him but he only took it out when no one else was around. Only Sabrina had seen it, the evening Tatiana had arrived.

After an hour of adding and calculating, Gareth stopped and rubbed his head again. Things weren't adding up. Someone had to be skimming profits, but who? Each of his employees felt like family to him. The thought of one of them stealing made his head ache. One by one he went through the list. Jill? No, that wasn't her style. Bobby Sue? She'd sooner cut her wrists than steal. Finally, he had dismissed all of them but two. He drained the mug of beer and ran his thick fingers across the relief design on its side. The ceramic felt cold under his fingers, cold like the lump in his gut.

Tatiana was the new girl, which made her an obvious first suspect. He knew so little about her, but since she had walked though those doors two months ago, she had done everything she could to make improvements and fix things. Equipment didn't break down. The livestock stayed healthy and became more productive than ever. Even he had felt more energetic. Gareth wasn't sure whether it was because of the herbal teas she made or her mere presence. Gareth shook his head. Tatiana couldn't be the thief. Everything she did and said, every action showed she cared more for other's needs than her own.

No matter how he looked at it, he always came to the same conclusion. His stomach twisted in anguish at the thought. Only one person worked here who had the opportunity and desire to take more than she was entitled to, but he didn't want to believe it. He remembered the day Sabrina had wandered in so self-assured and bold, only a few weeks after he'd given Tatiana the food. Since that day, Gareth had watched Sabrina grow from a young girl into a beautiful and enterprising woman. He was a good businessman and a decent bargainer, but Sabrina had a gift, a way of turning every conversation to her favor. When she wanted to separate the store and tavern, he did, and their profits increased. When she suggested building the living quarters and guest rooms off the back and above the tavern, he built them. Gareth had a hard time saying no to any of her requests. It seemed absurd for her to steal when she knew he would give her anything she wanted. Yet he couldn't picture anyone else doing it. To think that he'd been so blind not to see it happening made his stomach clench.

"Gareth?"

The voice broke through Gareth's melancholy and made him smile. No matter how bad things were, Tatiana always made his problems seem insignificant. He waved her over to the empty chair to his right but Fifi beat her to it. The dog's tail swished back and forth as she scanned the table.

"Sorry, pup. Bobby Sue's already scrubbed down all the tables and swept the floor." He ruffled the fluffy white fur on the little dog's head.

"I heard things didn't go well with the council today," said Tatiana. Her voice sounded soft and distant. She scooped Fifi off the chair and sat. "Do you think you'll be able to convince them to repeal the new tax?"

Gareth snorted and took a drink. The liquid left a slight burning in the back of his throat.

"Not with Mako in charge. Mr. Zook was furious when he found out they had pushed the tax through during another special session he wasn't informed about. Mr. Herr didn't know either. It wouldn't surprise me if Mako tried to cut the farm representative positions on the council. They're the only thing keeping him in check. If things keep going like this, Mako will end up owning every business in town. Would you believe he offered to buy this place again and hire me on as proprietor last night?" Gareth laughed nervously. "Why would I want to work for someone else when I can run my own business?"

"It's a control issue. He can't control what you do and that makes him uneasy. If you give in to his demands, he'll only ask for more until you have nothing left."

"You're pretty insightful for such a young woman."

"I've seen his type before."

Gareth didn't miss the dark shadow that fell across Tatiana's face or the fact that she now looked at the table instead of at him. He longed to ask where did she come from, and where she'd disappeared to for all those years, but he hated to pry into people's pasts until they were ready, and he didn't think Tatiana was ready to share that yet.

"I wondered why you lit out of the room so fast last night. You were nothing but a blur. Mako squeezed his cup so tight after you left, I thought it would break, and that laugh of his gave me the chills. He looked like a beast stalking its prey. Be careful when you go outside. It wouldn't surprise me if his so-called deputies were out there prowling around."

"Thanks," said Tatiana. Her hands were clasped together on the table. "I'll be careful."

Fear flickered in her deep blue eyes. A moment of panic gripped him. He took her delicate hand in his big clumsy callused one and held it gently. She looked vulnerable, but he knew there was so much more to her. No one could survive these days without a good amount of inner strength.

"What's troubling you?"

Tatiana sucked in her lower lip, a nervous gesture he had seen her do often. "I know bookkeeping is Sabrina's domain, but it bothered me that we didn't seem to be earning much lately. Daily sales have been good when I've worked in the store, and other than the last few nights, the tavern has done very well. It worried me, so while you, Bobby Sue, and Sabrina were in town today, I looked at the records."

Gareth frowned. Sabrina was supposed to be running the business when he went out, not gallivanting around town. An icy lump formed in his gut. He had entrusted Sabrina with the bookkeeping for years, and there had never been a problem. "Tell me what you found."

"I've noticed inventory disappear. Sometimes just a few items, other times an entire shelf. There are no records of any trades. When I looked at the sales I made, I noticed that some of the transactions were recorded incorrectly. We took in a lot more than it says."

Tatiana's words confirmed his suspicions, and a deep pain gnawed at his heart. "Thank you for telling me this, Tatiana. Why don't you go turn in?"

"Gareth..."

"Go."

The pain and concern he saw in Tatiana's eyes made his heart skip as she left the table. He forced himself up and shuffled to the bar as she and Fifi left the room. Numbness leached into his bones and he wandered back to the table with his mug. As the liquid in the tankard vanished, the warm, tingly feeling that flowed over him only accentuated the hurt he felt.

Chapter Twenty-Six

Four Years ADR – August

An earthy loam smell permeated the air, but it was desecrated by the scent of blood and sweat. Bits of stone and twigs dug into Tatiana's back where she lay, hazily registering in her consciousness. Pain shrieked through her entire body and shame at what had happened crushed her mind. Tatiana's tormentors had left satiated and laughing. They'd left her to die here, alone. Part of her wanted to die, to shrink and wither away into the soil. How could she face them? How could she face any of the others, knowing what they had done? One tiny spark inside her cried out in indignant rage. It demanded retribution. Another piece of her mind feared for Fiona's safety. Somewhere in the back of her mind she knew the little girl had been with her the whole time. She had to live. She had to protect her bonded. With one great heave, she strained against the ropes that held her. Darkness crept over her mind from the effort.

Tatiana

Weeds, weeds! They were everywhere. Tatiana pulled more of the annoying greenery from the garden and dropped it into a basket. With an irritated swipe she pushed several wayward strands of hair off her face. No matter how often she tended the garden, there always seemed to be more weeds. They were frustrating, but not the real source of her vexation.

"I should have told him sooner," she thought.

It was almost noon and Gareth remained locked in the tavern where she had left him last night. The last of their boarders had left early this morning without a goodbye from Gareth. It wasn't like him, and that worried Tatiana.

Everyone busied themselves with chores, but they all seemed

on edge. Even Sabrina carried an air of anxiety when she slipped out after breakfast, leaving Bobby Sue in charge of the store.

"I don't like it, Fifi," Tatiana said. Perched daintily on a small lawn chair in the shade, the dog flopped her tail a couple of times. "I'm worried about Gareth."

"So am I."

Tatiana spun toward the voice, so tense she knocked over the basket of weeds. Bobby Sue knelt beside her and helped gather the scattered vegetation.

"Does she ever answer you?" asked Bobby Sue, who clutched a large leather-bound book in one arm.

Tatiana turned away, ill at ease. It wasn't what Bobby Sue asked, but how she asked it that bothered Tatiana. A cold lump began to form in Tatiana's gut.

"She knows."

That familiar voice whispered in her head. *"She's your friend."*

"Not in words," Tatiana said, with some hesitation, "But we understand each other."

Bobby Sue seemed strangely cautious as if she wasn't sure what to say. One thing about Bobby Sue, she had never been at a loss for words. She'd also been nothing but honest. Tatiana's icy lump grew and her palms began to sweat.

"Please, not now. I like it here."

"It shouldn't make a difference."

Tatiana bit at the inside of her cheek as her heartbeat quickened. Fifi scampered into her lap. With a slight tremor in her fingers, Tatiana began to stroke the animal. The feel of Fifi's soft white fur was soothing, but fear still churned insider her, tightening around her chest.

"You still miss her, don't you?"

Tatiana unconsciously intensified her hold on Fifi. Her throat felt dry, swollen, and she had to force her words out. "Miss who?"

"Fiona."

Tatiana's head snapped up in panic and her head rung with the sound of her heartbeat. There was no chance of hiding the fear she felt. Her chest constricted. Air barely squeezed into her lungs.

"He told her. I should have left as soon as I knew he was here. What will she do?"

"She's your friend. Trust her."

On her lap, Fifi snuggled closer. Her tongue began to gently caress her skin. Bobby Sue placed a hand on Tatiana's shoulder revealing the title of the book she held, *August the twelfth through October the thirty-first, year four ADR*. All hopes for a new novel to read were dashed. Tatiana felt the blood rush from her head leaving her dizzy, and tears blurred her vision. Year four After the Day of Reckoning, as the League of the Stars called the Cataclysm, was a time Tatiana wished she could forget. She wanted to flee, but a numbness born of terror kept her rooted. People got hurt when they knew about her past and what she was. Deep inside, she felt the power bubbling. With one burst of energy she could escape before Bobby Sue had time to stand.

"No."

"It's okay, Tatiana. I won't tell anyone who you are, but you can't hide forever. You have friends here."

"Told you so."

"I need to leave. It's not safe," she said as she uncoiled her body and jumped to her feet. "I've stayed too long already."

Bobby Sue dropped the book and moved to block her path. "Everyone has a past, Tatiana. You can't change it, but you can learn to accept it"

"Accept what?" snapped Tatiana. "That I'm a fool who likes to look at stars? It's my fault Fiona's dead. If it weren't for me she would be here with me now and the riots would never have happened."

"You don't know that, Tatiana."

A pain, greater than any physical injury could cause, jabbed at Tatiana's heart. Tears streamed down her face. She'd never spoken to anyone about what happened that night, not even Fifi. It felt as if a dam had burst. She began to shake. "You don't understand. I shouldn't have gone out that night. I shouldn't have gone alone. If it hadn't been for my arrogance and selfishness, they wouldn't have caught me like that. Fiona wouldn't have seen what happened."

"Listen, Tatiana," Bobby Sue held her by the shoulders. "The fault lies with the people who attacked you. You ain't to blame for what happened to you, to Fiona, or anyone else. People make bad decisions all the time. If the riots hadn't happened then, somethin' else would have started them later. Humans are just fickle, jittery creatures. Stop punishin' yourself for somethin' you couldn't control. It's time to let it go."

Being an only child, Tatiana had never experienced sisterly affection except with Fiona, and her death still haunted her dreams. The love Tatiana felt now in Bobby Sue terrified her. She couldn't bear to lose another close friend any more than she could bear losing Fifi. How could she stay here? Someone else could find out and come after her. Bobby Sue and the others would be in danger, and Tatiana couldn't allow that. Trembling, she pulled away from Bobby Sue and tried to run, but a large brindled canine blocked her way. Caught off guard, Tatiana stopped. Fifi didn't change without some kind of a threat. She looked around fearfully, but there was no one else in sight. No angry mobs. Not even Brother William. Behind her, Bobby Sue let out a gasp of surprise, but wonder mixed with the emotions. No fear emanated from her. Tatiana stared at Fifi, confused. The dog didn't growl or show her teeth; she just stood there looking at Tatiana, blocking her path.

"It'll be okay," Bobby Sue said softly. "You don't need to run no more. I'm here for you. We all are."

A soft whimper escaped Fifi's mouth and Tatiana crumpled to the ground shaking.

Chapter Twenty-Seven

Gareth

Only a single candle guttered in the near dark tavern. It disappeared into a diminishing pool of wax. Gareth stared at the pathetic wisps of light that struggled past the shuttered windows as he sat half sprawled across the table with his head resting on one arm. His mouth felt like a rat had made a nest in it, but he was too lazy to refill the mug still grasped in his other hand. Morning had long since come and gone but he had no idea what time it was now. Everyone had knocked at the door, pleading with him to come out, everyone except the person he wanted to talk to. That absence made his heart ache even more. Footsteps echoed across the room, the sharp clacking made his head throb. He lifted his head as Sabrina neared and looked at her through puffy bloodshot eyes. Her image wavered in and out of focus as she clucked her tongue and shook her head.

"Gareth, what have you been doing to yourself?"

Like a mother fussing with a small child, she helped him sit up and straightened his rumpled shirt and apron. After a minute, his eyes focused more clearly on the deep frown that creased her face. Emotions churned in him. Love and anger wrestled for his attention.

"How'd you get in here and where have you been?" He didn't mean to growl, but the words burst from his lips before he could stop them.

"With the keys you gave me, of course. As for where I've been, saving your ass and this business like I usually do. I spent all day arguing our case to the council. After much deliberation and persuasion, they finally agreed that the tax was inappropriate. It's been lowered to three percent of income and will be collected every three months. More importantly, food items are exempt from the tax. I managed to convince them that alcoholic beverages were food, so we only pay for room rentals and sales in the store. Isn't that wonderful?"

Sure it sounded wonderful, but a nagging little bug nibbled at his mind. Even innocent looking smiles could deceive. He'd seen how she looked at Mako and he at her. That snake wasn't even close to good enough for her.

"There are things missing from the storeroom."

Her eyes grew wide and for a brief second Gareth though he saw anger flare behind them. "Gareth," she said, her voice pleading and mournful. "I know you don't approve of this kind of thing, but it was the only way to keep our doors open. The council passed a health code for kitchens last month. They threatened to close us down because of that dog and all the chickens. I know I should have told you about it, but I didn't want to trouble you."

"You bribed the council?" he practically yelled the words making his head throb even harder. He had hoped to do away with corruption, not feed it.

Sabrina lowered her eyes, her voice sad and contrite. "I'm sorry, Gareth. I'm really sorry."

"About what?" he snapped. "The bribery or not telling me about it?"

"For not telling you about it. There really wasn't any other way."

"And the other evening with Mako?"

"Well..." she hesitated a moment, her lower lip pushed out into a pout. Her hands began to shake. "I know how you feel about him and I was so afraid he'd hurt you. I figured if I, you know, softened him up a bit we'd avoid an incident."

Gareth stared at her for a moment, then started to laugh. "Sabrina, you're incorrigible."

"Is that what this was all about?" she asked, indicating the empty mug. "Oh Gareth, I could never hurt you. You're the only family I have."

Tears streamed down her face as she threw her arms around him. The guilty noose tightened around Gareth's heart. How could he have doubted her?

"Sabrina, I'm sorry. I didn't mean to accuse you. It's just that display with Mako nearly made my heart stop. I've told you, you don't ever need to sell yourself like that, to anyone. You're bright, beautiful, anything you need, just ask me. As for Mako, he's bad news, and playing games with the likes of him is liable to get you bit."

Her arms squeezed tighter, almost as though she were clinging to a life raft. Tears dripped down Gareth's face as well.

Chapter Twenty-Eight

Four Years Two Months ADR – October

*For days she lay as if dead, staring blankly at the ceiling.
People came and looked at her wounds. They spoke, but the
words were meaningless, like whispers in the wind. The voices
came and went as time passed, but still she wouldn't respond.
Emptiness dwelled in her heart, a hole where a piece of her once
lived. It was more than the loss of innocence; Fiona's death had
left an unquenchable chasm of loneliness and failure. If only she
hadn't gone out that night, Fiona would still be alive. It was her
fault this had happened. She had been unable to shield the child
from things she was too young to bear, unable to save her. And
so she lay there, waiting and hoping for death to take her as well.*

*Over the din of rioters, as they pounded at the door of the
building, Tatiana heard a soft whimper. Perhaps a soft thought
would better describe it, for it wasn't a sound that could have
been heard in even the quietest of rooms. The pleading sound lit
a spark in Tatiana. Outside the building, people shouted and
brandished torches. They had but one purpose, to destroy all
who were star-touched, those who could call up the very fires of
hell. Until that moment, Tatiana would have gladly surrendered
to them and ended the pain she felt inside. But that whimper
called to her. For the first time since the attack, Tatiana moved.
Muscles ached with protest. Ribs still tender drove sharp
daggers of pain into her side.*

*Tatiana's resolve didn't waver. She had a purpose now.
Onward she struggled, forcing her limbs out of bed and into
clothing left by an unknown visitor. The clothes were worn and
ill-fitting, but it mattered little to Tatiana. She passed out the
door like a shadow. The doctors and nurses in the run down*

hospital were too worried about the mob outside to notice.

She felt numb as an inner voice guided her out a window in an unwatched corner of the building. Pain forgotten, she skimmed down the drainpipe as easily as a squirrel descends a tree, into the alley below. The whimper came again, weak and distant, another empty soul seeking fulfillment. Though a throng of people stormed the streets, Tatiana managed to avoid being noticed as she slipped out of town.

Hours passed and still she pushed on, leaving the riots far behind. Unfamiliar roads and trees passed her as a blur. Nothing else mattered except heeding the call for help. How far she traveled she didn't know or care. There was urgency in the cry as time ran short. When she finally drew near, her heart leaped. Muddy with matted fur, the dog lay unmoving on the ground. Blood crusted its delicate white muzzle. Despair draped over her like a shroud. She was too late. Tatiana laid her hand on the dog's cold and stiff chest. Blood pooled beside its head from a bullet hole. A whimper reached Tatiana's ears, her real ears, not the ears in her mind. She looked back at the dead dog. Its nipples were swollen. There would be puppies nearby.

Tatiana cast around, listening and searching for signs of a den. Only eight feet away, under a dilapidated house, she found a hollow from which the sound emanated. Three tiny bodies lay twisted and broken near the crudely dug entrance. The cry became stronger now. It knew she was near. Tatiana raced to the opening. She reached inside past the scraps of shredded cloth. Tucked away in the back, behind the rags, survived one impossibly tiny creature. The moment she touched it, a tingle of energy warmed her. Her heart leaped with joy. Where there had once been a huge empty chasm poured a flood of joy and love. Tatiana cradled the little pup and gently rocked it as one would a fussy infant. She sensed its fear subside as it faded from her own heart. Tatiana had a purpose now, a reason for being.

Tatiana

"Could one of y'all please pass the stuffin'?" said Bobby Sue. "Cook, I swear you've outdone yourself this evenin'."

"I concur," said Gareth. Joy seemed to float around him.

Only a few hours ago he'd been sulking in the tavern.

Tatiana pushed the food around on her plate and chewed slowly at the same bite of green bean she'd been grinding for the past several minutes. It wasn't that she didn't like the food. She was just too drained to appreciate it. Talking about Fiona had opened up old wounds, but somehow they had begun to heal. With any luck this time they wouldn't fester. Unfortunately, as exhausted as she felt, everything she put in her mouth felt like sand. If Bobby Sue hadn't been there to urge her on, she probably wouldn't have eaten anything. As it was, she had slipped bits of her chicken to Fifi when no one was looking.

This little impromptu feast had been Gareth's idea. A sign outside declared the tavern closed for a private affair, just so they could have one big family dinner. So here they sat, Sabrina at Gareth's side, smiling as everyone ate. It just didn't feel natural.

"Tatiana," said Sabrina, when they had cleared, washed, and put away all the dishes. "It's been a long day. Why don't you mix up one of your special teas? I think we could all do with something warm and soothing."

"I already have some steeping in the kitchen. I'll be back in a minute."

Sabrina's face remained calm, but Tatiana noticed the anger and anxiety that flared behind her mask. The woman pretended to study the tavern walls as she went to get the tea, but Tatiana wasn't fooled. At least everyone else seemed relaxed and happy, especially Gareth. It was good to see his worry lines faded some. When she returned with the tray of mugs and steaming pot, Sabrina met her at the door.

"You've done enough work for today, Tatiana. I'll serve the tea."

Spoken through semi-gritted teeth, the words were for Gareth's benefit, not Tatiana's, but she was so used to Sabrina's behavior at this point that she didn't even pause. Who knew when she'd get a chance to be served by Sabrina next? Sabrina put the tray on one of the unused tables, then poured the tea like a Victorian hostess, offering sweetener and cream to each person. She even poured tea for Fifi, although she asked one of the others to place the cup on the floor.

Sweet hints of mint wafted in the air and Tatiana breathed in the pleasant aroma. Some of the strains of the day seemed to fade with each sip. Conversations rambled amicably around her. Even Sabrina appeared happy for once. The tea was almost gone when Jill's eyes began to droop. A moment later, her head flopped onto the table.

"I feel so sleepy," said Sabrina, with an exaggerated yawn. "I think I'll turn in for the night."

"Me too," said Bobby Sue. She yawned behind her hand. "It's been a long day."

Bobby Sue never left her chair, but slumped back into it. With a dazed and sleepy look, Sabrina also collapsed. Tatiana looked around the room, confused. Everything felt sluggish and dreamlike. But somewhere, like a distant echo, someone's nerves leapt and jolted with anxiety. But where were they coming from?

"Just leave the dishes," said Gareth, as he stumbled to his feet. He teetered slightly, as if he were drunk. "We can take care of them in the morning."

With one last look around the room, he took four steps toward the door, and fell to the ground. Tatiana jumped at the thump and pushed away from the table. The room spun as she moved in Gareth's direction. A heavy fog descended upon her as she sunk to the ground.

Chapter Twenty-Nine

Four Years ADR – August

A moist and gentle tongue caressed her cheek, removing the dry and crusty remains of her tears. Eyes swollen almost completely shut struggled through the pain to open. The doe paused in its cleaning, as if acknowledging her existence, before resuming its task. At the same time, Tatiana became aware of something furry and warm brushing against her hands. Occasionally, tiny sharp objects slid across her skin near where her hands were tied, but never caused any harm. All the while, the sound of steady nibbling echoed in her ears. She tried to move, but the pain sent her tumbling back into oblivion.

Tatiana

It felt for a moment as if she floated, yet a heavy blanket covered Tatiana's mind. Her tongue felt thick in her mouth and a strange, sweet taste lingered. Panic nipped at the edges of her consciousness. Numbness, bordering on tingly pain, stretched from her fingers to her toes. Confusion fogged her mind as the darkness slowly faded from her eyes. No matter how hard she blinked, her vision wouldn't focus.

"Where am I?"

She lay on a firm, padded surface, but it wasn't her bed. It didn't feel right. Coarse cloth made her itch, causing the hairs on her arms to stand up.

"Where are my clothes?"

A musty smell filled the air, only barely masked by a strange perfume. She tried to move her arms. Pain shot through her

151

wrists and shoulders. Her hands were stretched over her head, firmly anchored.

Desperately, she tried to piece together her memories. The last thing she remembered was drinking a cup of tea.

"Where am I? How did I get here?"

"You've been drugged." Even the voice sounded distant.

Panic grasped Tatiana, its icy grip suffocating. For the first time in four years, she couldn't sense Fifi, and Tatiana's bubbling source of power had disappeared into a deep crevasse. Her heart raced.

"Not again, please God, not again. Where is Fifi?"

Tatiana ran her tongue over her dry lips and tried to shift her weight, ignoring the fiery tingles. No amount of twisting could free her hands or feet, and after a while she forced herself to lie still, gulping air in ragged breaths. Finally, though her vision appeared blurred, she made out some of the details of the room which was empty save for the bed she lay on. The only light came from a cracked window shutter. A door stood in the center of the opposite wall and a bare, unlit bulb hung from the ceiling.

The door creaked open and Tatiana froze. She blinked as the ceiling light flicked on. The face she saw seemed from a distant memory, an old nightmare. But this was a new nightmare. Mako Scaffeld stepped into the room with a smug look on his face. Duval and Diddler, the two bodyguards who had accompanied him to the tavern, trailed behind. Tatiana couldn't stop her body from shaking.

"Ah, I see our new toy is awake at last."

Tatiana cringed as Mako came closer. There was nowhere to escape to.

"You really are quite lovely," he said, running a hand through her long black hair, which splayed over the mattress. The look in his eyes as he examined her only added to her terror. His hand slid onto her shoulder and lingered over her breast before it drifted down her side. She fought back a wave of revulsion that made her stomach clench.

Mako returned his hand to her hair and slowly wound a thick clump until it pulled taut from her scalp. She bit her cheek to contain the cry that threatened to escape her lips. If Mako noticed, he ignored it, but his grip on her hair remained firm. He leaned over close, and his warm breath tickled her ear as he whispered.

"We call this our education room. It's where we teach our new acquisitions how to behave. We also make sure they know what is expected of them."

"Fifi. Where is Fifi? Why can't I feel her?"

"With all the fuss Joe made, I half expected you to have claws and fangs."

Confusion ate at Tatiana's mind. How would Joe know who she was? They'd never met. Mako began to laugh.

"You have no idea, do you?" He released her hair and began to caress her cheek. "Joe followed my boys home after they picked you up last night. Thought they had that luscious redhead. One look at you and he went crazy. Took a bit of prying to find out why. Seems he worked at Abuda before they shut it down. Pity I can't let him go now. But don't worry, I still have a use for him."

Tatiana felt the blood drain from her face. Sweat made her skin cold and clammy. Tremors rattled her arms and legs. Joe knew who she was, what she was. All this time she had kept her identity hidden. Now everyone knew. Bad things always happened when people found out. She squeezed her eyes shut and swallowed, praying she would wake up in Gareth's place.

"Fifi, I need you."

"Joe's proved useful in the past," he continued. "That old fool, Gareth, has no idea I've been hiring his nephew all this time. Joe will do just about anything for a drink, or a hit, not to mention that red head. Very easy to manipulate. I arranged things so he could rescue her. Knew she'd never go for him. It didn't take much to get Joe to charge that League guy the other day. Couldn't have Gareth poking his head into my council business."

Mako tapped her cheek until her eyes opened. His leer sent shivers down her spine. "I've dealt with your kind before. You don't frighten me. In fact, I have a very special buyer for you. Oh, I took the precaution of giving you another dose of sedatives, one that will keep your star-touched powers in check."

He held up a gold coin, just like the one she gave Gareth. Tatiana's heart jumped. Anger flared in her, making some of the fear melt away. "Where did you get that?"

Mako laughed softly, an oily sick sound. "You have a bit of fight in you. Good, a challenge is always more entertaining."

"What have you done with Gareth?"

"Pretty, isn't it," he said, ignoring her question. "Sabrina said you gave it to Gareth when you arrived. Funny thing about gold coins, they're like fish, they like to school together. Gold may not have a practical use, but it is a valuable luxury item and I like luxuries. Where are the others?"

Tatiana's emotions swirled around in a flurry of fear and anger. She clamped her jaw, refusing to answer. Mako nodded to Diddler, whose face twisted into an evil look of pleasure. A sharp pain flashed across her side as the man jabbed something at her and her body arched. When the pain eased, she lay gasping for breath. Her side felt like it was on fire, like a thousand tiny needles prickled her.

"You can make this easy on yourself, or very painful," said Mako. He stood and handed his suit jacket to Duvall. "Tell me what I want to know or your stay here will be very difficult. Where are the other gold coins?"

Anger overwhelmed her fear, and for a moment she felt a small surge of energy. "I have no others," she spat between clenched teeth. "I only took one."

"I doubt that very much."

Mako stared at her for a while, waiting for her to respond, and then nodded to the guards. "Very well. Put her up. We'll have to teach her obedience the hard way."

Rough hands dragged Tatiana from the bed. Pain shot through her feet as they slammed into the floor. She tried to wriggle free, but her body felt sluggish and the guards held her firmly. They tied her hands together and slipped the rope over a hook that hung next to the bulb. Mako watched with a satisfied grin as her body swung from side to side, lust glinting in his eyes. Now she saw the strange device they were using on her, fueled by a jury-rigged battery pack. Pain bit at her again as it touched. Memories of that other night flashed though her mind. Pain and terror overwhelmed her and tears streamed down her face, leaving her limp, drained.

A firm hand grabbed her chin and squeezed until she opened

her eyes. "I suggest you answer quickly. Where are the other coins?"

"No, no, don't tell him anything." Hate swirled with the voice's words.

"Why not? They're long gone from where they were."

It had been years since she and Fifi had sheltered in the cave with the gold coins. The original paved entrance was probably buried during the Cataclysm. A half collapsed side tunnel had led them to the stockpile. But they hadn't explored beyond the coins. Tatiana didn't want to risk her pursuer catching up, but she left a clear trail to the stash to slow him down. The lure of gold was like a drug to some people. People like Mako.

"I only took the one," she whispered in a shaky voice that seemed to echo from far away.

"Why only one?"

"It was all I needed."

"Selfish animal. He doesn't deserve even one."

"So there are more."

Tatiana nodded weakly. Her head spun. Two parts of her battled with each other. One wanted to hide, the other to fight.

"If I tell the pain will stop."

"No it won't. He'll take what he wants and demand more."

The walls of the room drifted in and out. They seemed to bend and change, adding to her confusion.

"Where am I?"

She lay in a wooded grove. Thomas and his friends grinned. She struggled to free herself. Pressure on her jaw snapped her back to reality.

Mako's fingers dug into her face. "Where? Where are they?"

"Where were what?"

"Gold coins, shiny, pretty, and bright. Why do people place such a high value on something so useless?"

"Make it stop. Make it go away."

"You were a pricey piece of merchandise. Tell me where those coins are or you'll repay me in other ways."

Other ways. Tatiana knew what those other ways were. How many times had she relived that nightmare? She longed for Fifi's gentle soothing, longed to wake from this bad dream.

Pain ripped through her body again and Tatiana descended

into her dreams and nightmares, no longer able to distinguish them from reality. Past and present merged. Roots dug into her back. The odor of musty loam from the forest floor filled her nostrils. They were there, forcing themselves on her. Pain ripped through her body.

Her mind screamed and the voice was silenced. *"Make it stop."*

Chapter Thirty

Gareth

Gareth rubbed his eyes and moaned, praying for the pounding in his head to ebb. It took a few minutes before he realized he lay on the tavern floor and another before he noticed everyone else sprawled around him. "What the…" He began to struggle into a sitting position, but a sudden urge to empty his stomach interrupted the action.

"Huh? What's going on?" said Jill, whose head had been lying on the table where she had collapsed last night. The rounded bowl of a spoon appeared embossed in her cheek.

"Good question," said Gareth, finally getting his gut under control.

The others began to stir. Sluggishly, Gareth pulled himself to his feet and helped Bobby Sue up. Sabrina remained the only one still unconscious, and Gareth raced to her side, unsure for a moment if she still breathed. Finally, she gasped as if in pain.

"Oh my head." A look of confusion filled her face as her eyes darted around her surroundings. "What happened? Why…" Her composure suddenly changed. It looked as if a light had come on in her mind. "That little wretch drugged us!"

"What?" asked Jill, who still rubbed her eyes. "Who drugged us?"

"Tatiana and her damn tea!"

Gareth looked around the room, noticing Tatiana's absence. His mind struggled to comprehend the implications of what Sabrina said. He watched as she staggered to the cashbox he kept behind the bar. After opening it, she slammed it shut with a loud clank and glared across the room.

"It's empty! She must have planned this for months."

Out of some instinct, Gareth reached into his pocket. He felt as if he had been kicked in the gut as his hand searched in vain for the gold coin. Disbelief left him numb. Tatiana couldn't have done this.

"Oh, Gareth," said Sabrina. She rushed over to him and wrapped her arms around his big frame, stroking his back. "I warned you the day she arrived that girl was trouble and that thing she gave you, it was a ploy, a trick to get you to trust her while she planned her theft. I'm so sorry this happened, but I'm here for you, always. You can count on me."

Weight seemed to press in on Gareth and he felt his chest tighten. "I know I can, Sabrina. You've always been here."

"Quick, all of you," said Sabrina. "Check the store and the house to see what else the ungrateful brat took."

"This is ridiculous," said Bobby Sue. Her head shook back and forth, and her eyes declared her conviction as they narrowed. "Tatiana wouldn't do this."

"Well, the evidence says otherwise. You two looked all buddy buddy last night. I guess she had you duped as well. Now go check the store like I told you."

Gareth sat in a chair, drained by this emotional rollercoaster. Who would be next, he wondered. After a while, the other girls reported the safe opened and empty, food missing from the pantry and supplies missing from the storeroom.

Deep furrows creased Bobby Sue's brow when she returned. Her nostrils flared angrily, but her eyes glistened with worry. She clutched a small tattered paperback in her hand. "Tatiana's things are gone."

"See, I told you," said Sabrina, with a self-righteous tone.

Gareth didn't want to believe Tatiana had anything to do with this, but it all seemed to point to her. Something in Bobby Sue's eyes kept him from any further musings. She glared at Sabrina with more anger than he ever remembered seeing, even more so than yesterday with Joe. His gut did another flip.

"I found this under her pillow." She held the book up for everyone to see. Gareth hadn't seen it before.

"So she forgot a stupid book," said Sabrina. "She was probably too loaded down with the rest of the stuff she took."

"This isn't just any book, Sabrina," Bobby Sue spoke with an icy tone impossible to miss. "It's Tatiana's favorite, one her mama and papa used to read to her. She wouldn't have left without it."

"Don't be ridiculous," said Sabrina. A nervous quaver shook her voice. "It's just a book."

Gareth rubbed at his head. His eyes still felt heavy, but not as heavy as his heart. "Bobby Sue..." His throat felt so tight the words barely croaked out. "Sabrina's right. Tatiana's gone. She's probably miles away."

"Like hell she is." The anger in Bobby Sue's voice felt like a slap. "Somethin' ain't right here and I'm gonna find out what."

"Now I know your feeling hurt, Bobby Sue, we all are, but..."

"Gareth! Gareth!" Jill dashed into the room. Tears rolled down her face.

Although streaked with dirt and blood, the white fur clutched in her arms was instantly recognizable. Gareth jumped to his feet, but Bobby Sue was faster. She took the limp canine from Jill.

"I heard something by the compost and went to look," said Jill. Her voice sounded as choked as Gareth felt. "I found her struggling out from under the muck, half buried. Who would do this to her?"

Who indeed, thought Gareth? He held his breath as Bobby Sue put the tiny dog on the table to examine it. With a slight shudder, Fifi's blue eyes popped open. They looked dull and confused, and she whimpered weakly.

"She's hurt pretty bad," said Bobby Sue. The scowl hadn't left her face. "It feels like a couple a ribs are broken. One thing's for sure, Tatiana didn't drug us or steal any money. Someone else is behind this. They wanted to make it look like Tatiana ran off."

"How can you be so sure?" said Sabrina. "She probably got ticked off at the little cur."

The pitch of Sabrina's voice sounded a touch higher than before. It was subtle, but taken with the nervous twitter, a terrifying thought began to eat at the back of Gareth's mind. Sabrina stood with her arms folded across her chest, and he could see her fingernails dig into her palms. In the four years he had known her, he had seen her both angry and afraid, and he could tell the difference. Despite the angry, indignant front she put on, Sabrina was frightened, just like the time the wild dogs ran through town. She'd pretended not to care in front of the other girls, but Gareth knew she'd been terrified. Only one thing could be scaring Sabrina this time.

"I know for a fact," he growled, "That Tatiana would never hurt Fifi in any way. That dog is her life, like her child."

"She's more than that," said Bobby Sue. "William filled me in on the details Joe left out about Abuda. Those boys that were killed four years ago weren't trying to calm that girl. They were gloatin'. She told the truth about her friend. They attacked her."

"What are you babbling about?" snapped Sabrina.

Gareth held up his hand to silence her, his throat felt even tighter than before.

"Tatiana was the little girl's friend," continued Bobby Sue, ignoring Sabrina. "They was kinda soul bonded. So is Fifi. They're both star-touched. There's no way they'd ever hurt each other."

It all made sense now. No wonder Tatiana had been afraid to stay when he first met her four years earlier. She had been fleeing for her life, trying to stay one step ahead of the mobs who were killing every star-touched they could find. He could still see her image in his mind - pale, tattered, bruised, and afraid. And Fifi, he should have known a normal dog of her size couldn't have survived.

All the little things over the past two months came together. No one had been ill. Jill's speedy recovery, Old Henry's improved behavior, his renewed energy. Anger burned in Gareth. Not because Tatiana and Fifi were star-touched, but because he finally realized who had been playing him. At that exact moment, Fifi struggled to her feet, wobbling dizzily. Her right rear leg hung limply and her breath came out ragged and raspy. Bobby Sue gently caressed her with one hand, while steadying her with the other. Fifi whimpered and closed her eyes. Gareth expected her to pass out again, but instead, the dog's eyes opened wide and glowed with a strange inner light. It happened so quickly that Gareth wasn't sure if he had really seen it. Only the soft gasp of surprise from Jill reassured him that he had.

Without warning, Bobby Sue sat heavily in a chair, as if exhausted, and Fifi stood steady on all four legs, eyes intent on Sabrina. If he hadn't seen it for himself, Gareth wouldn't have believed it was the same dog that had been half dead, crying in pain a moment before. A growl formed deep in Fifi's throat and she began to stalk across the table. Sabrina backed away, a look of horror on her face.

"Keep it away from me!" she shrieked.

"What's the matter, Sabrina? You afraid of a little fur ball?" asked Jill. An angry sneer filled her tear-streaked face.

Fifi's fur stood up on her back, making her look bigger than Gareth knew her to be. The growl deepened as she walked, but the biggest shock came when she leaped off the table. By the time her feet hit the floor, they were the size of saucers and her body became a huge bristling mass of muscles. The other girls, who only just reentered the room, squealed at Fifi's transformed size. Bobby Sue, on the other hand, didn't look surprised at all. Gareth could only blink as Sabrina backed herself up against a wall. Growls and snarls grew in intensity as Fifi advanced. Her eyes were the same height as Sabrina's. He wondered how such a small creature could get so big.

It took a moment to find his voice again, but it felt strained. "What did you do?"

Terror filled Sabrina's face as she stood face to face with the behemoth canine. Tear streaked and hysterical, she crumpled to the floor. Words babbled from her mouth as incoherent as an infant's. Her eyes pleaded with him as she shook her head.

"Sabrina."

"Keep it away from me. Please. Don't let it eat me. I had to. I had no choice. Don't you understand? She was ruining everything, all my plans. She and that demon had you twisted around her finger. I…"

Gareth had to scream above her rants to be heard. "Sabrina! Where is Tatiana?" Sabrina gave no indication that she had even heard him and he was losing patience. He seized the raving woman by the shoulder and shook her. "Where the hell is Tatiana, Sabrina? What did you do with her?"

She stared at him for a moment, with a look of utter

confusion, and then cried out as if in pain. "I sold her to Mako." She crumpled into a sobbing heap. "I had to. She was stealing you."

Fifi raised her muzzle to the ceiling and let loose a long bone jarring howl that made Gareth's chest reverberate. Outside, a chorus of howls filled the air. He turned his attention back to Sabrina, and shook his head with disgust. He'd known she was ambitious. He'd known her morals could be sketchy, but to sell another human being was unthinkable. His throat felt dry. All this time, he never noticed how jealous and insecure Sabrina had become. After a moment he turned away and walked behind the bar. Every eye in the room watched as he pulled out his shotgun, checked the chamber, and stuffed a handful of extra cartridges in his pocket. Sabrina's face paled.

"Lock her in the cellar."

Gareth looked at the shotgun and shook his head. A fine weapon for fighting off a couple of crooks, but for what he planned, it would be ludicrous. The floor creaked under Gareth's feet and his heart leaped. He was probably crazy, but he didn't see any other options and the longer he delayed the longer Tatiana remained in danger. No one said a thing as he began to pull up the floorboards. It took several minutes to clear them away. With a grunt, he pulled out the wooden crate Marty had left with him. This sure fit the description of an emergency to Gareth. He pried the lid off and rummaged in the straw, uncovering the contents.

"What's all this?" gasped Jill, as he lay the semi-automatics and extra munitions on the bar.

Gareth looked up and let his breath out slowly, hoping he still remembered how the things worked. His stomach churned. "Marty asked me to watch these for him. This seems like a good opportunity to check them out. I'm going after Tatiana."

Bobby Sue held Fifi, who had returned to her normal size, as Gareth moved out from behind the bar. He gave the dog a tender caress. She looked ragged and helpless now and her eyes seemed to plead with an intensity that made his heart ache. "I'll get her back for you," he said. "The rest of you stay here."

"You're not going alone!" said Bobby Sue. Fifi winced as she jumped to her feet. "Mako's goons'll rip you to shreds before you get in the front door. I bet Snider is already waitin' in ambush."

There was a fierceness about her that startled Gareth. Her thoughts were echoed around the room, but he shook his head.

"It's too dangerous."

"I don't care," said Bobby Sue. "And if that scum, Mako, thinks he can just waltz in here and snatch up anyone he pleases, he's got another thin' comin'. Jill, you're the fastest runner. Wake up Mr. and Mrs. Burns. Tell them what's happened. Then go to the League of the Stars' house and tell them. We have friends in this town, Gareth. It's time we called on them to stand up."

Gareth blinked, shocked, unable to argue. Beneath Bobby Sue's curvy nineteen-year-old exterior were solid muscles and determination. Her lips were pressed thin and her green eyes seemed to dare him to say no, but he knew her mind was made up. The others stood beside her, already armed and ready to rescue their friend. Jill had dashed out the door so quickly, it made him dizzy. A proud smile crept over his face as he handed the shotgun to Cook. This was his family. The rest of the world might have turned upside down, but somehow they had remembered right from wrong.

Chapter Thirty-One

Four Years One Day ADR – August

"Dear God Almighty. Wha'ave they done to you, chil'?"
Terror gripped her heart at the sound of the male voice, but quickly passed as she recognized the tone of concern. It wasn't one of 'Them.' The voice sounded older. Something warm lay close, keeping the chill from her body. Light played on her eyelids, the first pale light of morning. How long had she lain here? Where was Fiona? She reached out with her mind, but was too weak to reach the churning energy that allowed her to connect with her bonded. Her limbs were no longer bound, but even the slightest movement filled her with agony. Pain wracked her body as she forced her eyes open, fearful of what she would see. Along with a raccoon and several other woodland creatures, a doe lay next to her, keeping her warm. In the midst of all stood a stringy old man leaning heavily on a twisted wood cane like an ancient sage. His hands were gnarly and bent. Wrinkles covered his frail looking face, and his heavily patched clothes hung loose on his thin frame.
"Easy thair'," he said softly, kneeling at her side. "We're's here to help ya."

Tatiana

Something broke through the confusion in Tatiana's mind, through the pain. Hope flared in her heart, and tears of relief rolled down her cheeks.
"Fifi. Fifi is coming, with help."
Energy flowed into her body, and the power that had felt so

distant edged closer. She opened her eyes and glared at the man before her. His face still flickered between Thomas and Mako, but she could tell which was which now.

"He hurt me."

So did those boys, snapped the voice.

Anger boiled within her and she felt the power begin to surge.

"He's going to hurt me again."

You know how to fight back. Use the power.

Flames filled her mind, and the memory of pain and terror screeched through her. How could she unleash that horror?

"NO!"

It's the only way to stop them.

She could still feel the cannibals burning. She could still feel the boys burning. And she could still feel Fiona being consumed by that same power.

"I can't do it."

You must.

Tatiana shook her head.

"There has to be another way."

Mako's face loomed closer, only inches away. She felt his hand glide over her skin and cringed with revulsion.

You know what he wants. They're all the same.

Anger and fear gave Tatiana the energy she needed to bring her feet up and kick Mako away.

"Don't touch me!" Her throat felt tight.

The move caught Mako off guard, and he stumbled against the wall. His laughter wasn't a pleasant or happy sound. One corner of his lip curled into a snarl as he moved toward her. Before she could bring her knees up to kick him again, something hard and cold smacked her shins. Her legs throbbed, and fear enveloped her once more. That fine line between now and then faded again, as Mako patted her cheek.

"It seems you need a bit more educating."

Chapter Thirty-Two

Bobby Sue

Bobby Sue cradled Fifi in her arms and rushed to keep up with Gareth. The dog trembled and whimpered with every step, evidence that she was only partially healed. Bobby Sue was no expert, but Fifi's raspy breathing and speckles of bloody foam around her muzzle hinted at a pierced lung. Why she had taken the injured dog on this rescue mission baffled her. It didn't make sense. Neither did the strange connection she felt to the little dog or the tingly surge that rippled through her back at the house. Bobby Sue was sure she had been the source of energy Fifi used to heal herself, contrary to everything William had told her about the star-touched. One second Fifi was near death, and the next Bobby Sue felt drained. There was no time to wonder how or why. Fifi was in need and Bobby Sue gave freely. Now images seemed to jump into her head - people, places she'd never seen.

Gravel from the town square crunched loudly under their feet. Only a few people, mostly merchants, were on the streets. Their eyes stared at the grim look on Gareth's face and the guns he and Cook carried. Whispers followed their party, but Gareth didn't appear to notice.

Once beyond the square, they covered the remaining three blocks quickly. Out of the corner of her eye, she saw a few dogs lurk in the shadows and sensed other dogs behind them. The thought that the wild dogs had returned chilled her. Overhead a hawk screeched and she saw Gareth glance up and grip his gun harder.

"I don't remember seeing birds of prey here before," he muttered. A frown creased his brow.

Before she could respond, he quickened his pace. Unease

nibbled at her consciousness. Packs of dogs, predatory birds, and Gareth charging across town like a bull—it didn't make sense. Something was happening. Then, unbidden, reassurance flowed through her. The animals were all there to help. The knowledge eased her worry but couldn't completely dispel it. Gareth's actions still troubled her.

When he ground to a halt, Bobby Sue almost ran into him. He stared at Mako's estate with a stunned look on his face. It had been the former mayor's house before the Cataclysm, back when the town could afford such a luxury. Only half of the original building had survived. Mako had rebuilt it with lavish extras. Carvings of sharks adorned the white painted house. Columns flanked the steps leading to the front porch which lay across a well-manicured lawn.

"When the hell did he rebuild this place?" asked Gareth. She heard disgust in his voice.

"You haven't been down this way in a while, have you?"

Gareth shook his head. "I wonder whose funds and materials the bastard used."

"I don't think she's in the mansion, Gareth," said Bobby Sue. "Why not?"

She nodded toward a three-story house to the left of the mansion that housed Mako's brothel and its adjoining saloon. Fifi growled at the building. Gareth nodded. Some of the frantic urgency cleared from Gareth's eyes. For the first time since they'd left the tavern, he looked more like himself. Worry creased his brow. It was a relief to see some rationality after his mad dash.

"You look pale, Bobby Sue. Are you okay?"

"I'll be fine. Fifi drew energy from me to heal herself."

Before she could say any more the hawk screeched again. Bobby Sue glanced up at the bird but turned back at Gareth's sharp intake of breath. Across the street the dogs converged on them, and down the block, a crowd of people had gathered, moving in their direction. Bobby Sue recognized many of them from the town square and could just make out Mr. Burns running to catch up.

They were coming to help. She knew they were, but before she could tell Gareth, he turned and rushed toward Mako's brothel.

"Gareth! Wait!"

Bobby Sue raced to catch up as Gareth reached the large wooden door. She glanced at the half columns flanking the door and blushed at the carvings of naked women and men entwined in various erotic acts. Gareth stood with his teeth clamped. His hand froze inches from the breast-shaped brass doorknockers. Face, bright red with more than rage, he grabbed the door handle, cast in the likeness of a penis. The door should have been locked at this hour, but it swung open easily. Bobby Sue's heart quickened. Something felt very wrong.

Chapter Thirty-Three

Bobby Sue

Bobby Sue followed Gareth into the brothel with trepidation, expecting to be challenged. Guards should have greeted them, but none were in sight. Surely Mako wouldn't have left the doors wide open and unprotected. Thick pillows made of plush, red fabrics decorated the candle-lit reception room. More of the decadent cloth draped the walls and doorway. She almost gagged from the heavily scented rose perfume that filled the air, and the silence made her even more uneasy.

"Gareth, we should wait for help. I saw Mr. Burns. He's bringing others."

"No! There's no time! We have to hurry! Which way do we go?"

Gareth's gruff, urgent reply left a queasy feeling in Bobby Sue's gut. It sounded as if someone else spoke. Cook stood next to him, pale and trembling, her eyes oddly glazed. In the back of her mind, Bobby Sue felt herself being drawn along, as if someone were pushing her, forcing her forward.

"That way," she said, indicating a hallway to the right.

The words were out before she could stop them, and she looked on in disbelief as Gareth and Cook charged down the corridor. That insistent urging came again and Bobby Sue glanced at Fifi. Was the dog meddling with their minds? "Stop that," she hissed, and rushed to catch up. Fifi's head lowered and a feeling of guilt licked at Bobby Sue's consciousness.

The pull in her mind ceased, but it clearly still affected Gareth and Cook who raced down the hallway. Bobby Sue glared at Fifi, with the intent of ordering the dog to end the manipulation, but stopped, confused. The dog's image seemed momentarily overlaid with the image of a blond-haired child. The smoldering fire in the girl's eyes belayed her fragile build.

"Fiona!" Bobby Sue stumbled at the revelation, and almost dropped Fifi. The dog yelped in pain and the vision vanished. Meanwhile, Gareth and Cook dashed farther ahead.

An agonized scream echoed from upstairs. Gareth and Cook quickened their pace and Fifi leaped from Bobby Sue's grasp. Red streaks marked her arm where the dog's nails raked it. A second later, Bobby Sue grimaced as a sharp cramp immobilized her right hip and her side exploded with pain. Tears filled her eyes and a wave of dizziness made her stumble again.

Fifi raced up the stairs, followed closely by Gareth and Cook. Bobby Sue clenched her teeth and staggered after them as fast as she could, pausing only a moment to catch her breath at the top of the third flight. Gareth and Cook were already halfway down the dimly lit hall, their footsteps echoed ominously in the empty stillness. The only other sounds emanated from a room at the end of the hall. Fifi had fallen behind, her breath once again heavy. Why hadn't the little dog transformed?

Gareth kicked in the door, his face twisted in a snarl. "Get your hands off her, you bastard!"

Bobby Sue gasped at the sight of Tatiana, who hung naked and limp from the ceiling. Ugly red marks covered her back and her hair hung in sweat-drenched strands. For a moment, Bobby Sue thought she was dead, but then her head lolled. Tatiana's eyes were closed, but her lips moved as if she mumbled to herself. It was clear her mind drifted elsewhere. Beside her stood Mako and his bodyguards.

Mako spit curses and dove behind Tatiana's swaying body as Gareth fired, leaving his bodyguard to take the bullet. Pain streaked across Duval's face and he clasped his upper arm. Blood oozed out from between his fingers. The injured bodyguard dove out of the line of fire only seconds before Mako fired back with a small handgun.

Diddler, who had lurked out of sight, jabbed Gareth with a strange, two-pronged stick that sparked and sent him to his knees. Gareth struggled to his feet and lunged, planting the butt of his gun in the man's groin. With a grunt, Diddler dropped the stick and fumbled for a gun, his face pale green.

Bobby Sue watched Fifi dive into the chaos of flying bullets. A second later the dog yelped. Head spinning in pain, Bobby Sue grasped the doorframe. Every muscle in her body ached but the pounding in her head overshadowed everything. What was happening? The ringing in her ears resolved into thunderous footsteps. She glanced down the hall and prayed it was Mr. Burns coming to their aid, but her heart sank. She hollered a warning to Gareth and stumbled into the room. Fifi lay in the far corner, her white fur marred by a streak of blood.

Ignoring the sound of gunfire, Bobby Sue ran to Fifi. She bent protectively over the little dog as four guards charged into the room. Before Gareth could react, a guard blindsided him. Another grabbed the gun from his hands while a third pinned his arms behind his back, binding his hands firmly. In seconds, Cook was likewise disarmed.

"It's about damn time." Mako brushed off his shirt casually and stepped out from behind Tatiana, an annoyed frown on his face. "You were supposed to stop them before they reached the third floor. Take care of this old fool and put the women in the other room. I'll deal with them later." He nodded toward Cook and Bobby Sue. "Thanks for bringing the women, Gareth. It saves me the trouble of fetching them myself."

With an angry curse, Gareth knocked the guards aside and lunged for Mako. A sharp blow to the back of his head knocked him to the floor where he lay still. Bobby Sue scooped the unconscious Fifi into her arms, unsure what to do. She stood, numbed with shock, as the men dragged Gareth out the door and down the hall while Cook screamed and struggled with her captors. Diddler, recovered from his encounter with Gareth's gun, leered at Bobby Sue with a deranged look of pleasure that made her stomach twist. Bile rose in her throat. Where was Mr. Burns? Where was Jill? Had she reached William?

Diddler put away his gun, picked up his stick, and closed in on Bobby Sue. Sweat prickled her skin as she shrank back flat against the wall. Beneath her hands, Fifi twitched. Anger surged through Bobby Sue's mind. It blocked out her fear. Only sheer will kept the fury from overpowering her. Then, just like back at the tavern and in the hallway, it felt as if someone reached into her gut and sapped her energy, only much stronger this time. Sharp needles prickled her skin, sending a small trickle of fire through her spine. She gasped and collapsed, unable to do more than watch events unfold.

Deep red glowed in Fifi's eyes when they snapped open and a rabid snarl shot from her mouth. Transforming in midair, the dog launched herself at the advancing bodyguard. Diddler had no time to react. He staggered back and crashed to the floor as Fifi ripped his throat open.

Blood dripped from Fifi's muzzle and huge teeth. That, combined with her blood-curdling howl, gave her a crazed demonic look. Duval took one look at the massive dog and fled, slamming the door shut behind him. Outside, Bobby Sue heard a cacophony of barks and howls which grew louder by the second, until they seemed to echo through the halls.

With one snap of her jaws, Fifi shattered Diddler's stick and let the pieces fall as she advanced on Mako. Across the room Mako blanched, his mouth open and twisted in terror. Fifi launched herself at Mako's throat with such force that they left an indention in the wall before crashing to the ground.

The sharp crack of a gunshot echoed in Bobby Sue's ears. She clutched her chest, a scream caught in her throat. It felt as though a knife had pierced her heart. Across the room, Fifi lay sprawled across Mako's chest. Mako struggled out from beneath the behemoth canine, wisps of smoke rising from his gun. Before he was completely free, Fifi returned to her normal form, a small, limp, white mound of fur that slid off Mako's chest like an old rag.

Energy surged through Bobby Sue as Fifi's body hit the floor. Pain vanished and her limbs felt numb and tingly. Silence blanketed the room for a split second; then the most anguished sound she had ever heard rang in her ears. Everything went cold, and the charged smell of a summer storm filled the air. Bobby Sue shrank down as small as she could, sensing danger.

A fiery bolt shot from Tatiana's hands. It severed the ropes which held her to the ceiling and pierced the roof. Tongues of fire began to spread, but Bobby Sue hardly noticed. Tatiana's eyes glowed red and she had a look of madness about her. More flames leaped from her fingers, enveloping Mako who writhed and screamed in agony.

Tatiana stood within a pillar of fire, but more than fire surged around her. Fear, anguish, anger, and pain swirled through the room unlike anything Bobby Sue had ever felt. The emotions were raw and unchecked, visually transformed into flames. The room felt like a furnace as Bobby Sue crawled toward the door.

"Go back. You have to go back to her."

The words echoed in her ears over the roar of the fire. William stood just beyond the door, his hands held up to shield him from the heat. Dark bruises mottled his face, accentuated by the unusual paleness of his skin. He gaped at Bobby Sue, eyes wide and fearful. His body trembled with such intensity Bobby Sue expected him to pass out. Wisps of terror, in visual form, swirled around him. The stark imagery of his fear shocked her. So did the sudden realization that while fire surrounded her, none of the flames came close. They seemed to part as she came near.

Brother William's voice was tight and strained. "You have to stop her. She can control the fire. She's done it before. If she doesn't, it will destroy her."

Fire still leaped from Tatiana's hands and her eyes blazed with fury. The thought of getting closer to that inferno horrified Bobby Sue. She looked back at Brother William and shook her head.

A.L. Kaplan

Chapter Thirty-Four

Six Years Nine Months ADR – May

Pain. She could hear the man scream as flames licked at his flesh. The sound felt like nails on a blackboard. Tears streamed down her face. Small minds, a small town, and a miss-applied bible were a dangerous mix. Only hours earlier she and Fifi had escaped the same fate the man faced now. Smoke filled the air. The smell of burnt cloth and burnt flesh assailed her nostrils. Even after all she had experienced, that could they do this to another human being shocked her.

"We have to help him, Fifi. We can't let this happen."

The little dog growled in agreement, then the two of them charged the crowd that surrounded the burning man. Anger gave birth to a ferocious war cry, and power rippled through her. Fifi drove the crowd back like a large brindled demon, clearing a path.

Tatiana stretched her arms toward the flames and let the power guide her. Heat seared her hands as she drew the fire to her like a vacuum, consuming the flames. Wind whirled around her, tossing her hair and sucking the air from her lungs. With an effort, she held steady until the fire died to cold embers, then sent a blast of energy to shatter the chains holding the man to the pole. She caught him as he fell, being careful of his damaged skin. With the power still flowing through her, she dashed away, carrying him as if he weighed nothing.

The man moaned in pain as she laid him on the ground. Only a few patches of pink remained amongst his blackened and blistered skin. All of his hair had been burned away. Without help, death would be slow and painful. Fifi whimpered, sensing the man's anguish.

Tatiana had to help. The pain in her hands was

inconsequential compared to his need. Once again she drew on her well of power. She sent it deep beneath his skin, triggering his own body's healing abilities. Slowly, the blackened bits fell away, revealing new pale pink skin in their wake. Ears grew back to their original shape from melted lumps. Scorched and soot-filled lungs were cleansed. The man's breathing eased into a more natural flow. No scars would mar his features.

At last Tatiana drew back, weak and light-headed. Her limbs shook so badly she could barely crawl. Never had healing drained her this way. Was it worth it? Would he stop following her? Part of her wanted to stay until he woke, to ask why he tracked her, why every time she turned around, he stood there. Her heart raced fearfully. What if he asked about her past? What if he already knew? Tatiana shook her head. She couldn't risk that.

Shaking with fatigue, she crept away from the unconscious man and hid in the brush. In moments she fell into a deep slumber. When she awoke, the man was gone.

Tatiana

Fire filled the room.
"Let it burn. Let him burn."
Tatiana's heart cried in agony. Losing Fifi, losing her bonded again was too much to bear.
"Let Fifi go."
"No!"
"You must."
Flames lashed out at the one who had hurt her.
"Let it go."
"No!"
"Stop using Fifi as a crutch the way Fiona used you."
Mako's torso twisted and convulsed on the floor.
"What have I done?"
Fire enveloped the room.
"You must control the power."
"I can't. It's too strong."
Flames licked at her skin, leaving behind scorched blisters. She could feel the power gushing, erupting from her in an

uncontrollable blast. It consumed Mako. It consumed the roof, and soon it would consume her. Her eyes closed, deep in the memory of another fiery blast. The burning came from within. This was how Fiona died.

Cool hands grabbed her wrists and yanked her into the present. Someone called her name. She opened her eyes reluctantly, ignoring the pain of her burning flesh.

"Tatiana. Put out the fire."

Bobby Sue stood before her, coppery hair billowed behind her from the force of the energy. She emanated only love and acceptance.

"Let go the anger, Tatiana. Let go the pain. It's time to heal."

Chapter Thirty-Five

Gareth stumbled outside, half carrying and half leading Bobby Sue. His eyes stung, and his lungs burned with pain as he gasped for air. The fire was out, but parts of the building were still smoke-filled. Bobby Sue leaned heavily on his shoulder. Hacking coughs made her body shake and her hands were covered in red and oozing black blisters that made Gareth cringe. He felt her legs tremble as he helped her lay down on the ground. She looked pale and weak.

"Gareth!" Mr. Burns tucked a revolver in his belt and hurried over from where Joe lay near the saloon a few yards away.

A magnificent white stallion stood near, and a young man with straight, black shoulder-length hair tried to examine Joe's injuries. In typical Joe fashion, he thrust his arms at the man until he backed away. Fresh cuts and bruises marked Joe's face and arms, and dried blood crusted his shirt.

"Gareth?"

Gareth ignored Mr. Burns. Instead he scanned the area for Brother William and Tatiana. Worry creased his face. They had been right behind him when they left the building.

"Tatiana. Where's Tatiana?" Panic edged his voice.

Finally, Gareth spotted Brother William lay Tatiana's limp form on the ground nearby. He swallowed hard. Tatiana looked half dead with her raven hair accentuating her sheet-white pallor. The thought of her dying crushed him like a breath sucking weight. He couldn't imagine a world without her.

"Gareth! For God's sake, man," said Mr. Burns "Why didn't you wait for us?" A deep crease in the man's brow emphasized the concern in his voice and he shuddered when he looked at Bobby Sue's hands.

"I don't know," said Gareth.

He rubbed his sore eyes. The fuzziness of the whole morning bothered him. Clouds seemed to obscure why he had charged into the brothel and confronted Mako so recklessly. A blurred image was all he had of being dragged down the hall by Mako's men, and a pack of dogs that had fought them off for him. Brother William and Mr. Burns had appeared out of nowhere, but by the time he made it back to Tatiana's room, the place was a blackened ruin. Gareth didn't know if being hit on the head caused the memory lapse or not. Whatever the reason, something had happened in that room with Tatiana, but he hadn't a clue what.

"You could have been killed. We would have been here in less than a minute."

"I know, but I couldn't stop." The foggy feeling in his head dissipated, but he still felt confused. Another wracking cough seized him. His chest felt like he had breathed in a cactus and the burning in his throat almost confirmed it. "I don't know what...what came over me..." he said, between gasps of air. "I saw you coming and knew I should wait...but something just kept pushing me forward. It felt like...well, it felt like someone else pulled the strings."

Townsfolk milled about outside Mako's brothel and across the street. First Street looked as crowded as high noon in the market square. Some people tried to help those who had fled the fire while others merely gaped at the scorched building. A cloud of smoke hovered above what remained of the roof on the right side. It sounded as if every watch post was signaling an alarm. Most people in town were early risers, but if anyone had still been asleep, it seemed a safe bet they were up now.

More than a dozen of Mako's 'employees' clustered nearby, far more than Gareth suspected. Both women and men looked confused and frightened, unsure of where they should be. Six dogs circled Mako's remaining guards, their growls ensuring that no one moved. Gareth couldn't tell who controlled them.

"Marshall! Rider! Thank God you're here," said Brother William.

The young man who had been trying to help Joe turned at the sound of Brother William's voice and rushed over. The stallion followed, pausing a moment to gently nuzzle Bobby Sue's head. Gareth sucked in a sharp breath. The horse's bright golden eyes had the same depth and intelligence he had seen in Fifi's. They had to be star-touched, both of them, but which one was Marshall and which Rider? Gareth watched the man place his hand on Tatiana's head while the horse caressed her hair with his velvety muzzle.

"Gareth?" whispered Mr. Burns, an uneasy edge to his voice. Gareth tore his gaze away from the stallion and looked at Mr. Burns. "Those eyes...are they...?"

Gareth licked his lips, not sure how to respond or if he should. He had only learned this morning that Tatiana and Fifi were star-touched. Mr. Burns was pretty liberal, but how would he react to knowing his only son had been slathered in licks from one?

The dark-haired stranger moved to Bobby Sue's side and held her hands. His brown eyes seemed to radiate light. Gareth felt his mouth gape as the blisters on her hands disappeared and a healthy glow returned to her face.

"Holy Crap!" exclaimed Mr. Burns. "How?"

There were several other gasps of astonishment from those close enough to see. Murmurs spread through the crowd. Both admiration and fearful whispers abounded.

"He healed her wounds," said Brother William, placing a hand on Bobby Sue's shoulder. She looked up at him and smiled with a look of wonderment. "These are my friends, Marshall Winters," he said, indicating the man, "and Rider."

"Here," said Marshall, laying his hand on Gareth's back.

Gareth felt a slight tingling in his chest as Marshall's eyes grew distant again. He took a deep breath, surprised to discover his pain and discomfort gone.

"Better?" queried Marshall. A hint of weariness slipped into his voice.

"Yeah," he said. "What about Tatiana?"

Marshall's face turned grave. "She's stable for now, but will need more healing, more than Rider and I can do for her at the moment, but don't worry. There are others on the way."

Gareth looked from Rider to Marshall as the import of the latter's words began to sink in. More star-touched were coming. He wasn't sure whether that was a good thing or not. Many in town still had reservations about their kind.

"Are you okay?" he asked Bobby Sue.

Bobby Sue nodded. "Fifi..." she said, exhaustion evident in

her voice, "manipulated you. Cook as well."

"What in blazes are you talking about, Bobby Sue?" said Gareth.

"I didn't realize what was happenin' until it was too late," she continued, looking at Brother William. "Fifi was terrified for Tatiana. She egged them on, rushed them to rescue her. It was…a powerful compulsion."

Marshall's eyes grew wide in surprise and Rider gave a startled snort. Even Brother William looked uncharacteristically speechless for a moment.

"Fifi's…gone," said Bobby Sue. She choked back a sob. "Mako shot her."

Brother William hugged Bobby Sue. "We can talk more on this later."

"Yes, of course," said Marshall as he glanced around the crowd as if sensing their discomfort. "Is there a place we can take the injured?"

"My tavern," said Gareth.

Anger gnawed at him as he climbed to his feet. He felt violated, betrayed. Fifi had gotten in his mind and forced him to act in a way he never would have on his own. Then his military training kicked in. It was time to act, not dwell on what might have been.

"Cook, help them to the house. Use the guest rooms. Keep Sabrina locked up until further notice and everything closed until you hear from me. I have some things to take care of here."

"Rider can carry the women," said Marshall, and then pointed at Joe, "but someone will have to bring that man separately. He won't let us near him."

"I'll deal with him," said Mr. Burns. "Joe's a handful."

"I suggest you send for the doctor if you have one. Your friend is bleeding internally, and I think his liver is failing. That's all I could determine before he made me stop."

"How in blazes did you learn all that in a few seconds?" exclaimed Mr. Burns.

"We're star-touched," he said, with a shrug.

Mr. Burns shook his head. "Until I saw you heal Bobby Sue, I thought that healing stuff was just rumors."

Marshal sighed, then explained as if for the four-hundredth

time. "No, it's not just rumors. We can heal injuries. Yes, we can also start fires, but there isn't a star-touched I've met that would do so unless there was absolutely no other choice."

"Why not?"

"Because they would be consumed by the flames," said Brother William. "Tatiana is the only star-touched who's ever been able to control fire."

Mr. Burns gave Gareth an uneasy glance. His eyes flickered back and forth between Gareth, Tatiana, and the burnt building. He said nothing, but Gareth noticed the sudden movement of his Adam's apple as he swallowed and the tightness in his jaw. Those near enough to hear the comments quickly spread the word.

Marshall ignored the growing agitation of the crowd. "Where can I find the doctor? Joe needs tending."

"I saw Doc Johnson helping some of the women." said Jill, who only just joined them. "I'll go tell her." She disappeared into the crowd again.

Marshall lifted Tatiana onto Rider's back, carefully supporting her limp form against the horse's neck until Bobby Sue climbed up behind her. Gareth didn't miss how tenderly Brother William looked at Bobby Sue, or the longing in her eyes. Perhaps he could convince the disciple to take Bobby Sue someplace safe, maybe even Penn-York. Marty had said things were safe there. He clamped his jaw as he watched them head down the street. First they had to survive this day.

Chapter Thirty-Six

Gareth

Gareth glanced at the gathered crowd. They were his neighbors, fellow merchants, and friends, but there were many he didn't recognize, including Mako's prostitutes. The brothel had been open over a year, yet none of the women were pregnant or holding babies. Either they had been extremely lucky, or Mako took care of any unwanted pregnancies. It was the latter that irked Gareth.

A young girl, barely eight years old, stood alone in the center of the group. Bright red rouge decorated the girl's cheeks and the lipstick she wore made her face look ghostly pale. She shivered in the provocative clothes that clung to her waif-like frame, and her wide, hollow eyes gaped at the crowd. A pretty olive-complexioned boy stood a few feet away. He didn't look more than twelve.

"Kiah!"

One of the teen-aged girls looked up and scanned the crowd. "Mama?"

Tears streamed down the girl's face as a dark skinned woman rushed forward and clasped her in a fierce embrace.

Rage rippled through Gareth and his fists tightened so hard his nails dug into his palms. Their interaction made it clear that the young woman hadn't been there by choice. Chances were, neither had most of the others, especially the children. How could he have been so negligent to allow this to happen in his own backyard?

A cluster of council members stood on the far side of the street near Mako's market. Hugh Hafley, Darren, and a few others looked his way. Suspiciously missing from the group were his friends John Zook and Abraham Herr. With all the alarms, they should have been here by now, even if they had been working in the fields. Gareth yanked his gun from the pile of weapons near the circling dogs and reloaded as he walked toward them. Townsfolk parted, clearing a path. Darren's eyes grew wide, his small mousey frame taut and poised to flee. Hugh, a short, brown haired man who had lived in Atherton for less than a year, stepped toward Gareth as he approached.

"You've gone too far this time, Gareth." said Hugh. His stout frame blocked Gareth's path and his condescending tone made his opinions clear. The hair on his head looked like a short-cropped greasy lawn. "How dare you attack the Mayor's place of business…"

"Shut up, Hugh," said Gareth, shoving him aside with unconcealed disgust. He wondered if the wide-eyed waif he had just seen was Hugh's personal toy. It was no secret the man liked very young girls.

"Where's Mako?" demanded Carlene, one of the few original council members. "What happened here?"

"Mako's dead," said Gareth, between gritted teeth, "and good riddance."

"Jesus, Gareth," said Carlene. "I knew you were bitter about losing the election, but I never thought you'd resort to murder!"

A thick hand yanked Gareth's shoulder and spun him around before he could respond.

"What the hell did you do?" said Neil, his round freckled face only inches away. Bits of spittle sprayed Gareth in the face.

"The question you should be asking is what your illustrious Mayor has been doing behind your back," said Gareth, wiping his face. "Or did you know about his plan to abduct Tatiana?"

"How dare you accuse…"

"Are you part of his little extortion scheme as well? Do you get a cut of every business he takes over?"

Neil's face grew red. "You have no right to toss around accusations like that."

"Mako brought prosperity to this town that we never saw while you led the council," said Darren.

The accountant-turned-weaver took another step back when Gareth glared at him.

"And drugs, and prostitution…"

"Which have been around since the dawn of civilization,"

said Hugh. He puffed up indignantly, his nose angled back so far Gareth could see clear up his sinuses.

Gareth ground his teeth. "Sex between consenting adults is one thing, Hugh, but children? You disgust me."

Hugh gave a soft snort and rolled his eyes. "This from the man living with seven women."

"As employees, Someone needed to keep them safe from the likes of you and Mako. See those people?" Gareth asked, pointing at the prostitutes. "Is that what you want our town to be, a place where people are used for others' pleasure? A world where people are snatched from their homes in the dead of night and forced into servitude? What's next, open slavery?"

"It's the price we pay for progress," said Hugh, a contemptuous sneer on his face.

"Hugh!" Carlene said.

Gareth shook his head. "I know most people think some of my ideals are old fashioned, and that's fine. But somewhere, you have to draw the line at common decency. Ever since Mako walked into this town, things have changed. Yes, there are more people. Yes, business is booming, though most of it is Mako's. It isn't worth the cost. Our friends and neighbors have been threatened and our women debased. Too many businesses have been coerced to hand over their profits to him. Darren, how many of your fellow weavers have come to you with complaints lately?"

"Um, well…" Darren stuttered, uncomfortably.

"Carlene, how many loaves of bread have the guards snatched without so much as a may I?"

"More than I care to think about," she replied.

"Troops need to eat," said Hugh.

"Yeah," said Gareth. "That's why we pay them. But do we need fifty hired guns? That militia is too big. He and that psychopath he hired to run it treat Atherton like their private domain."

Darren looked uncomfortable and turned away, but Hugh continued to glare. Of all of them, Hugh had probably gained the most from Mako's rule. He ran a store similar to Gareth's. Neil was surprisingly silent. Gareth hadn't heard of any disputes with the carpenters and woodworkers, but that didn't mean there weren't any.

"Listen, Mako is dead, but his cohorts aren't. It's only a matter of time before Snider makes a move to take over. His people are imported cutthroats and militants. They have no vested interest in this town besides profit. You've had to notice how they treat people. They're more a hindrance to our safety than protection. It's time you all decide whose side you're on, this town's or Snider's. I'll be damned if I'll bow to him. I'll die first."

Townsfolk grumbled their agreement with Gareth. The council may have turned a blind eye to Mako's slow takeover, but the townsfolk hadn't. They'd had enough.

"What the hell's going on here?"

Everyone except Gareth jumped at the gravelly voice. Gareth turned around, steeling himself for the confrontation. Snider, the militia commander, stood with his hands on his hips. A weapon hung across his chest in a casual fashion, but the eight thugs behind him had their guns at the ready. Several more stood guard around Mako's house down the block.

Snider's dark eyes surveyed the crowd. Duval stood there as well. He looked haggard and shaken, a contrast to his usual tough demeanor. A blood-soaked bandage was bound around his arm.

Gareth cursed silently. He had forgotten about Duval. The man must have slipped away during the confusion. There was no telling what other details had slipped his mind.

"Well?" asked Snider. "Tell me what this is all about. Duval here has been a bit incoherent. Keeps saying something about fireballs and monster dogs."

"Mako is dead," said Gareth. "So is Diddler."

"I figured as much, but that doesn't explain why you are all standing around here?"

"We're trying to help people, Snider. Why are you here?"

"To keep order, of course." His lips twisted up in a parody of a smile.

"You never have before. Why start now?"

Snider looked around the street. His eyes flicked between Gareth and the council members, but the only move he made was to spit a gob of brown phlegm on the ground. A few people scowled, but Gareth didn't react. He knew Snider was trying to bait him.

"Mako was right about one thing, Gareth. You're a troublemaker. I'm taking you into custody."

"On what charges?"

"Inciting the general populous to riot."

"Now you hold on a minute, Snider," said Carlene, "you work for us, not the other way around. Gareth hasn't..."

"Don't think you understood me properly," interrupted Snider. "I don't hold to Mako's version of the soft sale. My preference is for the direct approach. You either abide by my rules or suffer the consequences."

"What consequences? This is our town," said Neil.

"Not anymore. Now clear the street."

No one moved. One of his guards fired a single shot into the crowd. People scattered and a man fell to the ground. Shrieks from the injured man enraged the crowd and they soon lost their fear.

Gareth saw Snider's eyes narrow and sensed the general calculating the odds. His small group was better armed, but vastly outnumbered. Snider's lips curled in a sneer and he nodded at Gareth.

"This isn't over," he said softly.

With that, he and his men backed down the street toward the barracks, ducking stones as they went. Gareth breathed deeply. No, it wasn't over. Snider had over fifty armed men under his command. It wouldn't be long before he made his next move. Gareth just hoped he had enough time and the town had enough people who were willing to counter it.

Chapter Thirty-Seven

Four Years One Day ADR – August

Warmth soothed her body, and the pain felt less intense. She opened her eyes to see a small wooden shack. The old man sat in a weathered wooden chair, a doe and raccoon at his feet. Behind the chair a pair of rabbits nestled together. On the far side of the dimly lit space sputtered a small fire in a stone hearth. A pot simmered on a stand above the flames. Overhead hung a large tin cone, carrying the smoke outside through a round metal duct. The old man struggled to his feet and hobbled over to her cot carrying a bowl of steaming liquid. She couldn't imagine how he had transported her to his cabin if he could barely walk.

"Me friends 'er 'elped carry you," he said, as if reading her mind. "They's star-touched, liken you. They's did what they could fur you, but bein' critters and all, well, they's just don't 'ave all the 'uman know 'ow. 'Fraid I ain't good for much'n other than wrapping bandages and making broth."

Tears filled Tatiana's eyes at his kindness. At that very moment, a wave of fear and anger washed over the entire cabin. The doe jumped to her feet, her white tail raised high in alarm. Birds and other small animals that she hadn't noticed before shrieked and dashed about the room.

"What'n blazes..."

She never heard the rest of his words. Fire filled her mind, terrible uncontrolled fire. Tatiana gasped. She saw 'Them', the ones who attacked her, writhing in flaming agony. Their screams howled in her ears as if she stood there.

"Fiona! No!"

The power was too strong for Fiona to contain. Tatiana tried, but couldn't get through to her. She watched helplessly as Fiona flashed into flame and vanished, leaving a gaping hole in her heart.

Tatiana

"No!"

Light seared Tatiana's eyelids, blazing like the flames that took Fiona. Images jumbled through her mind, but what was real and what wasn't? Pain crushed in on her. Fiona was gone. Fifi was gone. That much was real. All around, anxious voices cried out, but the words seemed blurred unfocused. Her limbs felt heavy and sluggish. Tatiana forced her eyes open, blinking in the sunlight. The horse she rode swiveled its white head around. One large golden eye regarded her for a moment before it turned away.

"Shh," said Bobby Sue, holding her tight. "It'll be okay. You're safe now."

Tatiana glanced to her left, focusing her eyes on the dark-haired stranger walking beside her. Wispy black hairs covered his chin. Beyond him, people hurried down the street. When she looked to the right an all too familiar profile greeted her. Her heart began to race. It was him, Brother William, the shadow that wouldn't leave her be. As if he knew she was looking, he turned and cast his hazel eyes on her. Panicked, Tatiana jerked away, slipping out of Bobby Sue's arms. A pair of strong arms caught her as she toppled off the horse.

"Careful. You'll undo my healing," said the stranger. "You need to rest."

A faraway look filled the stranger's brown eyes. Slowly, her heart eased its pounding. Then the heaviness returned to her body and darkness filled her vision.

Chapter Thirty-Eight

Gareth

"You," Gareth called to one of Mako's prostitutes who stood outside the brothel. She looked more alert than the others. "What's your name?"

The woman's hazel eyes narrowed, their gaze intent, intelligent. Unlike the others, she seemed at ease in her tightfitting turquoise bustier, completely unabashed at the amount of cleavage it exposed. He could almost see her mind clicking away, trying to decide whether to trust him or not.

"Sharon."

"Sharon, are there any more, ah…workers besides the ones here?"

"No one's left in the building, if that's what you mean. The lucky girls are in there," she said, pointing to Mako's house. "He likes to keep a couple of his favorites close to his quarters. Gives them private rooms and all. The unlucky ones are in the barracks, if they're still alive. No one has ever come back from there."

"There's not much I can do about them now," Gareth said. "Bring everyone you can to the town square. We'll see about finding new accommodations for anyone who wishes."

Sharon looked skeptical, she but began to herd the dull-eyed prostitutes down the street. Most of them stared at their feet as they walked. A few looked fearfully at the people they passed, others with hope. He wished he could do more, but Gareth had already had his fill of rash actions for one morning. Charging into Snider's headquarters or Mako's personal quarters wasn't on the agenda. No one questioned his authority as he barked out orders and sent people to watch the militia's movements. It felt as though he were back in the military, with subordinates jumping at his command.

"The rest of you, if you value your freedom, come with me."

It didn't take long for the council building to fill. People stood shoulder to shoulder, and a few of the younger folks shimmied up into the rafters of the large, high-ceilinged, single story structure. No one bothered with the long wooden benches stacked against the walls. They would have taken up too much space. Those who weren't fast enough to get a spot inside crowded the town square. Several hundred people pressed into the market square just outside. Their nervous chatter drifted in from the open windows.

Angry and anxious shouts permeated the building. Gareth heard the words star-touched and Tatiana tossed about with both shock and suspicion. Fear and resentment flitted across Hugh's face as he stood on the platform. His back pressed against the simple wood wall in the back with the other four council members to make room for more people. Darren looked terrified. His eyes darted from face to face. Neither John nor Abraham were present, which worried Gareth.

Silence descended as Gareth climbed onto the narrow table that separated the council from the crowd. Then everyone began shouting at once. Gareth couldn't discern a single question from the deafening chaos. Finally he held up his hand. As the voices settled down again a few queries became clear.

"What happened?"

"Who started the fire?"

"Is one of your girls star-touched?"

"Is she safe?"

"What happened to Mako?"

"Tell us what's going on."

Gareth waited for complete quiet. It only took a moment to relate Tatiana's abduction and subsequent rescue for those who hadn't heard. The people who frequented his tavern knew her well and grumbled loudest.

"But is she star-touched?" someone asked

Gareth hesitated a moment, steeling himself for whatever their reaction might be. "Yes."

"How long have you known?"

"Is she dangerous?"

"I just found out this morning that she's star-touched." said

Gareth. "She doesn't like to advertise. As for her being dangerous, how many of you have met Tatiana?" Dozens of hands went up. "Did she seem dangerous to any of you?"

"Well, no, but..."

"There is no but," shouted Mr. Burns from the back of the room. "Tatiana is one of the sweetest, nicest people I know. And that other star-touched guy, the one with the big white horse, I saw him heal Bobby Sue's hands. They were covered with third degree burns. Now they're as good as new."

New rumblings sprung up around the room. Gareth ground his teeth. Necessary as it might be to share this information, they didn't really have time. Snider was probably deploying his troops already.

"Enough," said Gareth, his deep voice commanded silence. "Whether Tatiana is star-touched or not is not the concern right now. Mako is dead. Unless you want Snider ruling Atherton, we need to act now to stop him."

Before Gareth could continue, a hubbub ensued in the back of the building.

"Out of the way!" a voice shouted. "Let us through."

The crowd parted to reveal a slight, brown-haired thirteen-year-old girl wearing a simple light blue dress with a dark smock. One of the scouts Gareth had just sent out had his arm around her waist and struggled to hold the girl upright. She looked dirty and exhausted. Wisps of brown hair hung across her face and the small white cap on her head sat askew.

Gareth's stomach knotted. She was one of John Zook's grandchildren. Someone scooped her up and carried her the remaining distance and set her down on the table.

"Alma," Gareth said, taking her hands. "What happened?"

"Papa, they killed Papa," she said. Tears streamed down her dirt-streaked face.

"My God," someone exclaimed. "Thomas Zook is dead!"

"Were they raiders? Why didn't the militia stop them?"

"I heard a couple of gunshots earlier, but didn't hear any alarm. Thought someone put down a cow," said a man near the front.

"Quiet, all of you," yelled Gareth. "Who did this, Alma?"

"Soldiers," she said between sobs. "Militia men. They came

at dawn, just as we were about to leave the house. I was in the root cellar putting away the butter. They didn't see me hiding behind the potatoes. I heard a gunshot and Mama screamed for Papa." She paused to wipe her face. "The door caught on the rug after they searched the cellar and I peeked through the crack. That man was there, the one with the big scar across his face. He ordered his men to take Papa's body outside. Then he left. Said something about checking on the Herr's. I slipped out when the alarms sounded. There were soldiers in the fields."

Shouts of dismay erupted around the room at this news. Snider's men had to have been on the move long before Gareth woke to Sabrina's little charade. He cursed out loud. Mako must have known he would charge to Tatiana's rescue, giving Mako the perfect excuse to get rid of Gareth.

"Alma," said Gareth. "This is very important. How many soldiers did you see?"

Alma wiped her face with her sleeve again and her lips quivered as she spoke. "There were a dozen, but most of them left with the scarred man. I saw four at the house when I left and six in the fields on my way here."

Gareth did some quick calculations. Snider only had fifty men. Eight came to the brothel and he had seen at least six farther down the street near Mako's house. If he went after all four major farm families and left four at each of the farms and a dozen, maybe more, patrolling all the fields, he only had eight more in reserve.

"Burns!" called Gareth. "Take ten men to the Herr house."

"I'm on it."

"I need volunteers to check on the Yoder and the Bunderman families and to secure grain storage."

"Wait a minute," said Hugh, who had been mercifully silent until now. His voice had a slight tremor, but Gareth wasn't sure if it was fear or anger. "Who put you in charge?"

"Oh for God's sake, Hugh," said Carlene. Her sharp tone echoed Gareth's feelings. "I make a motion to let Gareth take over security."

"I'll second that," said Neil.

"All those in favor say, aye."

The resounding 'aye' made the floor boards vibrate.

"All those opposed say, nay."

Everyone stared at Hugh, but he remained silent.

"All right," said Gareth. "Do we have any volunteers?"

Dozens of people stepped forward. They all knew that the farmers were the life blood of Atherton. If Snider controlled the farms...

Chapter Thirty-Nine

Gareth

"Tatiana and Bobby Sue are resting," said Doc Johnson. "Who knew turning into a blowtorch and then putting out the fire took so much energy. Brother William and Marshall will keep an eye on them. I've made Joe as comfortable as possible, but it doesn't look good. Cook's watching him. I'll let you know if there're any changes."

"Thanks, Edna," said Gareth. Her grim prognosis of Joe made his stomach knot. As obnoxious as Joe behaved, Gareth didn't want him to die, especially not like that. "I appreciate you coming in person."

"Just try to stay out of trouble. You already have one lump on your head," she said.

Doc Johnson nodded to Carlene, who was helping coordinate patrols, before heading for the exit. Her shoulder length cornrows swung with each step.

Sheaves of papers lay scattered across the table, along with a map of Atherton. Gareth struggled to keep his face neutral as he turned back to the dozen or more other people that remained in the council building. The latest scout reports weren't comforting and he didn't want anyone to lose hope because he frowned at the wrong time. Their base of operations stood closer to the barracks than he would have liked, but the center of town was like a magnet for people, which made getting information easier. Both Marshall and Rider had been helping to deliver messages and to transport people and supplies all morning.

Things didn't look good. The entire Bunderman and Yoder families were Snider's prisoners, along with most of the Zook family. They were being held at their farmhouses as far as anyone knew, but Gareth couldn't be certain. So far, the town's defense remained scattered. Only a little over a hundred people were willing or able to fight. Too many hid in their houses, hoping to stay safe from attack. They needed to pull together quickly.

"What about the blacksmith?" asked Gareth.

A young dark-skinned man whom Gareth had never met stepped forward. "Ted Minto, his family, and the Herr family are secure, along with the herds. Apparently he was more prepared than Snider expected and had stockpiled a small arsenal of weapons. He's been making them for months. Our people are guarding the north gate to the town. I've already sent a cart to collect the weapons Ted doesn't need."

"Good."

At least there's some good news, thought Gareth, but Snider held both the south and west gates. Small skirmishes had popped up throughout town, and not just with Snider's men. Some of the drunken rabble that had moved in during Mako's regime were causing trouble. If they weren't brought under control quickly, Atherton would be tossed into the same chaos that followed the Cataclysm eight years ago.

"What about the southern part of town?"

"The weaving district to the east is ours, but most of the other craft halls in the west are spotty," said a middle aged woman. "Those League disciples are pretty good in a fight. They've managed to beat back several would be rioters, though they lost their house. Most folk had them pegged as wimpy tree huggers."

Gareth hid a grin. Brother William had sure proved himself against Joe.

"News from the east gate," shouted young Alan Burns, as he burst through the door. The ten-year-old boy's face was red and he gasped for breath as if he'd run hard. "We have visitors."

Garth waited for the boy to speak, but before he had the chance, the door to the building swung open again.

"Silly boy," said a tall, muscular man with dark brown skin. The stranger chuckled softly. "I would have given you a ride if you had waited but half a second."

A blond-haired man who looked sixteen appeared equally amused. The two seemed an odd pair, but not nearly as strange as the hawk that rested on the younger man's arm. The room grew silent as they approached.

195

"You must be Gareth," said the older of the two. "My name is Eric. This is Gavin and his bonded, Shea. My bonded, Iolana, is outside. We did not wish to leave your skies unwatched while Shea took a much needed rest."

Gareth's throat felt unusually dry. It didn't take much to infer that the newcomers were star-touched.

"Welcome to Atherton," he said, "You picked a heck of a time to visit."

"Indeed," said Eric. "Perhaps we can be of assistance."

"We can use all the help we can get,"

"Wait a minute," said Carlene. "How do we know we can trust them?"

Gareth shifted his feet uneasily. Easing everyone else's worries was hard when he was only just coming to terms with what he knew himself.

"I understand your concern," said Gavin. "But we truly have come to help you. This is the Lost One's home. We won't let it fall."

Carlene wasn't the only one who looked at him like he was insane. "What the hell's that supposed to mean?"

"It does not matter," said Eric. He frowned at the younger man. "If you will allow it, we will help defend your town."

"But..."

"He's referring to Tatiana," Gareth said. "The details are complicated." He turned back to Eric. "Have you seen her yet?"

"Not yet." We wanted to deliver our message first."

"What message?"

"Marty is on his way with reinforcements. They should arrive sometime tomorrow."

"The merchant?" said Carlene, a look of surprise on her face. "What can he do?"

"More than you think, Carlene," said Gareth. "Marty has a lot of friends. We served together in Special Forces and he's well-armed."

"But how..."

"Does it really matter?"

"If you don't mind, we'd like to see the Lost One now. Then we will return here to see what we can do," said Eric.

"Of course," said Gareth. "Alan can show you to the house."

"No need, Shea knows the way," said Gavin.

As they turned to leave, Shea spread her wings and screeched at Darren as he hurried in with another report. The former accountant fell back, startled, even more nervous than he'd been all day. With a slight tremor in his hand, he pushed up the glasses that had slipped down his nose.

"Shea!"

Eric helped Darren up while Gavin stroked Shea and made soothing sounds. Suddenly Gavin's face grew pale. Gareth recognized that distant look in his eyes. He had seen it several times this morning on Marshall's face.

"What did she see?" said Eric.

Gavin looked at Gareth, his brow wrinkled with concern. "Shea saw this man talk with some armed men in an alley not long before we arrived. The men were soldiers from the big building in the west, the one right next to the gate."

Darren paled. Sweat beaded on his forehead. Gareth reached him in two steps and grasped one of his bony wrists.

"What did you do, Darren? What did you tell them?"

Darren merely opened and closed his mouth like a fish. "For God's sake speak up," said Carlene

"Nothing. I...I...They're sending more troops to the granary."

"He's lying," said Eric, with a distant look in his eyes. "There is no movement by the granary, but there are troops heading north, toward the gate."

Gareth's jaw twitched as he grabbed Darren's shirt at the neckline and pulled the shaking man in close. Rage born of betrayal throbbed in his temples. He'd trusted Darren as much as he had trusted Sabrina. For years before the Cataclysm the man had done almost everyone's taxes in the town. He'd been chosen to tally the votes for the mayoral election because the whole town believed in him, respected him.

"Keep your damn misinformation to yourself. Now tell us the truth or I'll have you tied up and thrown to the mob."

"They want us to pull people off the town gate to protect the granary. They're going after the gate and the Herr family."

"What did you tell them?"

Darren's voice came out like a whiny whimper. "Where our

forces are weak and strong."

"How could you?" exclaimed Carlene. "Especially after what we know about them now? Do you really think Snider and Mako planned to leave us alone after they got control of the farmers? We'd have been obsolete, expendable."

"I...I didn't have a choice. Hugh made me."

"Hugh! What does that son of a bitch have to do with this?" demanded Gareth, his face twisted into an angry scowl. The contemptible man had fled to Snider's side not long after Gareth was elected chief of security. Hugh hadn't been seen in two hours, two hours without his snide and self-righteous comments. His defection didn't surprise anyone, but Darren's did.

"He knew...he knew what I did."

"What did you do?" grumbled Gareth through clenched teeth.

"Don't hurt me...promise you won't hurt me." The panic in his eyes verged on madness.

Carlene yanked Darren's head to face her. "I'm going to hurt you if you don't spit it out. Now what did you do?"

Gareth's stomach knotted again and his head began to swim. His tongue felt thick and dry as he spoke. "The election."

"Y...yes," Darren said with a slight whimper. "Mako didn't win. You did."

Gareth threw Darren to the ground with loathing, and not just at the man's actions. He had been so depressed by the election he never even questioned the results. It never occurred to him that Darren would falsify documents. If he had known...

Gareth muttered a few choice words under his breath and began jotting notes on scraps of paper. He needed to get messages out to people immediately. Beating himself up for his descent into disinterested despair wouldn't change what had happened. Right now there were more important things to deal with.

"I need to get a message to Ted, the blacksmith," said Gareth. "At the north gate."

Shea lifted her wings and screeched. Gareth looked at the hawk and shifted his feet. Beside him, Carlene took a step back. Gavin smiled, clearly amused by their reaction.

"Just roll the note up and hold it out. Shea knows the person you're looking for."

As soon as Gareth held the rolled up paper over his head, Shea leaped off Gavin's arm. Gareth gasped as the wind from her powerful wings rushed against his face. With the note clutched in her talons, Shea lifted into the air and shot out the door. Gareth held a second note out to young Alan, who had watched, wide eyed the whole time.

"Take this to your dad."

"Yes, Sir!" said Alan, before he dashed out the door.

"What do we do with Darren?" asked Carlene.

Gareth's eyes narrowed as he scrutinized the man. Darren crouched on the floor, clutching his legs in close and oscillating like a demented rocking horse. Tears streamed down his face. It was a pitiful sight, but Darren's betrayal was another on a long list. Gareth wasn't sure he could handle any more right now. Sabrina he would discipline himself. Darren would have to face the entire town. They had a right to know what he did.

"Lock him up somewhere secure until we can deal with him."

Chapter Forty

Tatiana

Images of the cannibals Tatiana had killed when her powers first appeared overlaid with Mako's body writhing on the floor, screaming in agony. Even the boys Fiona had killed haunted her. Tatiana jerked awake, heart pounding. Her powers killed…again.

A small lamp lit the room; one of Gareth's nicer guest quarters. Bobby Sue slept in the other bed, her hands still red in places. Tears stung Tatiana's eyes. No one was safe when she was around. It was best if she left before someone else got hurt, or worse, killed. She forced her body to move and rolled out of the bed, but as soon as she touched the floor her legs collapsed under her. Tatiana bit her lip to keep from crying out.

"Will I ever be rid of this curse?"

"It's a gift."

"For bringing death."

"And healing. Besides, they deserved it."

"Not like that. No one should suffer like that."

Tatiana grabbed the edge of the bed and tried to pull herself up, but all that did was drag the sheets down. Even reaching for the pool of energy garnered only a murky surge of strength. Sweat dripped down her back and fatigue tugged at her body.

Footsteps sounded in the hall. Renewing her efforts, Tatiana struggled to disentangle from the sheets. She had to leave, now.

"What happened?" Brother William rushed toward her and reached for the offending sheet.

"Leave me alone!" said Tatiana, pushing him away. Her hands started to shake. Tears streamed down her cheeks.

Startled, Brother William jumped back. "I was just trying to help."

"By chasing me across the country?"

"But…"

"Every time I turned around you were there," she said between sobs. "It almost got you killed. What do you want from me?"

"I…I'm sorry," he stammered. "I only meant to… Thank you for saving my life last year."

"You were gone when I woke," she whispered, remembering how badly he'd been burned. It had taken so much energy to heal him she'd passed out as soon as she'd finished.

He looked at her for a moment, lips pursed. "You were gone when I returned to your hospital room."

Tatiana turned away, her throat constricting with pain. She left for a reason, but not one she was ready to talk about.

"Maybe you should wait outside, Brother William," The dark-haired stranger stood in the doorway. "Tatiana needs more rest. You two can talk again later."

"Who are you?" said Tatiana, once Brother William left.

"If I tell you my name will you stay put for a while?"

Tatiana bit her lip and nodded. It wasn't like she had much of a choice.

"Marshall Winters," he said, as he scooped her up and gently placed her in the bed. "You know, Brother William really does mean well. He feel's guilty about losing track of you four years ago. The least you can do is tell him why you ran out."

"It had nothing to do with him."

"No, but he needs some closure. So do you."

"Smart man. Listen to him." said the voice

Marshall sprinkled some powder in a glass of water and handed it to her. "Doc Johnson left this for you. It'll help you sleep."

Too tired to refuse; she gulped down the liquid, grimacing at the bitter taste. In seconds her eyes drifted closed and she drifted off to sleep.

Chapter Forty-One

Bobby Sue

Bobby Sue sat propped up in bed where she stared at the whitewashed walls of the modest sized second-floor guest room. Across the room Tatiana mumbled in a fitful slumber. Hours had passed since Marshall healed their injuries. Glancing down at her hands, Bobby Sue marveled at the few patches of pink, all that remained of her burns. The new skin felt strange as she flexed her fingers, more so with the pain still fresh in her mind from this morning. Both Marshall and William had insisted that she rest. At first she had resisted, but the reality of her fatigue finally caught up to her and she had slept.

A pained whimper drew Bobby Sue's attention back to Tatiana. Perhaps if she could move closer it would help ease the demons that haunted her friend's dreams, or maybe some natural light. Thick green curtains covered the window. In her effort to reach them she almost upended the oil lamp that sat on the small end table under the window.

"I'll get that for you," said William, as he hurried in.

He placed a steaming mug on the end table and tied back the curtains. Bobby Sue was surprised to see the sun so low in the sky, too low for any of its light to shine on the brown and green oval rug between the beds. In one fluid motion, William pulled the single chair closer to her bed, sat, and took her hand.

"How are you feeling?"

"Better," she answered, relishing his touch and the caring look in his eyes. She tightened her grip on his hand. "What all's been happenin' while I napped? And don't you sugar coat things. I don't want to be kept in the dark about anythin' from you. Understand?"

"I wouldn't dare," he said. A half smile flashed across his face for a moment. It almost hid the worry in his eyes, but not quite. "Gareth is busy directing defenses but he sent word not long ago. Darren sold us out but is in custody. Snider's people have control of the grain storage buildings and have managed to garner support from a good chunk of townspeople. We're not sure if it's by choice or coercion. Either way, this isn't going to be easy, even with help from Marshall, Rider, and the others."

"Who else is here?" she asked, trying not to think about what a civil war would do to Atherton.

"Gavin, Eric, and Iolana arrived while you slept. You need rest to finish healing. We didn't want to wake you."

Healing. If only there had been something she could have done for Fifi. Pain pulled at Bobby Sue's heart. After her brief connection with Fifi, Bobby Sue couldn't imagine how Tatiana felt. For her, losing her bonded, again...Bobby Sue grabbed a strand of hair and twined it around her finger. Creases of sorrow wrinkled Tatiana's pale face as she slept, and her eyes twitched beneath the lids.

"They've done everything they can for her," said William. "She has to do the rest."

"What about Snider?"

"Gareth is keeping him busy. That man has many more tricks up his sleeve than I thought. Don't worry. We're well guarded here. Both Shea and Iolana are watching from above. No one will sneak up on us unawares."

Bobby Sue nodded. Before her nap he had identified Shea as the hawk that had circled above this morning. But how many more star-touched would arrive and how would people react?

"Bobby Sue." A strange, pained look crossed Brother William's face and he turned away. A quiver rippled through his hands. "About this morning."

The weight of Fifi's death hung over her, gouging a sharp pain in her heart. "What about it?"

"I should have helped you more, I should have..." His voice tightened and tears pooled in the corners of his eyes. "I was too afraid. I..."

"The room was an inferno, William! Of course you were scared. Anyone with an ounce of common sense would have been terrified. I sure as heck was."

William's face reddened as he bent to study a spot on the

floor. "I sent you in because I was too scared to enter. The fire...I knew you were safe...but..."

Bobby Sue put her hand on his shoulder. She'd never seen him like this. "It's okay, William. The fire couldn't hurt me, and if you hadn't pointed that out, Tatiana would be dead. You did fine."

"I..."

Bobby Sue pulled him close and pressed her lips against his. Life was too short to wait for him to make the first move. There was no way she was letting him come up with any more excuses. Happy butterflies flipped in her stomach as he returned her kiss without hesitation. Her lips quivered as they pulled apart, smiling. The glow in his eyes sent a rush of warmth through her. They both jumped at the sound of a voice clearing just outside the room.

"Gareth," exclaimed Bobby Sue. She felt her face flush hotly as he took in the scene. "You're back!"

An amused smile played across Gareth's face before giving way to a somber frown.

"Not for long. The militia has been busy. Doc Johnson already has a full house. Some of the injured are pretty serious. Marshall and the other star-touched are helping, but it's still bad. You look like you're feeling better."

"I am," she said, looking down to hide her flushed face.

Mumbling resumed across the room and Bobby Sue looked up. Gareth stood near Tatiana's bed. He gave the sleeping woman's hand a squeeze, then turned back to Bobby Sue.

"What happened with Mako?" he asked, pulling at a loose thread on his shirt. "What happened after they took me from the room?"

Bobby Sue chewed at her lip. She wasn't sure herself. Voices had echoed in her ears. Raw energy and emotions still burned in her memory, but that's all they were now, memories.

"Fifi did something."

Gareth's face clouded.

"Not like what she did with you and Cook," Bobby Sue quickly said. "Somehow we were linked. It was scary, the power she commanded, the power both of them had at their fingertips. But it was also exhilaratin'. I can almost understand how the two of them and all the other star-touched must feel...to have that much power...It's such an overwhelmin' responsibility. I only touched that energy briefly when Fifi died."

"Her life force must have bounced back to you," said a new voice. "Giving you brief access to star-touched power was Fifi's way of protecting you and Tatiana if things went wrong."

They all turned toward the door as a chestnut-haired woman entered the room. Her eyes were a dark brown and her skin a rich burnished bronze. She wore her hair cropped short and small, hooped earrings hung from her ears. A wide leather belt gathered a loose-fitting cream-colored shirt at the waist. Several brown leather bags hung from the belt. With her loose slacks and fitted boots, she looked like something out of an old swashbuckling movie only without a sword.

"Winona," said William, rising to greet her with a hug. "I'm glad you arrived safely. This is Bobby Sue and Gareth."

"Pleased to meet you," said Winona, shaking Bobby Sue's hand. "Gareth and I met earlier. He and Marshall filled me in on what's been going on."

Winona sat gently on the edge of Tatiana's bed, a sad expression on her face. She placed her palms on either side of Tatiana's head. Almost immediately, Tatiana's mumbling ceased and a tranquil look spread across her face.

"We're here for you, Tatiana," she whispered. "Never again will you be alone."

"What did you do?" asked Bobby Sue.

Winona placed a gentle kiss on Tatiana's forehead before answering Bobby Sue. "Just letting her know that she's with friends. It's all we can do."

"What will happen to her now?" asked Gareth.

"That's up to her. She'll always be welcome to come to our sanctuary and school, but I sense that may not be the best. She's been running for years. Here she's found acceptance and friendship. After such a long search, staying here seems a wiser choice. But that's Tatiana's decision to make."

"You're assuming here will still be around come morning," said Gareth.

Bobby Sue was startled by Gareth's words. Fear rippled through her.

"Bobby Sue, do you feel anything of the power now?" said Winona, ignoring Gareth's comment.

"Nothing," she said, forcing the words past the tightness in her throat. "Not since Tatiana put out the fire."

"You must be quite an extraordinary woman for Fifi to have forged a temporary bond with you as she did. That kind of connection with a non-star-touched is, well, it's never happened before."

Bobby Sue shook her head and flushed again. She didn't feel extraordinary. In fact, she didn't feel any different than she had yesterday or the day before. Unless, of course, you counted being more informed. Over the last few days she'd learned more about the star-touched than she had during the past eight years.

Bobby Sue twisted at her hair. "Well, Fifi was all full of firsts today."

Winona's lips pinched together and creases lined her brow. "Marshall told me about the manipulations. Reprehensible isn't a strong enough word."

"I'm inclined to agree, but I think I know why she reacted the way she did. Just after I realized what she was doing to Gareth and Cook...I saw something."

William took her hand. "What did you see?"

"It only lasted for a moment, but...well...I think I saw Fiona, Tatiana's first bonded."

"Fascinating," said Winona. "I never considered the possibility of reincarnation with our powers.

William shook his head. "I don't think anyone has."

Gareth's face paled. "Reincarnation? Are you telling me that Fifi was the same kid who started the riots?"

"Fiona didn't start the riots," snapped William as he scowled at Gareth. "Ignorance and fear did. People reacted without knowing the facts."

"Fiona never learned to control her powers," added Winona. "From what we understand, she wasn't mentally or emotionally stable. The attack four years ago sent her over the edge. If she and Fifi were the same spirit..."

"It would explain some of her reactions," said William. His anger deflated and his voice took on a sad tone. "Tatiana thought she protected Fifi, but it was the other way around. Fifi became so overprotective of Tatiana that I believe it may have hampered her healing. A little over a year ago, I was almost killed in a fire…"

Bobby Sue felt him quiver and gently touched his cheek. He placed his hand on hers and closed his eyes, leaning into her caress.

"I can still smell my hair burning," he whispered. "I used to wear it long, down my back and the villagers used it to tie me to the stake. I've kept it short ever since, as a precaution. I had followed Tatiana and Fifi to the village where I was attacked, but they had already fled. Tatiana returned and rescued me, healed my wounds. Marshall and Rider found me, not long after. They said they could sense another star-touched hidden nearby, but Fifi wouldn't let them approach."

Tears glistened in Bobby Sue's eyes as she wrapped her arms around William. Now she knew why he kept his hair so short.

Chapter Forty-Two

Gareth

Sweat dripped down Gareth's back and face, leaving streaks where it mixed with accumulated dirt and grime. Overhead the sun blazed, but it wasn't enough to evaporate the moisture that made his shirt cling uncomfortably.

"We need more ammunition," he called, peering over one of the makeshift barriers that crisscrossed Atherton. It marked the dividing line between Snider-controlled areas from those Gareth and his compatriots defended. This barrier was made from boards ripped from one of the Herr's' barns and only barely offered cover from their attackers. Assorted wagons and equipment made up other parts of the one-hundred-twenty yard section just north of the Atherton river. Behind Gareth lay the Herr's' house and barns, as well as the black-smithy, stable, and a herd of dairy cows. Gareth was positioned half-way between the river and the northern gate, with a good view of the wheat field that stretched into the distance. Most of the stalks near the barrier were trampled and crushed, some stained dark red. Somewhere out there, amongst the stalks and ditches, hid Duval and his commandos. On the other side of the closed gate was a squad of Snider's trained mercenaries, forcing the townsfolk to defend both sides of the town wall.

Gareth glanced to his left, wondering how things were going in other parts of town. He could just make out the top of the council building over the trees. It wasn't a great distance but might as well have been miles away. Snider controlled the eastern portion of Market Door Avenue all the way down to Peach Road. Walking the road was risky even with the barrier.

A dark-haired man in his early twenties named Bob gave him a weak smile. Bob worked in one of the woodcraft halls. Gareth returned the look with a reassuring nod. Many of his defenders were on edge from Snider's hit and run tactics last night. Nine other men and women were spaced along the barrier beyond Bob. A couple scowled across the wheat field, searching for targets. The rest just looked scared.

Ten more of his friends and neighbors stood to his right, and five of his best marksmen were in the tower next to the gate, guarding the big, wooden double doors. All of them were determined to defend Atherton. They were also ready to drop from exhaustion.

Gareth reviewed the defenses. Walls had been added to all the guard towers to protect the defenders from attacks from within the town as well as from outside the walls. The East and North gates were reinforced, with guards posted at all watch towers. Both Shea and Iolana watched from above.

Gareth hoped it was enough, but Snider was wearing them down. Most of their bullets were gone. Some defenders were left with only the blacksmith's modified sling shot contraptions and crossbows. Even Gareth was down to his last few rounds. Pretty soon they would be throwing rocks.

"Where's that ammo!" he shouted again, then rubbed at his eyes. It wouldn't do for him to doze at the wrong time. Duval was probably waiting for that.

A young man ran toward him, bent low to stay out of sight, a heavy bag slung across his back. Gareth quickly directed him toward the defenders holding the blacksmith's weapons, praying no one could tell just how worried he was.

"Make each shot count," Gareth reminded the defenders. "We can and will drive them back."

Since yesterday more people had joined the fight. At last count over two hundred townsfolk had stepped up to defend Atherton, and another hundred or so were helping in non-combat positions. A torrent of women and children had fled to Gareth's part of town as well, leaving behind almost everything to escape the roving bands of thugs in the southeast.

Unfortunately, for every fighter who had joined Gareth, another sided with Snider, leaving him with plenty of fodder to throw at Gareth's defenders. Gareth wasn't at all surprised that the majority of people who fought for Snider had arrived after Mako came to town. If Snider won this battle, Gareth would lose not only the gate, but the black-smithy, the main stable, and most of the dairy cattle.

Gareth muttered a curse as he spotted Duval ducking for cover in the field across from the blacksmith shop. A bandage was wrapped around his arm where he had been shot yesterday. A couple of bullets from the snipers on the tower whizzed over the man's left shoulder, but Duval didn't even glance up. He looked like he was waiting for something.

A sharp whistle from somewhere outside the gate triggered an instant reaction from Duval's group. Gareth crouched for cover as bullets buzzed overhead and into the barrier, showering him with splinters of wood.

"Damn," he muttered under his breath. "How much ammo do they have?"

The sound of shattered glass, quickly followed by the smell of alcohol, signaled a new phase of the attack. Adrenaline surged though Gareth.

"Water! We need buckets of water!"

Wisps of smoke slipped between the slats of wood that made up the outer wall and the barricade. The dry wood crackled as the fire gained purchase. Ignoring the flames, Gareth peered over the barricade again. Duval's men crept forward a little too confidently. With precision born of his military training, Gareth fired two shots. Curses erupted in the field and at least two bodies didn't run for cover.

"Where's that water?" Gareth shouted, as the flames became too strong to ignore.

Smoke momentarily blinded him and he moved away from the wall, coughing. Someone hurled a bucketful of water on the fire near him. It did little to quell the flames. The guard tower was completely engulfed. It must have taken a direct hit from the fire bombs. Gareth watched helplessly as the fire spread. There was no way to know if anyone had escaped the inferno.

"Watch out!" yelled Bob. "They're charging."

Gareth looked just in time to see one of Duval's soldiers leap over the barrier and thrust a sword into the man's gut. Blood gurgled from his mouth as his attacker pushed him off the blade with his foot. Wide-eyed, the young man fell to the ground.

"Stand your ground!" yelled Gareth as more soldiers

clambered over the crumbling barrier. The defenders began to falter. "Push them back."

Gareth pulled the trigger as sword man closed on him. The quiet click he heard in response made his stomach clench. Instinct took over. Swinging the gun, he caught the edge of the sword and then rammed his foot into the man's crotch. Without a second thought Gareth smashed the butt of the gun in the man's face and grabbed the sword. Blood splattered as the body fell to the ground.

The attackers surged over the barrier. Battle rage narrowed Gareth's world, moving him from one target to the next before the last hit the ground. Fighting surrounded him for what felt like hours. He was only vaguely aware of his defenders retreating from the onslaught or falling to the ground. Duval's forces seemed to pop out of the field like so many kernels on a cob.

A small break in the wave gave Gareth a moment of respite. He wiped his face with a hand that trembled from fatigue. Fires still raged around him and clouds of smoke filled the air. It took a few moments before he noticed that the gunfire from his people had faded to nothing. Even the crossbows had stopped. Through the inky mist Gareth saw three of his fighters fall and more of the enemy close in. Bodies littered the ground, especially clustered where he stood. His throat tightened. So much bloodshed.

With a sickening crack, the doors to the gate splintered inward and soldiers burst in, weapons firing. Gareth's heart sank. There were too many of them, and without ammunition his people didn't stand a chance.

"Fall back," he called. His voice cracked with emotion. "Fall back beyond the river!"

Snider's men came through the gate screaming, making no move to hide as they fired on the fleeing defenders. People scattered in all directions, seeking shelter as they retreated. There was nothing Gareth could do but dive for cover himself.

His lunge into the blacksmith shop sent him tumbling into the pile of scrap metal next to the anvil. Bullets splintered the bucket of water to his left, causing Gareth to scramble back to a two and a half foot section of wall on the west side of the building. The sword, his only weapon, sat entangled in several large springs.

Looking for a new weapon, he scanned the small shop frantically. The river stood less than twenty feet away but he knew there was no way he could reach the trees on the other side of its banks without getting cut down.

Duval's voice shouted over the noise. "He went in that building over there. Aim for his legs when you shoot. Snider wants him alive."

Gareth's jaw clenched as he heard footsteps converge. He grabbed a hammer off a wall hook. Laughter and taunts erupted from the attackers as they neared. He had a pretty good idea of why Snider wanted him alive, and it wasn't for a tea party.

"You may as well give up now, Gareth. You have no place left to run."

Gareth muttered a curse. Duval was right, there was no escape, but he wouldn't go down alone. He swung as hard as he could at the first body to come around the corner where he hid. A satisfying crack resounded as the hammer sank into the man's skull. Without a second thought he spun around and caught a second man in the face.

Gunfire increased in volume as the second body fell. Gareth held his breath. This was a different sound, a different kind of gun than Snider's men had been using. Startled shouts from Duval and the rest of Snider's men were nearly drowned by the roar of motors and the booming sound of the "1812 Overture's" final movement.

A grin spread across Gareth's face. He grabbed the gun from the hands of the man he had just killed and charged out of the smithy in time to see Duval dive for cover over the barrier. Marty's bus barreled through the gate with Marty himself working one of the machine guns on the roof. Snider's people ran for cover, completely routed by Marty's dramatic entrance. Duval was the first to vanish into the smoky wheat field.

Gareth leaned on the wall of the smithy as the adrenalin rush exhausted itself, watching two of Marty's people chase Snider's men on their motor bikes. With a rusty squeak the bus came to a halt in front of him, still blaring music. A young wiry man, who Gareth had only met once, drove the vehicle.

"Sorry we're late," said Marty. He slid down the ladder to greet Gareth. "Had a flat tire about thirty miles back."

"Better late than never," said Gareth

"Ewelard," said Marty. He pointed the driver up the ladder to keep watch with a young woman then turned back to Gareth. "Don't mention it. By the way, you look like hell."

"Thanks," said Gareth with a snort. "Who's your new friend?"

"That's Loni," said Marty. "Air Force gal. Met her last winter in Penn-York. I sent Thelma and Louise to the east gate with the other regulars."

"Good."

"And we brought more weapons and ammo."

Gareth glanced grimly at the wreckage around him, choking on smoke. Too many bodies littered the ground. Some cried out in pain, but most lay disturbingly still. Fires still burned, but those who weren't helping the injured doused the remaining barrier and outer wall with water. They'd almost lost this battle, but his people weren't ready to give up and neither was he. Gareth's eyes narrowed in determination and he felt a muscle in his jaw twitch.

"How many weapons and how much ammo?" he asked without preamble.

"Enough to beat that rabble, Sir!" said Marty, snapping to attention.

Gareth looked at Marty and raised an eyebrow. He wasn't sure if Marty was being serious or employing his odd sense of humor. Either way it didn't really matter. Gareth knew he could trust Marty to follow his command but still tell him if he was full of crap.

"Gareth."

Gareth looked up in surprise as Neil rode up on a chestnut horse with Gavin. Eric was right behind him on another horse. The two star-touched immediately ran to the closest wounded fighters and began to heal them.

"What are you doing here? Who's directing at headquarters?"

"Relax, Gareth," said Neil, his freckled face reddening. "Burns and Carlene have things under control. They have Thelma and Louise and a couple more of Marty's friends to help. Besides, those two star-touched guys said you needed help with the wall."

Gareth forced himself to relax. The man was right. The barrier and wall were in bad shape, and Neil was the best carpenter in town.

"Sorry, it's been a little rough out here. It's a good thing Marty showed up when he did." Gareth took another look at the battered defenses. "Do what you can. Let me know what you need."

"There should be plenty of wood in the barn to scavenge," said Neil as he surveyed the damage. "Looks like Snider sent most of his heavy hitters out here. It's been relatively quiet at the council building."

Gareth let out a sigh. "It won't stay quiet much longer. Especially once Snider gets word of what happened here."

As soon as Neil moved away, Marty slapped his arm around Gareth's back and began steering him down the road. "Exactly, so leave the gate to me for now and take a minute to catch your breath."

Gareth grimaced. Marty wasn't exactly subtle.

Chapter Forty-Three

Tatiana

Voices nibbled at the edge of Tatiana's consciousness, anxious voices. Gradually, some of them became familiar. One sounded feminine with a slight southern accent. Bobby Sue. A happy wave washed over Tatiana. Bobby Sue was her friend. A deep, masculine voice, slightly strained by fatigue and concern whispered, sending a fatherly embrace around Tatiana's soul. Gareth. One youthful voice pulled away from the cacophony, fear plainly evident, yet filled with undercurrents of determination. Jill. The others were strangers, yet not unknown. Many had touched her mind recently. Silver tendrils of concern and love twisted around Tatiana. They were waiting, waiting for her.

Gareth and Jill stood on the other side of the small room, near Bobby Sue, who sat propped up in the other bed. A chestnut-haired woman with burnished bronze skin stood near the door with a young blond-haired man. Her heart raced as Brother William's hazel eyes locked with hers. So many times, for so many years, she had run from those eyes, afraid of where they might lead.

Several moments passed before she realized the conversations had ended. All eyes looked in her direction and panic began to build. Emotions swirled through the room, but no fear, no anger, and no hostility. A man was dead, burned alive by her hand. The death left a stain on her heart that had to be visible, yet only concern and love emanated from the people around her. Tension seeped out of her body and her heart calmed. These were friends, family. There was no need to run anymore.

Gareth knelt by her bed and took her hand. "How are you feeling?" Dirt clung to his nails and fingers, and there were deep circles under his eyes. The clean clothes he wore didn't seem to fit his haggard appearance. "We've been very worried about you."

Tatiana's eyes flickered around the room. Bobby Sue held a tightly wound wad of hair with one hand, while her other clasped Brother William's. Strands of love seemed to spin around the two of them in a delicate yet fragile web. Life, family, friends, they were all as precarious as that web.

"Tat?" Gareth whispered.

Another wave of love washed over her. He was so much like Papa. Gently, she closed her hand around his. A tear ran down her cheek.

"I'm okay now," she said softly.

"Fifi…"

Tatiana nodded, unable to force words though the tight knot in her throat.

"This is Gavin and Winona," Gareth said, indicating the newcomers. "I believe you know Brother William."

Brother William took a tentative step closer. Fear flashed in his eyes, but it didn't seem to be directed at her so much as for her. If she chose to run, would he continue to follow? "Why did you leave the hospital?"

Memories of pain and fire rippled through her mind. Angry voices shouting in the halls. The walls seemed to close in on her. Then she felt everyone's emotions wrap her in a warm blanket. He was there so long ago.

"I heard a call for help. I heard Fifi," she whispered.

Tears flowed freely. Little, defenseless, overprotective Fifi was gone. Her very existence had been a contradiction. Tatiana couldn't remember when their roles had switched. At first Fifi had been the one in need of protection and nurturing, giving Tatiana the will to live. Sometime, over the past four years, Fifi had begun to protect her. She had come to rely on that guardianship perhaps a little too much.

The mood in the room shifted. Tatiana wasn't the only one to feel her loss. Their sadness was unmistakable. But no amount of mourning would bring Fifi back. The hole in Tatiana's heart was vast, yet filling it didn't seem insurmountable this time. Already love trickled in to fill the expanse.

"Listen," said Gareth. "I can't stay."

"Why?" Tatiana asked as panic edged in and made her heart pound. "What's happening?" She started to sit up, but Gareth pushed her back into bed.

"Snider's causing trouble, but we'll handle it. You rest and feel better. Just promise me you won't run off."

"He's so like Papa."

"He would be heartbroken if you left. They all would."

She had promised Papa to watch over Mama, a promise she couldn't keep. Dare she make another? A heavy silence filled the room. They were waiting for her reply. They were waiting for her to choose.

"Hold tight, Tatiana. Don't give up."

A drop of moisture fell on her fingertips as she caressed the tangle of wiry whiskers on Gareth's face.

"They aren't afraid of me. They aren't angry."

"They love you."

"I promise," she said at last.

Chapter Forty-Four

Gareth

Gareth glanced up at the sky, then back to Eric, who had that faraway look in his eyes again.

"All is clear. There are no guards in sight."

Gareth nodded and gave the signal to move in closer to the Zook family's farmhouse. Thanks to Marty, the farmland north of the river was free, but the farmers were still prisoners in several locations. Located just south of the tree-lined river, the Zook home was the easiest for them to reach. So while Gareth and his team carefully crept up to the front of the house, Thelma led a second team from the other side with Marshall.

This rescue mission marked the first time any of the star-touched had done more than heal and carry messages. Eric, Marshall, and Gavin had surprised Gareth when they volunteered, but he wasn't going to turn down help. Reasons for their sudden change of heart didn't matter to him. With Eric orchestrating communication, they were able to coordinate their attacks. He'd sent Gavin with Thelma's twin, Louise, to free the Yoders. If all went well, both families would be free before dusk.

"Thelma and Marshall are in position now," said Eric. "As are the groups with Gavin."

"Good. Tell Gavin and his group to proceed on their own. Now you're sure your bird..."

"Iolana," said Eric, with a patience that bore no hint of patronization or irritation. "Her name is Iolana."

"Yeah, sorry," said Gareth, silently berating himself. "You sure Iolana will be okay getting that close to the building? It's going to put her in the front line."

"She understands and wants to help."

"Then send her in," said Gareth, still wondering what had made the star-touched suddenly so willing to fight.

Gareth watched the small dot in the sky that was the bald eagle dive. It happened so quickly and silently that he was surprised to see her a moment later perched on a woodpile, as she peered into a window on the eastern side of the house.

"She sees two men with guns," said Eric, his eyes unfocused. "They sit near the front door at a long wood table. The room is approximately forty feet long and fifteen feet wide. Two doorways stand next to the fireplace. One leads to the kitchen. The other to the room and stairs you told us about earlier. Many adults and children sit on the floor. Most are on the far side of the room. They face the two men and appear to be tied at the feet, perhaps at the hands as well. Not all of the prisoners appear part of the Zook family."

"Probably field hands and some of the smaller farm families," said Gareth.

Eric nodded. "The guards have a very good view in this direction."

"I knew those windows would be a problem."

"Do not worry. Iolana will distract them as planned." A frown suddenly creased Eric's face and a muscle twitched on his jaw. "A third man, an angry man, just came into view. He grabbed one of the women and is taking her out of sight."

Gareth's head snapped up and his hands tightened on his gun. They needed to get in there. "Damit. Make him stop."

Eric's eyes narrowed to tiny slits. "Gareth, do not EVER ask me to do such a thing. Do not ever ask this of any star-touched. We will do what we can, but not that."

The venomous tone in his voice made Gareth flinch, but there was no time for apologies. With an ear piercing screech, Iolana launched herself into the sky. It was time to move. Gareth and Eric charged the front door with a freckle faced young carpenter. If all went as planned, Thelma and Marshall would enter from the back next to the kitchen.

The doorframe shattered as Gareth kicked in the front door. Without hesitation he fired at the guard nearest the window, taking the man out before he could react. The other headed toward the prisoners. Eric's knife sliced the edge of the second guard's shoulder, but the carpenter only managed to hit the wall behind the man as he dodged away. Before anyone could get off another shot, the guard grabbed a boy and held him up as a shield. Gareth was a good shot, but he wasn't willing to risk the child.

"You son of a…"

In that half second hesitation a bullet whizzed by Gareth's head, and someone shoved him aside. He rolled over the wood table and hit the ground with a loud thump, wrenching his shoulder. Eric staggered back from a shower of shotgun pellets before collapsing. With a surge of adrenaline, Gareth upturned the thick wooden dining table, barely getting it down in time to block another hail of buckshot. He couldn't see where the other shot came from, but suspected it was from the back room where the third guard had disappeared. Blood spread across Eric's chest, and his breath sounded ragged and raspy. He lay only a few feet from Gareth. The young carpenter crouched just outside the front door, trying to unjam his gun.

Spewing curses with every shot, the two guards continued to fire. There was little Gareth could do under the barrage. Breaking glass and more gunfire erupted from the other side of the house; he prayed that the rest of his people were doing better than he was. At a pause in the gunfire, the carpenter, his gun finally unjammed, fired toward the back room. Gareth used the opportunity to pull Eric behind the table.

"Damnit, Eric," said Gareth. "Why the hell did you do that?"

A loud avian shriek rent the air. Startled, Gareth peered over the edge of the table to see the second guard, still clutching the boy, look around with a panicked expression. The man fired randomly at the ceiling, continuing even after several empty clicks sounded.

"Damn you crazy bastards," he said, as he threw the gun aside and drew a long knife. "Anyone make a move and I'll gut this brat."

"Let my boy go, I'm begging you," cried one of the prisoners. Her face twisted in horror. "Russell!"

"Mama!"

The boy's whimper and the expression on the mother's face set Gareth's teeth grinding again. "Let the boy go."

"Not a chance. Gus! Where the hell are you?" he said. The man's eyes were wide, and took on a slightly crazed look when his friend Gus didn't answer.

A weak whisper gurgled from Eric, who lay still, eyes closed. His voice was so soft, Gareth barely heard it. "Let him leave. The boy will be safe."

Mixed feelings churned in Gareth's mind. The man edged toward the side door, knife pressed firmly to the boy's throat. At least one of his people stood on the deck outside the door. If their aim was off even a fraction, Russell wouldn't make it. But even if they let him go, it was doubtful the guard would allow the boy to live.

Eric's voice sounded strained, as if every breath was a struggle. "Tell your people to let the man leave. We will not allow the child to be harmed."

Every instinct told him no, but Eric's confidence in the boy's safety won him over. "Fall back. Let him leave."

Startled protests came from the prisoners as the guard backed out the door and down the porch steps. He grinned in victory, pointing his knife towards Gareth. Without warning, a flurry of wings and feathers engulfed the man, then leaped into the air leaving only the boy, wide eyed but unharmed. The knife clattered on the stone walkway.

Gareth gaped at the spot where the man had stood. Icy chills ran down his spine. "What the hell was that?"

"Did anyone else see the size of that eagle?" yelled Thelma. She stood out on the deck, staring at the sky.

Blood soaked Eric's shirt, never a good sign. Gareth saw his eyes flick open and the corners of his mouth turn up. "Fifi is not the only star-touch who can transform," Eric whispered.

"Damn fool," said Gareth. "Last time I looked, even star-touched weren't bullet proof. You trying to get yourself killed?"

"No, just trying to get you not killed."

Gareth shook his head, trying not to think about Eric's statement. Eric had saved his life, damned if he was going to let him die. He pressed his hands on the wounds in an attempt to staunch the bleeding. It was like sticking a finger in a dike.

"Forget about the eagle, Thelma," he shouted. "We need Marshall in here. Now! Hang on, Eric."

Marshall ran into the house before he finished speaking and immediately fell into a healing trance. Tingles brushed Gareth's fingertips before Marshal slid them away. It wasn't until Iolana's anxious chattering reached his ears that he realized the eagle stood next to him, rocking her body side to side. Moments later Gareth was surprised to find his own blood-drenched hand clasped around Eric's.

Several men righted the table he had so casually flipped over, allowing Gareth to scan the room more closely. The prisoners were being untied and Magdalena comforted the dark-haired woman who had been taken to the other room. Russell snuggled safely in his mother's arms. Emma, Alma's mother, headed in his direction with a bowl of water and clean rags. An all too familiar clenching tugged Gareth's gut. John Zook was nowhere in sight, and neither was his second eldest son.

The haunted look in Emma's eyes said it all. In the past seventy-two hours she had seen her husband murdered and her family terrorized. There was one question he knew he could answer.

"Alma is safe."

Emma almost dropped the bowl. Tears of relief rolled down her face. "Praise the Lord. I've been worried sick."

"She told us what happened to Thomas. I'm so sorry. We came as soon as we were able."

Emma nodded, pain flashing across her face. "They took John and Clayton away. I don't know where."

"We'll find them, I promise."

"Alive?" she choked.

Gareth turned back to Eric, afraid to answer. He had no way of knowing if they were alive. Eric seemed to be breathing easier, but looked ashen, clearly far from healed, so Gareth was surprised when Marshall's eyes fluttered open.

"Iolana, tell Winona I need her help. Rider is already on his way."

"What's wrong?" asked Gareth.

"He's stable, but weak and I can't remove the shrapnel. One of them is near his heart. Winona has studied medicine and is a much stronger healer than I am. It'll take both of us to save his life."

Gareth squeezed Eric's hand. "You stay with us, Eric. That's an order."

Soft feathers rubbed against Gareth's bare arm and he saw Iolana studying him. Her round black eyes looked deep into his soul.

"Thank you," he said. "Thank you for your help and for saving the boy."

Iolana nodded her head then resumed nuzzling her bonded.

"Is there anything else we can do?" asked Emma, as she cleaned the still open wounds on Eric's chest.

Marshall sighed and shook his head. He looked exhausted. "You could pray. I've stopped the bleeding for now, so until Winona gets here, that's all any of us can do."

"Gareth," said Thelma. "The buildings and surrounding fields are clear. Looks like those three were the only ones here."

"Good. Any other injuries?" he asked as he stood, wincing as his shoulder began to throb.

Thelma glanced at Eric, doing a quick assessment of his condition, then shook her head. "Just some minor cuts and bruises. What should we do with the two bodies we still have?"

"Two?" asked Emma. "What about..."

"I don't think our friend here dropped the other man anywhere nearby," said Magdalena, looking directly at Iolana. The woman looked exhausted and far older than her fifty-four years. "Thank you for your help. We're indebted to you. I'm sure your bonded will make a full recovery in time."

"How did..."

"Come now, Gareth," she said with a grim smile. "Our faith in God hasn't changed, but our acceptance of this new world has. We aren't so cut off that we don't know of the star-touched. John told me what happened between that dog and Fifi last month. And that horse didn't heal himself. He suspected the first day he met them that Tatiana and Fifi were star-touched. The incident with the dog just confirmed it."

Gareth felt a pang of sadness and shook his head. "Then he knew before anyone else did."

"Did he now?" she said, clearly surprised.

"Fifi is dead," said Marshall, without warning. "Mako killed her."

Magdalena put her hand on her chest and gasped. "That's horrible. Is Tatiana...?"

"Tatiana will be all right," he said, looking at Gareth. "She's in good hands."

Magdalena pulled Gareth aside as Winona rushed in and began to pull supplies out of her medical bag. She and Marshall worked silently, as if each knew exactly what the other was thinking, their eyes focused on something no one else could see.

"Emma," said Magdalena, her voice conveying authority. "Bring clean hot water and bandages. Donald, keep the fire stoked. The rest of you clean up this mess, see to the livestock, and stay out of the way. And you," she said, rounding on Gareth. "Tell me everything that has happened in the last three days."

Chapter Forty-Five

Tatiana

Tatiana jerked herself awake. Sweat soaked her bed sheets and her body shook at the memory of that day four years ago. Pain still ached in her heart, but she was coming to terms with it. She couldn't have stopped Fiona that day, and playing the 'what if' game would change nothing. Fiona was gone. Fifi was gone, too. Nothing could change that, either.

A cup sat on the small end table. Tatiana grabbed it, thankful for the cool feel under her fingers. Water sloshed over her hands as she brought the cup to her lips and drank deeply. She lived, and there were people here who cared for her. To give up now would be a disservice to them and herself.

"Here, let me help you," said Winona. "Bobby Sue stepped out for some fresh air before it gets dark. How are you feeling?"

"Better," whispered Tatiana. There had been something unsettling about her dream, something she had noticed this time that she hadn't noticed before. Some seemingly insignificant detail that wasn't insignificant at all.

"Not a very reassuring, 'better.'"

"Something's not right."

Winona nodded, an understanding look on her face. "Death. We can all can feel its approach in the air."

Tatiana looked up, fear tightening around her heart. "Is Gareth hurt?"

"Gareth's fine," Winona said, shaking her head. "But Eric was injured. Marshal and I healed him as best we can. He just needs rest. It's Gareth's nephew, Joe, who's dying."

Joe. She had never even met the man, yet his name made her feel so uneasy. "He was at Mako's place."

"Yes. He got hurt pretty bad there, but that's not all that ails him."

Thoughts flashed through Tatiana's mind, memories of Mako's torture. She shuddered. Mako had told her that Joe had been at Abuda, but she got the impression that Joe was too old to have been a student.

"I need to see him," she said softly.

Winona's brow wrinkled and worry swirled around her. "Why?"

"I'm not sure. I just need to see him."

"I don't think that's a good idea. Neither of you is in good shape. Besides, he hates all star-touched. Absolutely refuses to be treated by 'the devil's magic' as he put it."

"But you've been treating him, haven't you?"

Winona smiled. "Only with conventional medicine. He doesn't know I'm star-touched, and I won't use my powers on him against his wishes."

"I still need to speak to him."

"Why?"

"Because he was at Abuda when Fiona died."

Winona said nothing, merely studied Tatiana for a moment, then nodded her assent. Struggling out of bed, Tatiana slipped a robe over her shift. Her legs felt weak and a mild dizzy spell made her abruptly sit again.

"Maybe this isn't such a good idea. Rest a little. See him in the morning."

"Is he going to make it that long?"

Winona sighed and pursed her lips. "Probably."

"But not for sure. I need to see him now, if he's aware enough to talk."

"I'll walk with you, but you're on your own in the room. Be careful, he's not particularly stable."

"I understand."

The walk down the hall to Joe's room felt like a mile. Tatiana couldn't remember when she had felt this weak. She should have been well rested after two and a half days, but instead her breathing was heavy and labored by the time she reached the door. Doubt muddled her thoughts as she waited to catch her breath. Would seeing Joe change anything ... for either of them? Perhaps letting him die in peace would be best.

"No, I've done enough running. It's time to face my past."

With trembling hands, she turned the knob and pushed the door open. Joe's bed jutted out from the center of the far wall. His skin looked a ghastly shade of yellow and the rise and fall of his chest was barely noticeable. Death hovered near, leaving a bitter taste on Tatiana's senses. She waited patiently, almost ten minutes, before Joe's eyes opened. Their yellow gaze flickered around the room before focusing on her.

The change was instantaneous. His eyes widened with recognition. Emotions hung in the air like a heavy scent, issuing from every pore on Joe's body. The room suddenly reeked of fear, hate, and something else...guilt.

A barrage of images flashed though Tatiana's mind. She remembered him now. She knew him. The room swayed, and Tatiana leaned against the wall in shock. Anger washed over her with a wave of heat. Energy grazed her fingertips. Killing him would be so easy.

"I remember you." The words hissed though her lips, and tears ran down her cheeks.

Joe pulled the blankets up to his chin in an attempt to shield himself. His body shook so hard he could barely hold the cloth. It only fed her anger. Tatiana's hands clenched into tight fists, but she ignored the pain as her fingernails bit into her flesh.

"You were the one who watched and did nothing. You saw them throw Fiona from the cliff and did nothing. How many other crimes did you witness, Joe? How many people suffered because you were too weak to speak up, because you relished the occasional bone they threw you? You may not have participated in their crimes, but your silence condoned them."

"They kept order," said Joe. His eyes took on a wild and crazed look.

"They hurt anyone that didn't do as they said, no matter how absurd the request." She moved closer to him.

Joe clamped his eyes shut and shook his head frantically. "No. That's not true."

"Tell me Joe, did you enjoy watching them beat me near to death? Did it give you some perverse pleasure?"

His eyes popped open. "Stay away from me! I don't know what you're talking about."

The room began to spin again and Tatiana grasped the edge

of Joe's bed to steady herself. Could it be that he really didn't remember? No, the look in his eyes was denial, not confusion.

"You watched them that night," she said, blinking back tears. "I saw you in the distance sipping the cheap booze they always gave you. It was the last thing I saw clearly before the attack. Answer me at least this. Did you know what they planned to do after everyone else left?"

Joe's face went from pale yellow to ashen. Faced with her truth, he had nowhere to hide.

"No," he croaked, sweat dripping down his face. "I swear, I wandered off with the rest of the kids and passed out in front of the commons."

When she looked into his eyes, she saw guilt piled upon guilt hiding just behind his mask of hate and wall of fear. Tatiana shook her head. She had only pity for the empty shell of a man who cringed on the bed before her. The anger that had filled her only moments ago faded away. Joe didn't cause her misfortune. And while his silence may have contributed to her tormentors' continuing free hand, he wasn't to blame. Nor was he to blame for Fiona's death.

"Did drowning your memories in liquor really help, or only push them into a temporary blur? That's why you drink so much, isn't it, to forget."

"I drink because I like to."

"Is that so?"

"What do you care? It's none of your business what I do."

"Do you really want to die?" she said softly. "I've had my heart torn from my chest twice now. Somehow I've found the will to live. Soon you'll be beyond even our abilities to heal. Is this how you want to go?"

Joe stared at her, his face twisted with indecision. His guilt and pain was as visible to her as Brother William's painted star. Years of fear, hate, and booze had kept it buried, but there it remained. She was a reminder of what had happened, and now he had no choice but to face it.

"Yes," he whispered at last. "I want to die. I want it to end."

"Then be at peace, Joe. I forgive you for your part in what happened. It's up to you to forgive yourself."

"Where are you going?" said Joe, as she turned to leave. The surprise in his voice echoed in the swirling emotions.

"Back to my room, to rest. I'm tired."

"But..."

"No, Joe. I'm not an executioner," she said, as the meaning of his unspoken question dawned on her. "I can ease your pain if you want, but I won't end your life. Neither will any of the others."

"But...at Abuda...the other girl..."

A cold lump stuck in Tatiana's throat and a tear trickled down her face. "Fiona was a child, Joe. A terrified eight-year-old child who saw things she never should have seen. It overwhelmed her. Once she lost control of her powers, there was nothing I could do to stop them."

Tatiana left without another word. One hand trailed the hall wall as she walked, the other leaned on Winona. The other woman said nothing as she climbed into bed. Tatiana didn't know whether her words made any difference with Joe, but seeing him had helped her.

Chapter Forty-Six

Gareth

Gareth slipped wearily out of Joe's room, rubbing his shoulder as he walked. With all the people in need of healing, he didn't want to take energy from any of the star-touched. Besides, he was healthy and it was just a bad bruise. If only Joe would let them near. At least he had seemed calm. Too bad it took so long for the man to come to peace with himself. Both Doc Johnson and Winona agreed that he probably wouldn't last another day. If he lasted through the night it would be a miracle. Gareth drew his hand across his eyes, removing the moisture that had begun to pool there. No matter what he had become, Joe was still his sister's little boy, family.

"How's Eric doing?" asked Gareth when he saw Winona in the hall. The pellets buried in Eric's chest had taken several hours to remove. Despite the risks of moving him, Winona had wanted him here in case of complications.

"As well as can be expected," she said. Perspiration dotted her forehead and she wiped it away. Even with every window open, the hallway was sweltering. "It may take a while before he's up and running. Iolana is watching him."

Guilt churned in Gareth. He still owed Eric an apology, and a thank you. "Thank goodness no one from Louise's team was seriously injured. They rescued the entire Yoder family without any problems. I don't think Snider has many men left."

Winona shrugged. "I'll feel more reassured when the fighting stops completely.

"Yeah," said Gareth. "We all will. I'm heading to the kitchen for a little break. Care to join me?"

"Sure, but not for long. I need to check on a few people."

Gareth's home had been transformed from an inn into a hospital. The injured filled every bed, with more camped on the floors.

"Any sign of your friend John or his son?" she asked after a few moments.

Gareth shook his head. "Nothing. My guess is Snider has them at or near the barracks with the other prisoners. A lot of people are unaccounted for."

"Atherton is a big town."

"Not as big as it was a few days ago."

"And the prisoners your people have taken? What's to become of them when the war is over?"

Gareth glanced at Winona as they walked. Many of the prisoners she spoke of were townsfolk who had sided with Snider. He knew now that some of them had been coerced. For now they were tied up in one of the barns, carefully guarded by the butcher's sons and a dozen other people. "I don't know yet. It's something the town council will need to decide."

They continued through the empty hallways to the kitchen in silence. Gareth grabbed two bowls of the stew that simmered by the fire and some dark bread. It wasn't much, but more than a lot of people had. With all the fighting, and extra mouths to feed in the house, supplies were running low. At least they had most of the livestock secured. Crops were another story, but until they dealt with Snider, they couldn't get a good assessment of them.

They sat in a corner of the common room. There were too many people camped out in the tavern area to go in there. Winona set right to eating, but Gareth pushed his food away after only a few spoonfuls, and rubbed his callused hand across his face. Too many questions raced through his mind for him to eat.

"Winona?"

The woman's dark brown eyes peered up at him. After a moment she put her spoon on the table and folded her hands in front of her. "Go ahead, ask."

Gareth blinked, momentarily startled by her bluntness. "What happened between Tatiana and Joe?"

"They talked."

"I know that," said Gareth, trying not to let his irritation show. "What did they talk about?"

"Did you ask them?"

"Yes."

"And what did they say?"

"That it was in the past."

"Then I suggest you leave it at that. They've made their peace. So should you."

A scowl creased Gareth's face. "You're a lot of help."

"Gareth, what happened between Tatiana and Joe is none of my business, or yours. Ask me something I can answer freely."

"Fine. Fifi changed into a behemoth, long-fanged dog. Iolana grew big enough to carry a grown man into the sky. Can all star-touched change like that?"

"Fifi may have made it look simple or easy, but that kind of transformation takes an incredible amount of energy. It can't be sustained for long."

"That didn't answer the question."

Winona shook her head. "No. Humans can't change."

"So Shea…"

"Grows as Iolana does."

"And Rider?"

Winona studied Gareth's face for a moment before answering. "Rider's transformation is a bit more dramatic. I'd rather you ask Marshall for details."

"That's fair," said Gareth. "Are any more star-touched coming to Atherton?"

"None at this time, but if we send word more will come."

"For how long?"

"Don't worry, Gareth," Winona said with a smile. "If you and the people of Atherton ask us to leave, we will. We aren't like Mako and Snider. Anything else?"

"One more question," said Gareth. "Why did Eric, Gavin, and Marshall decide to join the battle? You were all content to sit on the sidelines and heal until last night."

Winona put her elbows on the table and folded her hands together. He could feel her eyes on him, peeling away layers of armor. "I think you know the answer to that question, Gareth."

Gareth sighed. Only one reason came to mind…Tatiana.

Chapter Forty-Seven

Gareth

Gareth slammed face first onto the ground, then tumbled several times before he finally came to rest against the side of a building. He hardly noticed the gash on his head over the pain in his left leg. Heat seared his back, and a loud ringing filled his ears. Nothing moved around him in the predawn light except flickering shadows cast by the inferno behind him. Pain ripped through his chest as air raced back into his lungs. Shielding his eyes with his arm, Gareth rolled to his back, grimacing as he moved. He stared numbly at the long jagged piece of metal imbedded in his thigh, wondering how it got there and where he was.

Something dripped into his eye. He wiped at it and his hand came away red and slick. Gareth looked around, trying to clear his head. A charred body lay several yards away and debris littered the ground. Flames soared into the sky from the tattered remains of a bus, hungrily licking the nearby buildings. Memory flooded back into Gareth's mind and his heart lurched. There had been at least four men on the bus when it exploded. Hunting Snider, they had traveled a few blocks west of the town square when they were ambushed. Gareth only hoped that Marty and the other members of the team had been clear of the blast. He struggled to see through the increasing smoke, searching for any signs of life.

Another explosion shook the ground. Gareth's heart sank further as more flames shot up to the south of town. Thick oily smoke swirled around him, filling his lungs. Coughing and gasping for air, Gareth dragged himself away from the burning bus, hoping he would clear the smoke before it overcame him. He barely made it around the corner before another wall of flames sprang up. If he didn't move fast, he would be trapped.

All he could do was grimace and keep moving.

Coarse hands grabbed him before he even realized anyone was near. Instinctively, he reached for a weapon, but the man with the cloth-shrouded face swatted his hand away. Some distant and garbled sound punctuated the loud buzzing in his ears, but Gareth couldn't make it out. He continued to resist until a damp cloth was wrapped around his face. The eyes staring back at him finally came into focus. He knew this man. A moment later, Ted tossed him over his shoulders like a sack of grain.

Sounds of chaos flooded into Gareth's ears, and his eyes blinked open. He lay on the ground outside the council building. Gavin, eyes lidded, crouched over him. Pain shot up his leg as Sharon, the woman from Mako's brothel, tied a bandage around it. People ran every which way, without any obvious direction. Voices shouted and cried around him. It seemed as if everyone had lost all common sense.

With a muttered curse, Gareth tried to move, but Gavin shoved him back down.

"Hold still and let me finish with this head wound."

"My head's fine," he said, ignoring the throbbing pain. "How long have I been out and what the hell is going on? Where's Ted?"

"About ten minutes," said Gavin, moving to his leg. "The city is on fire and Ted is looking for survivors from the explosions."

Gareth's hands clenched, catching dirt and gravel from the road. Most of the buildings in Atherton were made of wood. They would be nothing more than kindling.

"Leave the leg," said Gareth, pushing Gavin away and sitting up. "Sharon took care of it. She's a fine field medic."

"But it's still bleeding."

"Go mother someone else, damnit. I'm fine." Gareth stood and staggered away, grabbing the first person to run past. "Find me Burns and any council members you can."

Gavin looked at Gareth sharply for a moment before backing away as ordered. Within a minute Burns was there along with several other people.

"Status report," said Gareth, choking on a cloud of smoke carried by the wind.

"There were two explosions and at least three fires," said Burns. "One from Marty's bus and one to the south, probably the distillery."

"The son of a bitch set fire to grain storage as well," said Neil, his brow wrinkled in fury.

"Gareth," said Burns, his voice strained with concern. "There are people still hiding in their houses. They're afraid to come out. The wind is blowing in this direction. If they don't move quickly..."

"Get a team together. I don't care if you have to rip the doors off the hinges, get those people out of there, now!" said Gareth, rubbing his head as Burns ran to follow the order. "Neil, grab anyone you can and start moving the wounded to the other side of the river. Go out the east entrance if you have to. Kurt, hold back that fire as best you can. Abraham, you're on crowd control. I don't want anyone trampled."

"What about the prisoners?" asked Neil.

"Get civilians out first. If there's time to go back for those traitors do it. If not..."

"Gareth," said Gavin, running up, his brow knitted.

Gareth glared at the young man. "I told you I was fine, Gavin. Find someone else to heal."

"But this is good news. Shea spotted Marty and several others down by the Bunderman farm. They're okay."

"And Snider?" asked Gareth, not letting his excitement show.

"Nothing." Gavin, shook his head. "Shea is having trouble seeing thorough the smoke. She's lucky she spotted Marty."

"And the fires?"

"Out of control. With the winds like they are from the west no amount of bucket brigade is going to stop it."

Gareth ground his teeth in frustration. He could feel the muscle on the side of his head pulse. If they didn't move now, the inferno would kill everyone in its path. He put his hand on Gavin's shoulder and leaned into his ear.

"Call the other star-touched. Meet me at my house in five minutes."

Chapter Forty-Eight

A white mist shifted at Tatiana's feet. Clouds swirled and billowed around her, forming momentary walls and hills. To her right appeared the ashes of an old doorframe, a few charred stumps near the ground were all that remained. To her left another pile of rubble emerged. A huge door grew out of the white swirling mist only two feet from where she stood. Its marbled surface towered above her. Energy bubbled and crackled in the air making the hair on her arms stand up. Tatiana took a step back, her throat thick and dry. Her heart pounded in her chest. Is this what she wanted? Is this where her path led? Her hand shook as she reached for the door. It was time.

Tatiana

Images from the dream still clouded her mind as Tatiana ran down the stairs. She had been sound asleep during the first explosion. The second had sent her scrambling for her clothes. Now the shadows cast by the distant fires made her chest tighten. The sun just crept over the horizon, yet the fire's intensity threatened to overshadow its light.

Throughout the house and outside, Tatiana heard panicked screams and running feet. An acrid smell filled the air. Anxiety clutched at her heart. Everywhere Tatiana looked she saw the frightened faces of the injured and people who had taken refuge in Gareth's place. No one knew what was going on. Neither Gareth, Bobby Sue, nor any of her other friends were visible in the chaos.

"Tatiana! Tatiana!" called Jill. The teen pushed her way through the crowded tavern. Her dark eyes were wide and she spoke almost too fast to understand. "The town's on fire. Someone said Gareth got blown up! Bobby Sue's gone too.

Cook's out front. Everyone's running around like the hens after old Henry's been at'em. What should we do, Tatiana? What..."

Tatiana put her finger to Jill's lips then held her close, struggling to contain her own anxiety which expanded like a balloon. Gareth couldn't be gone. "Calm yourself, Jill. We'll find them."

Every head turned as the door crashed open. Gareth charged in, bringing with him a cloud of smoke. Cook and Bobby Sue were right behind him, their expressions both frightened and relieved. Sobbing, Jill threw herself at Gareth and held him tight, ignoring the blood drenched bandage that covered his leg and the huge, partially healed gash, crusted with dried blood on his head. Soot, dirt, and scrapes covered the rest of him. The look in his eyes made Tatiana's throat tighten in panic.

Her voice wavered. "What's happened? Gareth, what's going on?"

Gareth pulled her into a tight hug, then pushed both her and Jill back to address the room full of people. There were tears in his eyes.

"Snider's set fires around the town and the prevailing winds are bringing them in this direction. We need to evacuate everyone. Help those who can't walk on their own. There's no time to argue, move."

"Tatiana," he said, guiding her out the back door toward the kitchen area. "Listen to me. Rider and Marshall are outside. They've agreed to take you and the rest of the women to safety, but you have to leave now."

"Leave? To go where?"

"To Penn-York. To the other star-touched. You'll be safe there."

There was a frightening note in Gareth's voice that reminded her of the days immediately following the Cataclysm. He had a look that usually preceded a stupid and reckless action. Panic surged through Tatiana and she could feel her head spinning. No more. She couldn't lose any more family. She wouldn't allow it.

"I'm not leaving you," she said.

"Didn't you hear me, Tatiana? There's no time to argue. You're not safe here. You have to go."

"No, Gareth," said Tatiana, wiping a tear from his cheek.

"I've been running for too long. It's time for me to make a stand. It's time for me to be who I was meant to be."

"Half the town is in flames! We have no way of stopping it."

"You don't, Gareth. But I do."

Chapter Forty-Nine

Tatiana

Out on the street, people fled past Tatiana, pushing and nearly tripping each other to escape the descending inferno. Smoke stung her eyes as she continued forward, and even with the dripping cloth stretched across her nose and mouth, breathing remained difficult. Beside her walked Marshall and Gavin, determined to keep her from being trampled. She knew what needed to be done and they were resolved to help any way they could.

They advanced as far as the town square through the searing heat and smoke, guided mostly by the feel of the road beneath their feet. Tatiana stopped and closed her eyes, ignoring the caustic smell and roaring fire around her. The air felt thin and oxygen-starved.

In her mind, Tatiana saw the door from her dream, still surrounded by billowing white clouds. This time she didn't hesitate to fling it open. Tears of joy filled her eyes as an onslaught of calls hit her. There were thousands of star-touched and every one cried out to her. *We are here for you. We will stand by you.* Gavin and Marshall stood like statues alongside her, two sentinels casting a protective shield.

Their energy, their life force surged around her. *This is who I am. This is what I am.* Tatiana reached out to all those voices, and held them in her embrace. With a rush of energy, she flung her hands wide and guided a vortex of power toward the fire. Wind whipped through the streets, sending dust and debris swirling in every direction. A slight twist of her wrist drew the flames back toward her, a cyclonic firestorm with her at its center. Heat assaulted her flesh, but could not make its way past Gavin's and Marshall's shield. Fire, suddenly deprived of oxygen, shrank to mere embers, a thousand blistering hot points.

Tatiana, already nearly exhausted, pulled in more energy, drawing heavily on Marshall's and Gavin's reserve to cool the cinders. One by one, they winked into nonexistence.

As the last spark vanished in the swirling winds, Tatiana brought her hands together over her head, shutting the door on the torrent, but dust continued to spin around her, slowly coming to rest at her feet. Exhaustion sent Tatiana wavering to the ground, where she was startled to find her legs buried to her knees in debris and soot.

"Gavin, Marshall!" she choked, rubbing at her sore, soot-filled eyes. Dust billowed up as she moved, coating the now dry cloth over her face.

"I'm fine," said Marshall, breaking into a coughing fit.

Gavin sat up a moment later, gasping for air, blond hair blackened with soot. "Must have...passed out for a moment there."

"Are you okay?" she asked.

"Just give me a..."

A startled intake of breath was the only response Gavin gave before he collapsed, still half buried. Tatiana turned her head in time to see Marshall fall over as well. A small dart protruded from his neck. It wasn't until she felt something whizz by her ear that she noticed the approaching figures.

"Son of a bitch," said Snider. He smacked Duval with a lightning fast punch that sent the man sprawling. "How the hell did Mako ever put up with your incompetence?"

Tatiana's heart threatened to burst out of her chest as Snider ripped off his protective mask. He, along with most of the nineteen men with him, wore fireproof gear like the old firemen used to use. Snider, his face twisted in a scowl, turned his wrath toward the two men on either side of him. "Shoot her, and don't miss or I'll sell you too."

Understanding dawned on Tatiana as the two men raised their crossbows. Each weapon sported a small dart, probably holding the same drug Mako had used on her. Helpless, again. She struggled to extract her feet from their tomb, but had no energy left, not even enough to reach that bubbling pool.

Shrieks of anger rent the sky. Before the men could fire, they were snatched into the air by a huge eagle and hawk. A split second later, Gareth leaped from the back of a massive black winged apparition. The creature cast its red eyes on the remaining men as Snider and Gareth grappled on the ground.

One look at this entity's four clawed limbs sent most of Snider's men fleeing like mice. A few attempted to aim their weapons during the triple aerial assault. Their screams, as talons ripped into their flesh and lifted them into the air like dolls, echoed in Tatiana's ears.

Tatiana, still weak from dousing the fire, finally pulled her legs free from their prison of debris. She gasped for breath through ash filled lungs and watched the battle anxiously.

The two men, now coated in gray, continued to exchange blows. Snider's teeth gleamed bright in contrast as he pulled a long jagged edged blade and swung it wide. His maddened, battle-crazed look made Tatiana shiver. Gareth jumped back. A thin red gash appeared across his chest.

"Gareth," called Tatiana, her voice barely a croak.

Snider's blade slashed and twisted, driving Gareth away from Tatiana. She looked around desperately at the empty town square. In the distance she could hear shouts and the sounds of battle, but no one was in sight. Even Iolana and Shea had disappeared. Finally she spotted the butt of a gun protruding from the ash not far from where Garth had leaped from Rider.

Gareth continued his retreat toward the charred but intact council building as she struggled to reach the weapon. A slight movement in the shadow of the doorway caught Tatiana's eye and a chill ran down her spine. Knife in hand, a lone mercenary grinned as he inched toward Gareth. Snider renewed his attack, forcing Gareth closer to the weapon aimed at his back.

Gareth was too focused on Snider to see the danger. Tatiana tried, but couldn't get a sound past her parched mouth. Panic gripped her. She was too weak to draw on that pool of energy, too weak to grab what was needed for a burst of speed, but there remained one thing she could do. Her friends were out there. She could reach every star-touched with her link. Where her voice and body failed her, Tatiana's mind screamed. Multiple replies echoed in her mind and ears. Rider roared from high above. She saw Gareth's eyes widen in surprise and he twisted away just as the hidden assassin struck. The two mercenaries had no time to recover and Snider's knife sunk deep into the other man's chest. Snider staggered back from the dead weight, before he shoved the assassin to the ground.

Gareth used the momentary opening to smash his fist into Snider's face and snatch the dead man's knife. Blood streamed down Snider's face as they renewed the battle. Flashes of steel twisted and dodged. Still yards away from the gun but unable to continue, Tatiana lay stretched out across the ash. She watched with growing anxiety, flinching as a new wound sliced open on Gareth's chest.

His foot twisted as he jumped back, and he went down in a cloud of dust. Snider jumped on Gareth in an instant, planting a knee in his gut and knocking the knife from his hand. The two of them struggled for control of the remaining weapon, and quickly disappeared in the swirl of debris.

Tatiana strained to see through the haze, her stomach twisted in knots. Shadows grappled on the ground amid grunts of exertion. It felt like an eternity before she heard a final gasp and then silence. A single figure stood and walked toward her, a long object grasped in his hand. Tatiana held her breath. Relief flooded through her when she saw Gareth emerge. He knelt beside her. Blood ran freely from a dozen new cuts, and his leg and head wounds had reopened. Hot tears stung her eyes as he wrapped his arms around her.

"Are you okay?"

Tatiana could only nod.

"I heard...," said Gareth, a look of wonder on his face. "I heard someone scream in my head, warning me of that other man. I saw a picture of it in my mind as clear as if I'd seen it with my own eyes." Gareth looked at the council building and the dead man who would have killed him only moments earlier. "Was that you? This is the angle and distance that image came from."

Tatiana shook her head, her voice barely a whisper. "I can only communicate with other star-touched. The image was mine, but it came to you by way of Iolana. It was her voice you heard."

They both looked up as Shea, back to her normal size, fluttered weakly to Gavin's side and flopped on his chest. Rider practically fell from the sky a moment later, crumbling to his knees next to Marshall, sides heaving with exhaustion and sweat. His coal black coat returned to snow white, only to be coated in gray ash.

Tatiana watched the remaining transformation wearily. His leathery black wings vanished, long claws withdrew to delicate hooves, and fangs shrunk to equine length and utility. Glowing red eyes resumed their golden color and met hers for a moment, twinkling with a satisfied glint. Then, he too lay his head on his bonded's chest and closed his eyes.

"Are they okay?" Gareth asked.

"Gavin and Marshall were hit by tranquilizer darts. Shea and Rider will recover with rest."

Gareth's brow furrowed. "Why didn't they just kill them? Why bother with drugs?"

"That's a question I'd like to ask," said Marty.

He limped toward them, an M16 resting on his right shoulder. A nasty burn ran up his left leg almost to his hip and ugly, blackened splotches covered his arm. He tried to hide it with a smile, but Tatiana could see the pain flicker in his eyes. Thelma and Louise were a step behind. A bound and bleeding Duval stumbled between them. Marty glanced at Marshal and Gavin and sighed.

"I suppose a bit of healing is out of the question right now," he said, as the corners of his mouth turned up.

Gareth looked up at him and laughed. "Marty, only you could find something to joke about at a time like this."

Chapter Fifty

Tatiana

A tear rolled down Tatiana's face as she closed the door behind her and leaned on the wall. She squeezed her eyes shut and tried to stop the flow. Images flashed through her mind, making her head buzz. So many injured, so many dead. John Zook and his son were found dead this morning in the barracks, their last hours clearly marred by torture. The search for dead and injured in the rubble continued. Most of the surplus grain was gone and with it hopes for feeding the town through winter or seeding in spring. Tatiana felt the despair that hung over the town. They'd survived Snider, but the future remained uncertain.

This morning Gareth had met with the remaining council members along with Burns, Ted, and Magdalena to discuss the fate of the one-hundred-seventy-two prisoners. The vote was surprisingly unanimous; execute Snider's six remaining men and have juried trials for the rest. Included in the count were Darren, whose miscount of the election put Mako in office, and Sabrina. Gareth had returned from the meeting, silent, pain and anguish twisted around his body like a shell.

"Tatiana?"

For a moment, Brother William's voice sent Tatiana's heart racing, and the urge to flee almost overcame her. She took a deep breath and opened her eyes. Brother William stood a few feet away. She hadn't heard him approach.

"Are you okay?"

"This is my fault," she whispered, her voice tight with emotion. "All of it."

William put his hand on her shoulder. "I thought you were going to leave all that guilt behind. This isn't your fault."

"But it is. If I hadn't come here..."

"Mako would be running the whole town now and Gareth

would probably be dead." His voice had a stern and forceful tone. "You know what fate would have befallen the other women here, too. This war would have happened with or without you."

"More than two-hundred people are dead."

"But those that survived are free. Tatiana, you have to accept that you can't save everyone. We can't control everything around us, especially people."

Tatiana nodded and wiped her eyes. Understanding what Brother William had said was easy. Living with it was going to be the challenge.

"Thank you."

"Don't mention it."

"For everything."

Brother William looked at her with one raised eyebrow.

"Some of my memories of what happened four years ago are a little foggy, but I remember seeing your face in the hospital. I'm sorry I ran out on you."

"That's all in the past, Tatiana. Tomorrow is a new day."

"There's something else I remember," she said after a moment. "An old man, in the woods. He helped me. I never had a chance to thank him, or even ask his name. Do you know what happened to him?"

A fleeting look passed William's face and Tatiana sensed the sadness in him. Tears filled her eyes as he spoke, already knowing what his words would be.

"No one knew his name, or even how long he'd been living on that mountain. They called him the old hermit. Kept to himself long before the Day of Reckoning, going into town only for supplies. He told me where he found you and how." William paused. When he resumed, his voice sounded tight. Tears glistened in his eyes.

"When the riot started in Abuda...well, some of the men that went on the search party to find you mentioned the animals that hovered around the old man. It scared people. Two days after we brought you back to town, a mob went up the mountain and killed him and any critters they could find. Burned most of the mountain to get them."

Tatiana buried her head in Brother William's shoulder and cried, letting the tears wash away the regret and guilt she'd carried for years. He was right. Nothing could have stopped that tide.

Chapter Fifty-One

Gareth

"What do you mean he escaped?" Gareth pulled his shirt on as he spoke. Any thought of sleeping fled as he felt rage reddening his face. "How the hell did that bastard get loose?"

The guard stood ashen-faced, twisting a ragged cloth cap in his hands. "I'm sorry, Gareth. We checked on him only an hour ago, right after weighing him for the hangman. When I went back just now he was gone. Somehow he sawed through the ropes holding his hands and unlocked the foot restraints. We think he's still wearing that iron collar Ted put on him."

"Lot of good that does us," said Gareth. A few less than polite words slipped out as well. "Why weren't his hands chained like the other mercenaries?"

"They were earlier today, but the cuffs wouldn't lock when we brought him back from the weighing. Those ropes were tied so tight his hands turned blue before we even sent the broken cuffs to Ted for repair. I don't know how he got away. We had that man stretched tighter than a pig on the slaughter table."

Gareth stormed out of the tavern muttering curses and praying nothing else would go wrong. Even after three days, the pungent scent of smoke lingered in the night air. The odor only added to the ominous weight on Gareth's chest. Of all the prisoners, Duval stood at the top of his list for execution. Not only was he Mako's buddy, but he personally participated in Tatiana's torture. Once again the man had slipped out of death's jaws.

"I swear, he didn't have anything sharp on him." The guard scrambled to keep up. "We checked him."

"Did anyone check the stall?"

"Of course we did. We even sifted the straw on the floor."

"Gareth," called Burns. He ran up, huffing for breath. "I just heard. We're searching the town. Any idea how he got loose?"

"No."

Burns shook his head. "That man should have been dead so many times. He must be part cat."

"When I catch him, his ninth life will end real quick," said Gareth.

Gareth made a circuit of the barn, personally checking the chains on the remaining five mercenaries before heading for Duval's stall. At least a dozen guards were now scattered about the building, closely monitoring the remaining prisoners locked in the other compartments. Marshall crouched on the floor of Duval's stall examining something when Gareth entered.

He kept his voice low enough that it couldn't be heard beyond the stall walls. "What did you find?"

Marshall stood slowly, his face creased in thought. "I'm not sure," he said, holding out his hand.

A small piece of shredded cotton lay in the center of Marshall's palm. Even in the dim lamplight, Gareth could see that the gray-tinged fluff was the same color as the rope used to tie Duval to the wall. Marshall shifted his feet, biting his lower lip.

"What's wrong?" said Gareth, trying not to let Marshall's behavior add to his unease.

"This rope," Marshall said, pausing to swallow. "It looks like it's been chewed through."

Gareth's eyes flashed to Marshall's face, as he tried to quell his growing agitation. What could have chewed though a rope in so short a time?

"A jagged stone would do the same thing," said Burns, studying the rope piece still attached to the wall. It felt as though he had read Gareth's mind.

"Maybe..." said Marshall.

"Sir," said a guard as she entered the stall. The woman snapped to attention in front of Gareth. "We found a perimeter guard unconscious just south of here and a makeshift ladder against the wall. I believe the prisoner is outside the city barrier."

The woman stood stiffly, waiting for a reply, her shoulder-length hair neatly pulled back with a butterfly shaped clasp. The formal stance and coarse work clothes she wore were a stark contrast to the delicate ornament, a small reminder of how this woman had lived in peace time.

"Send out a search party," said Gareth "I want that man found before dawn."

"I wouldn't waste the manpower," said Marty as he walked in. The burn scars on his left arm were still pink. "They're not going to see much in the dark."

"If we wait, we may never catch him."

"It's up to you, but they better have some good lamps or night goggles."

Gareth's eyes narrowed. Something about Marty's tone set off warning bells in his mind. He'd known the man too long not to notice the masked look in his eyes, and the slight tightness in his face. Their eyes met for a second before Marty turned away.

"What about Iolana and Shea?" said Burns, "They should be able to spot him."

Marshall shook his head. "Their night vision is lousy and so is Rider's. I hate to say it, but Marty is right. We're better off waiting till dawn."

"Find a hunting dog and search anyway," said Gareth, still looking at Marty. "Maybe we'll get lucky. In the meantime, double the guard on this building and increase the patrols along the wall. I don't want anyone else pulling a Houdini on us."

Gareth watched the guard hurry off to carry out the instructions, wondering what other surprises awaited him. The first execution was scheduled for dawn. If it couldn't be Duval, Gareth would damn well make sure the other mercenaries were hanged. The sooner they were done with them, the better.

"I still don't get it," said Burns. "Why didn't he try to free the others?"

"Cause when it comes down to it," said Gareth, "Duval looks after only one person, Duval."

Chapter Fifty-Two

Bobby Sue

People packed the ash strewn field that once teamed with merchant stalls in front of the council building, waiting with anticipation. Voices murmured with angry and expectant tones, but there was a sense of excitement as well. The noose loomed over the wooden platform. It swayed in a gentle morning breeze that did nothing to diminish the heat. Behind the platform stood the skeletal remains of five trees. Only the council building showed signs of repair, with new wood standing stark against blackened and blistered paint. Other nearby buildings, mere charred and fragile shells, remained desolate mementos of why they were gathered in the town square today.

Bobby Sue tightened her grip on William's arm as Gareth and the other council members climbed onto the platform. She and the other women had arrived early to find a spot not too far from the gallows. They stood near enough to have a clear view, without being on top of things. Tatiana had remained at the house to help Winona with the injured. At least that was the excuse she gave. Bobby Sue suspected it had more to do with not wanting to see any more death.

"You sure you want to be here, Bobby Sue? I bet Tatiana and Winona wouldn't mind some company."

Williams's voice helped calm her nerves and she loosened her grip. "Yes," she said, letting herself be drawn into his hazel eyes. So much had happened since he confessed his love for her only a week ago. He pushed a strand of auburn hair off her face and laid his hand against her cheek.

Bobby Sue closed her eyes. "If Tatiana won't witness their punishment, then I'll do it for both of us."

"Then we'll attest to their punishment together." He brushed his lips against her forehead.

A moody silence blanketed the square. She looked up as the first mercenary's footsteps echoed on the wooden steps. Two burly men gripped his arms, and several more guards followed close behind, crossbows ready for any sign of trouble. The prisoner scowled at the crowd as he walked, but struggled as the hangman placed the noose around his neck. A shiver ran down Bobby Sue's back. She recognized the thrashing man. He was one of the men who had tried to drag her into Mako's brothel last year. Bobby Sue continued to tremble as Gareth read off the list of offenses, and didn't actually hear anything he said. Visions of Tatiana hanging from the ceiling in that room flashed through her mind. Bobby Sue curled her free hand into a fist. Duval should have been up there first.

The wooden platform shook as the mercenary fell though the floor and a loud snap echoed in the square. He twitched for a few moments, then grew still. Scattered cheers rippled through the crowd but stopped when both Magdalena and Abraham glared. Bobby Sue and William remained silent as they watched the other executions. It took a little more than an hour to extinguish five lives. But no amount of punishment would bring back the two-hundred-forty souls who had been lost in the three day war. They were nothing but memories, some with no names or families to miss them.

She and William walked back to Gareth's hand in hand. Bobby Sue twined her hair with her free fingers. The mercenaries were gone, but many more would likely swing from those gallows, maybe even Sabrina. For Gareth's sake she hoped not. They were almost home when Gavin trotted up. A frown creased his face and Shea shifted her feet on his shoulder, her feathers unusually fluffed out. "Have either of you seen Eric today?"

"No," said William. "Why? What's wrong?"

"I can't find him anywhere. Iolana's vanished as well."

"Maybe he went out huntin' Duvall with Marty," said Bobby Sue. "Winona said he left before dawn. Against her recommendation, I might add. That was a pretty bad burn he got the other day."

"I suppose," said Gavin. "He just usually lets me know when he and Iolana are going off somewhere. He's only barely healed himself."

"I'm sure they're fine," said William.

"You sound like a nervous parent whose daughter's out on their first date," said Bobby Sue. "From what Gareth tells me, Eric's more than capable of takin' care of himself."

Gavin shrugged. "You're probably right. Eric's usually the one worrying about me. He's been my mentor for the past few years."

"Then just trust he knows what he's doin'," she said. "Let's go see what Cook's been up to all mornin' and what tea Tatiana's brewed. I think we all need somethin' to calm our nerves and get those hangin's off our minds."

Chapter Fifty-Three

Tatiana

Things were quiet this morning so Tatiana had slipped out to the small shed when no one was looking. She drew a curry comb over Winona's sturdy brown mustang. The animal leaned into her grooming with a contented sigh. If only Tatiana cold feel so content.

So much had happened in the past week. The mercenaries were gone, hanged and buried in a ditch outside of town along with Darren. Tatiana tried not to think about their deaths, or the trials for the other prisoners that continued daily. Rotating juries handled up to four cases each day. Not all of them had been sentenced to death, but many had. Those who were granted life faced a period of service. Several still had banishment to look forward to after their sentence.

Heavy footsteps drew Tatiana's attention from the horse and her thoughts. Gareth's feet dragged across the straw covered shed. His eyes looked sunken under his deeply furrowed brow. Ever since Duval's escape last week, Gareth had been sullen and irritable. It didn't help matters that Marty wasn't back from his tracking expedition with Eric. She didn't know what else she could do to help him. This morning his shoulders were bent as if he carried a heavy load.

"Good morning, Gareth," she said, making it sound more like a tentative question.

Gareth sighed and ran a hand through the horse's forelock. His fingers gently caressed the wiry hair, earning him a nuzzle from the animal. Some of the tension eased out of him.

"Not really," he said at last. "Four more executions this morning, and I'm on judge duty this afternoon."

Tatiana nodded. The council members were taking turns acting as judge at the trials, but all of them were required to be present at executions. Abraham and Magdalena had insisted on that stipulation. Council meetings occupied every evening, and last night's had gone almost to midnight.

"You're a good person. I'm sure you'll make the right decisions. How many more are there?"

Gareth shrugged "Dozens."

"Something else is bothering you."

"Bothering me?" said Gareth, his voice tight. "What could possibly be wrong? That sadistic bastard is still on the loose somewhere. There's barely enough food left to get through the winter, building supplies are too low to make repairs, and we have almost nothing to trade with other towns."

Tatiana put the curry comb down and hugged Gareth. "We'll find a way to make it work. I know we will."

At the mention of the word 'we', Tatiana sensed Gareth's mood lift a little. If only she could solve some of the problems plaguing Atherton. Even one less obstacle would improve the situation.

"Tat," he said, "I'm really glad you decided to stay."

"So am I," she said, with a shy smile.

Gareth had listed the town's woes, but he'd excluded one personal note. Tatiana chewed at her lip, unsure if she should broach the topic Gareth hadn't mentioned. She knew he had more on his mind than the town's problems. Everyone in the house avoided the issue, but it couldn't be ignored forever. Even Gareth's friends tiptoed around him. Pain seemed to swirl around him like a cloud.

"When are you going to speak with Sabrina?" she said, finally working up the courage.

Anger flashed in Gareth's eyes, immediately followed by hurt and worry. His back stiffened and she sensed a chaotic churn of emotions. Despite Sabrina's betrayal, he still loved her as if she were his daughter. The council had made it clear that Sabrina's fate wasn't in Gareth's hands alone. Some of the judges already had a reputation for showing no mercy. If Sabrina got one of them...

"Talk to her, Gareth," said Tatiana, holding his bearded face in her hands like she used to hold Papa's. "It's been almost two weeks and you haven't seen her. You haven't even spoken her name. I know it won't change what she did, or make it right, but neither will avoidance. It took me a long time to learn you can't run away from your problems. You have to face them."

"Have you talked to her?" he said with a snort.

Tatiana shook her head. "Sabrina is terrified of me, Gareth. It's part of what made her do what she did. Do you really think it's a good idea for me to visit her? You're the one she wants to see right now. She needs you."

Gareth turned away, fists clenched. "She lost that right."

"Have pity on her, Gareth, for your own sake," Tatiana forced her personal feelings of anger toward Sabrina aside. It left a cold sick feeling in her gut. "In her own way, Sabrina does care about you."

A tremor shook Gareth's hands. Tears glistened in his eyes as he slowly exhaled. When he spoke his voice sounded strained and taut. "I'll think about it." He took a few steps away, then paused. "Her trial is in three days."

Tatiana swallowed, a tight knot in her throat making the action painful. Neil Thrall's turn to judge was in three days. No wonder Gareth looked so miserable.

Chapter Fifty-Four

Tatiana

Tatiana hung back behind the other women in the small common room of Gareth's house where she had first met everyone. Six chairs were placed in two rows. A seventh sat at one end. Everyone was tense, voices quiet, expectant. Pressure rose, threatening to flood Tatiana's eyes as Gareth led Sabrina into the room. This was their little trial before the one for the town. Sabrina had hurt Fifi and dumped her in the trash like garbage, then sold Tatiana to Mako. Tatiana swallowed past the lump in her throat and closed her eyes.

The stench that assaulted her nose made her open them again. Beside her, Jill wrinkled her face. She wasn't the only one reacting to Sabrina's odor and appearance. Clearly, the washing materials provided hadn't been used during her two week imprisonment. Normally pristine hair hung matted and twisted, like an old doll. Grime covered every inch of her body, and what remained of her fingernails were caked in dirt. Gareth stood next to her with hastily swiped tears staining his cheeks.

The dark mass of hair shifted, revealing two bloodshot eyes. Sabrina looked at the assembled household, momentarily confused, then her sunken eyes widened. Her entire body trembled and she began an earnest examination of the floor. Tatiana could practically taste the fear emanating from her, sour and dry.

"Everyone please sit until it's your turn to speak." Gareth gently pushed Sabrina onto the empty chair. "Cook, repeat what you told me about your first week here."

Cook twisted a strand of curly brown hair that had slipped out of the clip she wore. Tatiana quietly moved her chair to the back, just behind Bobby Sue, so her view of Sabrina was partially obscured. The anger she had so carefully banked, for

Gareth's sake, fought against the dam.

"Well, Sabrina set me to work on scrubbing the floors as soon as I put my stuff down. I finished around sundown, but she said they weren't clean enough to have earned me a meal and made me start over. My fingers were red and blistered by the time I finished the second time. Sabrina had gone to bed and all the cupboards were locked so I didn't eat that night. In the morning she gave me a little crust of bread and sent me to wash the sheets and chamber pots. You know I'm not one for shirking my duties, but she was just never satisfied. No matter how good a job I did, all I got was scorn and a crust of bread in the morning. I didn't expect much, especially the way things were and all, but a person can't live on scraps for long. Not if they're going to be of any use. I was afraid to go to you, Gareth, because I was new. It was a week before she let me have more to eat. My performance hadn't changed one bit. It took another week before she let me do anything in the kitchen where I belonged in the first place."

Gareth glared at Sabrina. "Is what she said true? Did you really starve this woman for a week?"

Sabrina looked up for the first time and scowled, her eyes dark and defiant. "I gave her bread," she said, her voice sharp and snide.

"A scrap no bigger than my finger!" Cook said, holding up her hand.

"I had to show her who was in charge," said Sabrina. She smiled at Gareth as if nothing unusual had happened in the past two weeks. "I had to show all of them. I did it all for you."

"Enough with your lies!" said Gareth. His voice boomed across the room. "Everyone knew you were giving the orders. There was no need to behave like a dog dominating its pack. And if anyone had stepped out of line, one word from me would have them sitting in the dust."

Sabrina shrunk back into her chair and quivered like a small child caught stealing a cookie.

"Bobby Sue, your turn," said Gareth.

"I didn't get anythin' to eat the first two days because I didn't clean fast enough..."

Tatiana watched Gareth's face while Bobby Sue and then the others confronted Sabrina with her treatment of them. Gareth listened to all of it in stony silence. Only his eyes betrayed his anger and hurt.

"Tatiana."

Tatiana's heart began to race and as she stood, her face reddened with anger. Energy bubbled at her fingertips. It would be so easy to give in to her anger, give in to the pain. Tatiana met Sabrina's wide-eyed look with silent rage and saw her blanch. It reminded her of Joe. But did Sabrina feel remorse over what she had done?

"You weren't happy when I told you Gareth had hired me and said Fifi could stay," she said, somehow managing to keep her voice calm and steady. "Then you locked the doors to prevent us from reaching the common room before the deadline, a stipulation for being fed and sleeping inside. But Fifi and I knew your game and ran quickly to reach the last door before you could shut it. It made you angry that we made it in time and you grabbed my arm. The force of your fingers hurt me and upset Fifi, so she growled, to protect me. When you tried to kick her, she transformed.

"I know she frightened you, she meant to, but I would not have allowed her to harm you. I apologize for her behavior, and I did reprimand her. After that incident, I did everything you asked of me, kept Fifi away from you whenever possible and calm when you were near. What you did..." Tatiana swallowed and felt her lip tremble. "How could you hurt her when she lay helpless from your potion? How could you throw her out like trash?"

Tatiana paused and blinked back angry tears. It took a moment before she could continue, and when she did, her throat felt strained with more than anger.

"You know Fifi was star-touched, but do you really know what that means, Sabrina? Fifi was more than just a dog. She had thoughts, feeling, ideas, just like you and me. More importantly, Fifi was my bonded, part of me, my soul. Our bond was more than love. Our spirits were entwined, and losing her left a hole in my heart.

"If what you wanted to do was hurt me, well, you succeeded. But there is something you need to know. I am a survivor. And the love and caring I've given others has returned to me ten-fold.

The hole in my heart is filling. What has all your cruelty and backstabbing gotten you?"

Tatiana sat back down, her hands tightly clasped in her lap as tears ran down her face. She could no longer hold them back, but the anger flowed out with them. She couldn't stay angry for someone as broken as Sabrina. Bobby Sue swiveled in her chair and placed a comforting hand on her shoulder. No one said a word for a long time. Finally, Gareth shifted his feet and turned to Sabrina.

"Do you have anything to say for yourself, Sabrina?"

Sabrina shook her head, causing the tangled black mass to sway.

"You've abused your position here, Sabrina, by hurting the people I took into my care. You stole from me when I would have given you almost anything you asked for. You conspired with my enemy, for the sole purpose of usurping me from my livelihood, sold all of us out to him. But what hurts the most, Sabrina, is the lies. I can't trust you anymore. I can't have you in my house."

A single tear rolled down Sabrina's cheek. Finally, she understood. Tatiana knew she did, she could sense it. Gareth reached out and caught the drop on his finger.

"I wish I could believe these tears were real this time," said Gareth, his voice choked with emotion. "But you've faked them one too many times. Good bye, Sabrina."

"Gareth," she said, as he turned away. "I'm sorry."

"So am I, because it's not good enough this time. Your fate is out of my hands. Bobby Sue, make her presentable. They'll be waiting outside to take her to trial."

Sabrina's body shook as she wept. Longing filled her eyes as she watched Gareth's retreating back, but longing couldn't undo the past. Tatiana wasn't ready to forgive Sabrina, especially for her part in Fifi's death, but at least she could begin moving forward.

Chapter Fifty-Five

Tatiana

Tatiana waited, shifted in her seat with the other people who had come to watch the trials today. Sweat dripped down her back, adding to the smell that permeated the air in the over-packed council building. The mood was a mixture of anger, fear, and pity, varying with people's connection to the accused. Sabrina's jury deliberated in the back room while the next trial proceeded, but only a handful of people were paying attention to the present court case.

For two weeks Tatiana had managed to avoid the trials and executions, but Bobby Sue had watched a few and said that the room hadn't been this packed since Darren's. Even those council members not on judge duty were there, sitting with the spectators. Everyone seemed to have an interest in Sabrina's fate.

This morning's events churned in Tatiana's mind. After Gareth left, she had helped Bobby Sue bathe Sabrina, and for once, the woman didn't shrink away from her touch. They dressed Sabrina in a pretty blue dress that accentuated her raven hair and bright red lips. Throughout all of this, Sabrina moved as if in a daze, following directions numbly. She didn't appear to be aware of what was going on. All the preparations required physical contact, but it only took one touch for Tatiana to know that more was at stake here than Sabrina's fate.

"Sabrina's jury is coming back," whispered Bobby Sue.

The room hushed as the jurors filed in and handed a slip of paper to Neil. Tatiana had been so deep in thought she hadn't even noticed the other jury leave. She held her breath and kept her anger in check. Fifi was dead because of the woman. For that there should be punishment, but what kind remained a question. Tatiana bit at her lip and glanced at Gareth, who sat a few seats away. His jaw looked so tense Tatiana could see the muscles twitch. Despite the blank mask he wore, she knew his emotions were roiling just below the surface.

Neil looked at the note and nodded, barely waiting for the guard to pull Sabrina to her feet before speaking.

"Sabrina Williams, the jury finds you guilty of conspiring with Mako Scaffeld and selling another human into slavery. For these crimes you are sentenced to..."

"Wait," said Tatiana, jumping up. Her hands trembled. She already knew what Neil would say, the same sentence he had handed down to almost everyone. After what she had learned, Tatiana couldn't allow it. "Before you continue, I wish to plead for leniency."

Murmurs raced across the room. Bobby Sue looked at her, her mouth open in stunned disbelief. Even Gareth's jaw dropped. Eyes seemed to drill into Tatiana from every direction. The urge to flee pulled at her will and she had to grip the seat in front of her not to succumb.

Neil blinked, eyebrows raised. He looked from Tatiana to Gareth and back again several times. "But you were the one she sold."

"Yes," said Tatiana. "Which is why it has to be me who insists Sabrina not receive a death sentence."

"If it weren't for the shocked expression on Gareth's face, I'd say he put you up to this. Why on earth should we go easy on someone who nearly destroyed this town?"

"She may have sold me to Mako, but she didn't plan his takeover. I doubt she knew his plans for Atherton."

"That doesn't excuse her."

"No, and she should be punished, but taking her life will also harm another."

"Listen, Tatiana. I know how Gareth feels about Sabrina, but we..."

"I'm not talking about Gareth. Sabrina is pregnant."

If Gareth looked surprised, nothing compared to the look on Sabrina's face. Her eyes widened, and for the first time since Gareth threw her out, looked alert. She couldn't have known this early in the pregnancy, but Tatiana did. As to the father, only Sabrina could know that, but Tatiana suspected Mako. Murmurs echoed around the room.

Neil looked from Sabrina to Tatiana. Skepticism swirled around him. "How can you be so sure? It doesn't look like Sabrina has any idea what you're talking about."

Tatiana looked Neil in the eyes and held her head up high. "I am star-touched. This is who and what I am. I can sense life growing in Sabrina's womb. Ask Doc Johnson or one of the midwives to examine her if you need a second opinion."

Chapter Fifty-Six

Tatiana

"You did a kind thing back there," said Marshall, as Tatiana stepped outside.

Tatiana brushed the sweat from her forehead as she moved to where he casually leaned against the newly sanded siding of the council building. His brown eyes had a welcoming glint and the soft black downy hairs on his face seemed to stand out even more than usual in the strong afternoon sun. The warm smile he wore chased away some of her weariness.

"I did what I felt was right. Sabrina's child deserves a chance to live."

"You could have said nothing and no one would have known."

"I would have known."

Marshall's smile broadened. "I know. Do you think she'll be okay working on a farm?"

"Magdalena agreed to take her in. She'll keep her in line," said Tatiana.

"What about after the indentured term is up? After the baby is born?"

"Whatever happens, Magdalena will make sure the child is well cared for."

Tatiana glanced around the town square and sighed, wishing today's emotional rollercoaster would end. Her decision had been both difficult and easy at the same time. She'd done what she could for Sabrina and her baby. If only she could do more to help Atherton. Few buildings showed signs of repair. With most of their resources destroyed by the fire, they didn't have materials for a patch job, let alone a full restoration.

"You okay?" asked Marshall, a touch of concern in his voice.

Tatiana tore her eyes away from the blackened remains of a

house and nodded. "Just tired. It's been a tense day."

"There you are," said Brother William. He forced his way through the throng of people pouring from the council building.

"Nicely done," said Gavin. He flicked his blond hair off his face, making it bob like a sailor at sea. A huge grin split his face. "You really know how to make an entrance."

Tatiana sighed. The last thing she wanted right now was jokes. "I wasn't trying to put on a show, Gavin."

Gavin seemed to droop and she regretted her sharp words. He had his own worries. Eric was still missing.

"Did you know about this?" Gareth marched down the council steps and waved a crumpled piece of paper at Gavin and Marshall. Deep furrows creased his brow and his eyes swirled with suspicion.

"Know about what?" said Marshall, taking the paper.

Gavin and Brother William leaned in to read it as well. Gareth glared at the three men as they read they note. "Thelma gave that to me a moment ago. Said she was ordered to wait until after Sabrina's trial."

Marshall looked up, his face creasing with anger. His voice was barely above a whisper. "I swear, Gareth. I knew nothing of their plans."

"He didn't say anything to me before he left." Shock and hurt filled Gavin's face. "I didn't even know he was gone until Shea told me hours later."

"This is the first I've heard as well," said Brother William.

Marshall handed the note back to Gareth. The emotions whizzing around Tatiana made her feel dizzy. And the hushed voices put her more on edge than she already was.

"Would somebody please tell me what's going on?" she said struggling to keep her voice low.

Gareth took a deep breath and let it out slowly before speaking, making sure no one was near enough to overhear. "Marty arranged for Duval to escape with Eric's help. They think he'll lead them to whoever made the drugs that suppressed your abilities. They also want to know who's been trying to collect star-touched and why."

Tatiana turned and walked away from the four men, clenching her hands to keep them from shaking. Her mind whirled around a thousand thoughts and memories. Mako had talked about a buyer. Snider had drugged Gavin and Marshall. He had wanted to sell all three of them. And then there was Duval. He had been there with Mako and Diddler. He had helped them hurt her. Tatiana suppressed a shudder and stopped, surprised to find herself in front of the wooden gallows. The faint stench of blood and urine surrounded the structure. Tears stung her eyes.

"Tat?" Gareth said softly.

"How many more, Gareth?" she said through the tightness in her throat. "How many more are going to be hurt or die?"

"I can't answer that, Tat. No one can. And I may be angry as hell, but I know Marty, and I understand his reasons. He'll be back. They'll both be back."

"Then we can have a nice long chat with both of them," said Marshall.

Her mouth felt suddenly dry. Tatiana looked around the burned out buildings near the town square again. "Will there be people left in town for them to come back to? How are we going to survive the winter?"

Gareth put his hands on her shoulders. Their heavy weight lay like a comforting blanket. We'll find a way, Tat. We survived the Cataclysm. We'll figure this out too."

A smile crept across Tatiana's face. He was right. This place was home, her home. They'd make it work.

THE END

AUTHOR BIOGRAPHY

A. L. Kaplan's love of books started at an early age and sparked a creative imagination. Born on a cold winter morning in scenic northern New Jersey, A. L. spent many hours developing her ideas before translating them into words. Her stories have been included in several anthologies, including *In A Cat's Eye, Young Adventurers: Heroes, Explorers, And Swashbucklers, and Suppose: Drabbles, Flash Fiction, And Short Stories. You can find her poems in Dragonfly Arts Magazine's 2014, 2015, and 2016 editions, and the BALTICON 49 and 50 BSFAN.* She is a past president of the Maryland Writers' Association's Howard County Chapter and holds an MFA in sculpture from the Maryland Institute College of Art. When not writing, or indulging in her fascination with wolves, A. L. is the props manager for a local theatre. This proud mother of two lives in Maryland with her husband and dog.

LETTER FROM THE AUTHOR

To My Readers:

Writing is mostly a solitary endeavor with many hours spent alone typing at computer or curled over a notepad. Many thanks to my family for their patience and understanding, to my wonderful critique group for pushing me to write a better story, and to everyone at Intrigue Publishing for getting this book into your hands.

I hope you enjoyed Star Touched and would love to hear from you. Feel free to contact me via Twitter, Facebook, or Goodreads with any questions and comments, and visit me on my website. Don't forget to sign up for my newsletter to get sneak peaks and to find out about giveaways and other surprises.

Sincerely,

A. L. Kaplan

Website: alkaplan.wordpress.com
Newsletter: alkaplan.wordpress.com/newsletter/
Twitter: twitter.com/alkaplanauthor
Facebook: facebook.com/AuthorA.L.Kaplan